BEING BUSTED

BEING

Leslie A. Fiedler

BUSTED

𝔰𝔡 STEIN AND DAY / *Publishers* / New York

To My First Grandson:

SETH

Acknowledgment

I AM GRATEFUL for the advice and counsel given to me by my lawyer, Herald Price Fahringer, Jr.

PREFACE

THE READER OF the following account should be warned that it is more parable than history. He will notice immediately, for instance, that none of the characters who appear in its pages is called by name except for the author, and even he is most often referred to by the anonymous designation of "I." But "I" is, of course, the true name of us all, of the reader as well as the other actors in the book, or at least would be in the similar books each of us might write.

Essentially then, this is, despite its autobiographical form, a book not about me, or indeed individuals at all, so much as one about cultural and social change between 1933, when I just missed being arrested, and 1967, when I made it at last. Its true subject is the endless war, sometimes cold, sometimes hot, between the dissenter and his imperfect society. Its pages, therefore, deal with both the assault of the dissenter on the world —protests and demonstrations, revolutionary polemics—and the counterattack of the world on the dissenter—wiretaps and the planting of evidence, legal and social harassment. Since the battlefield for me has always been the campus, my book may seem to be basically concerned with the present plight of the university and the confrontation of old and young within its walls. But it is, in fact, concerned with educational policy and cops on campus only as one aspect of that *total war against privacy* which all attempts to stifle dissent inevitably become, and in which electronic surveillance is the latest and most distressing weapon.

My book is also, however, and in a sense most importantly of all, about places: cities and streets which have survived the events that occurred in them in fact and dream, and are therefore not only named but described in specific detail. I am convinced that much of the truth of what follows depends upon the precise evocation of setting and scene. For me, at least, time tends to blur everything else, and hopefully an autobiography is a triumph over time.

LESLIE A. FIEDLER

Buffalo, New York
June 1, 1969

CONTENTS

Part One

BERGEN STREET: 1933

BEING BUSTED is not so hard to manage, after all, certainly nothing to be proud of. Actually I might have made it at sixteen. But I didn't: because I ran fast, because I was lucky, unlucky—it's hard to say. As a matter of fact, I did run as fast as I could when I saw the squad car, the submachine guns, but that wasn't until later. When the first cop pulled his .38 and grabbed for the speaker on the rubbish box beside the curb, that speaker was somebody else, not me. I had just stepped down a minute before, and so it was my friend whom they got. And maybe that's why at fifty he was being a stockbroker in Texas (immunized, you see, once and for all), while I was being arrested in Buffalo: my first time, some thirty-four years too late.

A male child born since World War II, the statisticians tell us, has one chance out of two of being busted before he dies. I don't know what the odds were in 1933 for someone born in the midst of World War I. One in three or four or five, I would guess, since not quite so many things were forbidden (and required) of everybody in those simple-minded days; and as far as kids were concerned, it was assumed that someone would smack their asses —or, at least, that someone *should*—for things that now make the courts and the newspapers and Ph.D. dissertations on juvenile delinquency.

In fact, my own almost-arrest happened quite by accident, since cops hadn't yet learned to think of the young as their ultimate enemies. There were hunger marchers around then, for the Depression was still new, and Union pickets and Communists to work out on, so that a kid had to make a hell of a lot of noise even to be noticed. But that's just what we were doing, it so happened, two of us yelling as loud as we could from our perch on what we were still enough our parents' children to think of as a horseshit box. Another one of us was trying to gather a crowd with the help of a ukelele which he claimed to be able to play.

It was a hot night for so early in the season, and we had been walking up and down Bergen Street (this being Newark, New Jersey, before the Spades had taken over from the Jews the role of most visible disturbers of the peace) pretending we were looking for girls, though pretty sure we would have to settle for ice-cream cones. The stores—ice-cream parlors, Kosher delicatessens, shlag-houses crammed with cheap clothes—stayed open late on Bergen Street. And even people with nothing they really wanted, and no money to buy it with in any case, kept cruising up and down trying to look like shoppers, or at least like somebody with something to *do*. Not like the idle kids.

But kids or adults, everybody knew that the real point was that it was too hot to sleep, too hot to be anyplace but out. And so the street-corner political speakers were there, too, on their rickety little wooden stands, with the required American flag drooping beside them in the no-breeze of a Newark June. There must have been mosquitoes, as well, since there were always mosquitoes in Newark, up from the melted swamps of the Meadows, our first sad sign of spring. But you couldn't have heard them buzz before striking any more than you could hear the slap of bare palms against bare arms after they struck; any more than you could hear *any* single sound in the general roar of starting cars and banging doors and yelling parents and squawling children and dogs and cats and birds all making appropriate noises at each other. Least of all could you hear the speech of the Socialist Labor Party soapboxer, leaning his pale old face forward and flapping his lips in some standard denunciation of the system we all hated—to a handful of bystanders who didn't seem to mind not hearing him one little bit.

But we did. "Louder and funnier," we yelled, adding to his tiny audience five or six more hecklers than he deserved or knew what to do with. "Can't hear a word you're saying," we bellowed at him loud enough so he could hear *us;* and then went on to tell him what we would have found wrong with his remarks if they had been audible in the first place: something about his not understanding the true nature of the Soviet Union, or the proper

role of the Trade Unions, or the menace of F.D.R.'s fascist New
Deal. And after a while, the rest of his small audience began to
laugh—at him, at us, at themselves for just standing there. Nobody could have told for sure, but the speaker took it as a personal offense and raised his voice for the first time (as he had
not raised it against the indignities of capitalism) to suggest that
if we thought we could do so much better, why didn't we get
the hell out of there and start a street meeting of our own.

It was a notion that appealed to us, as it did, apparently, to
most every one else on the street: hoodlums, shrews, storekeepers, even the dogs and cats. The fact was, I suppose, that
right down to the animals, they were all bored, bored with what
they spent most of their time doing, and even more with what
they didn't do whenever they stopped. But mostly they were
bored by hearing nothing above the general noise of their lives
except the fat official voices of Lowell Thomas and Gabriel
Heatter telling them over the radio what was called "news," i.e.,
what was happening somewhere else to someone else.

They heard us loud and clear all right, the rattle of the ukelele,
the thump of our heels brought down on the metal trashbox for
emphasis, and the sound of our voices roaring out what started
in play but ended in rage: the joke of our rage and theirs, our
boredom and theirs, the lousy joke of politics and revolution, of
all promises made in a world that wasn't a bit of a joke. It was
real, after all, real while it lasted, like any demonstration, though
in a sense we were only playing. And how I loved the moment
when, standing up over the crowd, I could see for the first time
just how real it was—how different from high school debates on
"Shall we recognize the Soviet Union," with evidence cards and
speech teachers as judges.

I kept watching all those people who didn't even know my
name overflowing the sidewalk in a growing circle whose center
I defined; after a while, they were hunched together, shoulder
to shoulder and belly to back, out into the roadway, blocking
traffic as baffled drivers tooted their horns and leaned out of
open car windows to curse us. And then I stepped down, hearing
the crowd, silent until I was through and for a second or two
after, really let go: roaring half in approval, half in mockery,
glad and embarrassed at the same time, because there was some

one dumb enough, young enough, loud enough to stand up and yell for them. To tell the truth, I've never been able to stop yelling for them ever since; but that's another story, or rather, the rest of this story.

What happened at that moment was that just as the next speaker was begining to get into his stride, suddenly there was this joker at the very heart of the crowd, waving his gun in the middle of a circle that was opening up even faster than the earlier circle had closed around us: another kind of circle. He was, it turned out, only an off-duty cop who lived nearby making a trip to a local saloon to replenish his beer supply. He was out of uniform but packing a revolver, maybe so he wouldn't forget even for a minute just who he was. Seeing so many people shoulder to shoulder, at any rate, and hearing what must have sounded to him like hostile yells, he was reminded of his problem twice over; and so he drew, checking his identity as it were. Or perhaps he was only scared, as scared without his gun as all the rest of us at the sight of it. Everybody was pretty good at being scared in those days anyhow; along with being bored it seemed the thing to do.

In any case, once this cop had drawn his weapon he felt brave enough to make a grab for the speaker, hauling him down off his perch in mid-sentence. And at that point, the women—more audible once the pressure was on than the men or even the kids —stopped screaming safety instruction to their own young long enough to yell at him: "Let go of that boy. Take your dirty hands off of him. What do you think you're doing anyhow. You're *shicker*, that's what you are. So let go already." The word for "drunk" they put into yiddish out of instinctive caution, maybe, though all the rest of it they hollered in the tongue they shared with the (naturally) Irish policeman. I suppose the fact that they were Jewish was one reason they were able to hate cops so wholeheartedly, those women who were our mothers— even when they were not Socialists or Communists. They knew plenty of gangsters who were Jews (including the neighborhood hero who had made it up to number fourteen on the Most Wanted list, and whose mother, they never let the rest of us forget, wore mink), and lots of radicals also in trouble with the law; but who ever heard of a Jewish policeman? A Jewish Miss

America was more likely. And so they yelled at the cop with all the power generated by years of yelling at their own crazy kids and weak-kneed husbands.

But he wasn't listening, not even to the plain English, since he was in fact *shicker* enough to think he was in some movie about the Royal Mounties, instead of just on poor old Bergen Street. And so waving his gun in ever wider and more wobbly circles, he yelled, "Stand back, I'm a police officer and I always get my man." For some reason, only I seemed to find the remark funny. Certainly I was the only one who laughed, as the women fell to screaming and clutching their children again, and several of the men found voices at last—pressing around me with information about the constitutional rights of my poor friend (held hard, and scarcely even struggling, in the large left hand of the cop), along with pledges to march en masse to the police station in a demonstration of solidarity.

An instant later, however, they were all gone, as a siren roared and a long black touring car came screeching to a stop just in front of us, full of cops all buttoned up in blue to the rims of their tight red faces, Thompson submachine guns resting in their laps. "The riot squad," I heard someone more whisper than say; and they had all melted away, disappeared, the entire crowd. But just when I was about to shout after them in contempt, I discovered that I myself was at the far end of a dark alley I didn't remember entering, my heart pounding and my breath coming short as I stared down at a lidless garbage can and listened to my own voice saying, incredulously, "You ran, you schmuck. Goddam it, you *ran*."

It seemed hard to believe of one who had long (since reading Thoreau at twelve, Marx at thirteen) thought of himself as the declared enemy of the entire System served by cops and courts and who sometimes dreamed himself rising in the witness box to accuse his accusers, as the sentencing judge glared and the guards clapped on the handcuffs. Well, it is melodrama to be sure, and no kid of sixteen entertains such fantasies without considerable irony, knowing that even Thoreau let his friends bail him out of the clink in pretty short order. Still he had gone to prison, while I, in whose head his words repeated themselves at that very moment ("Under a government which imprisons any unjustly, the true place for a just man is also a prison"), had run away—afraid of cops and guns, afraid of jail.

A pattern had set itself though I would not know it for a long time. The events that followed, back there in 1933, should have convinced me that my encounters with the law were destined to eventuate not in melodrama but in comedy; certainly they have seemed comic in retrospect forever after, no matter how painful at the moment they occurred. I myself learned to look a little better than I had on Bergen Street (at least to myself); but, alas, the police never cooperated. And how can a man —at sixteen or twenty or forty or fifty or whatever—come on like Thoreau or Dreyfus, Joe Hill or Sacco and Vanzetti or Tom Mooney, when the cops fate has chosen for him are always straight out of some Keystone Comedy or nineteenth-century farce? I do not mean that I have not suffered on my own account since, and suffered the more when those around me have become targets of comic malice for my sake; but I have continued to feel that I am doomed to be robbed always of the final solace of finding my suffering noble, since what falls on my shoulders is likely to be a rubber truncheon, what hits me in the face a custard pie.

When I did pull myself together after my non-arrest and get as far as the Precinct Station, it was clear that no manifestations of mass solidarity were about to take place. In fact, not a single idler stood within range of the place—only a couple of cops, who looked past me without interest. So, ducking into a nearby drugstore, I called up the Republican County Committeeman from our district, a real estate lawyer who enjoyed beating me at checkers. And in half an hour my friend was sprung, remanded in the custody of the ward leader. He looked pretty glad to be out of there at first, even laughing at the lawyer's jokes. But by the time I left him, he was well on the way to believing himself a hero.

A couple of days later, he was actually claiming to anyone interested that maybe I had meant well, but he sure resented my interference for having deprived him of the experience of a night in jail—necessary to all revolutionaries. With a lawyer besides, and a Republican one at that—who needed it! But he was glad enough next morning when it turned out that the Republican lawyer and the Republican judge before whom he appeared had cooked up a deal between them: a big reprimand and no sentence. Anyhow he made the most of the short time when the kind of people at South Side High School who would never have anything to do with either of us before would chase us down the corridors, to slap him on the back and get the details right from the horse's mouth. He was so busy strutting, though, that I had to do all the talking.

"You bet your life," I would hasten to testify when called on, "the sonofabitch actually pulled out his gun. We thought it would go off any minute. But listen, do you realize that if it had happened one minute sooner, *I* was the one who would have—"

But at that point everyone would go away, or interrupt by yelling over me, "Stop feeling sorry for yourself and tell us about what happened in the courtroom. What did the judge *really* say?"

And I would tell it to them straight. "'I want you boys to remember this isn't Cuba,' that's what he said. 'We do things *our* way here, the American way. The ballot box, not shouting on street corners.'"

"And the cop?" they would ask over and over, never seeming to get tired of hearing it. "What about the cop?"

"'Well,' the judge asked him, 'if they were Reds, what were they talking about?' And he said, 'About Roosevelt, about the President.' 'And were they for him or against him?' the judge asked. And this jerk scratches his head and says, 'I don't know, the words were too big.'"

"The words were too big," my listeners would repeat in wonder, laughing and laughing.

And "The words were too big," I would say to clinch it. I had a winner and was determined to milk it for all it was worth; and, indeed, I have for three decades and a half.

But it never seemed to me all that funny, not for a long, long time, not for as long as I walked Bergen Street.

In a year or two, I had left South Side High for New York University, and four years after that for the University of Wisconsin; while my lucky friend who had managed to get arrested pressed his luck and inscribed in our yearbook next to his name, where all the rest of us had been content to put down more conventional goals like Harvard and Yale or City College, "Lenin-

grad U." Actually, he went to work first in a grocery store, then
in a hat factory, on his unsuspected road to Dallas, Texas. But
even in the grocery store just around the corner from where he
lived, he was already further from home than I managed to get
in the Bronx or in Madison; on Tremont Avenue or State Street,
I was still looking for the encounter I had somehow missed in
Newark, for my real meeting with real police.

It was a time for demonstrations and mass meetings and protest parades, that long gray stretch from the start of the Depression to the outbreak of World War II, from the beginning of
F.D.R. to the beginning of his end. And wherever the demonstrations and meetings and parades were, I tried to be, too: in
Newark's Military Park when the hecklers screamed, "Who's
paying you, Moscow gold?" and the speakers screamed back
over to them, "Who sent *you*, McCarter from the Public Service?"
Or across the river in Union Square, when the cops rode their
horses into crowds howling, "RED FRONT! RED FRONT! RED
FRONT!" and little old ladies risked getting trampled to press
palmfuls of pepper into the quivering nostrils of the policemen's
mounts; or on the boulevards of Washing.on, D.C., where we
chanted, *"N.Y.U. wants N.Y.A."* in processions blessed by the
wife of the President of the United States; or at a convention of
the American Student Union at Vassar (imagine, *me* at Vassar!),
when everyone went mad in a frenzy of Jap hating, and the girls
ripped off their underpants to toss them into a huge bonfire; or
on the parking lots and playing fields and auditoriums of otherwise silent universities, where I was one of a half-million students
crying aloud the pledge never to support the United States in
any war; or in the mass picket lines around a steel plant in some
gray and peeling suburb south of Chicago, where a week later
the police would open fire and there would be six, seven, eight
dead.

But somehow it all stayed for me a festival and an escape, a
kind of tourism into scenes scarcely imaginable from Bergen
Street, a way out into the large world—though not yet for keeps,
not quite for real. The trouble was that I, at least, always ended
by going home. Our line of march would be lined by hostile cops;
the speakers' stand would be ringed by them, bored and resolute;
sometimes there would even be a cordon drawn up between us

and our immediate goal: White House or factory gate or whatever. But when there was actual contact, it would always be somebody else who got whacked on the head, somebody else who was given the privilege of being arrested, since I was not distinguished enough, or innocent enough, or goyish enough to be placed in the front ranks.

No, when I had finished singing: *"Down the street we'll hold a demonstration. We'll hold it in November and on the first of May. And when they ask us what they hell we're doing, we're fighting for our freedom which is not far away!"* I would help stack the placards on their long poles into the waiting trucks, and take the subway, the Tubes, a bus back to Newark or back to school. Even that final demonstration against the threat of Fascism and the connivance of the West, the Civil War in Spain, turned out to be for me hopelessly vicarious. Two boys actually went from our Y.C.L. chapter, with false passports and great secrecy, and one of them died; while I—out of fear or inertia?— stayed behind to cheer at rallies, to collect money from faculty office to faculty office, to turn the mimeograph machine, and to sell my textbooks to help pay for an ambulance.

But how irrelevant those books seemed, even less meaningful at the moment of selling than at the moment of buying, and how doubly irrelevant the classes which were their occasion. Like most of my comrades, I worked hard for grades in those classes —certainly never considered for a moment the possibility of dropping *out,* because I could never believe that I was yet quite *in,* only that I might some day get there by virtue of making it in those classes, getting those grades and the degrees to which they would all add up in the end. With the B.A., M.A., Ph.D., I told myself, I would have a louder voice, more access to the centers of power, a better fulcrum and greater leverage with which to heave over the whole rotten mess out of which I had been trying in vain to crawl.

But meanwhile, it seemed necessary to take the curse off my apparent commitment by differentiating myself clearly from those who wanted only to succeed in the society dying around them: to qualify themselves as doctors or lawyers (what else could the sons of their mothers dream?), ready to tend the beneficiaries of that society, strangled by the fat around their

hearts, or to judge its enemies, putting on black robes and banging a gavel. And so I would go to English Department teas
wearing a "Vote for Foster and Ford" button; teach my charges
at Freshman Orientation Camp to sing the "Internationale"; slip
onto campus before dawn with leaflets attacking compulsory
R.O.T.C.; even join with my comrades to bust up one of their
formal reviews—or at least refuse to salute the flag they carried
past our jeers.

It even seemed possible to carry dissent into the classroom
itself by writing Marxist interpretations of Courtly Love and the
Elizabethan theater, or by rising in back rows with embarrassing
questions about the contradictions of capitalism after a lecture
on American History, or by lying in wait to distribute leaflets
outside the door of some eminent Professor of Labor Economics,
labeling him a fink and Social Fascist. At the day's close, however, there I would be back on the Lexington Avenue Subway
(as an undergraduate, I commuted daily between Newark and
the Bronx) taking one more aspirin tablet, and writing in my
battered blue notebook one more cry of loneliness and contempt
—in *French*. (Would you believe I used to write to myself from
myself, secretly, as it were, in bad French: i.e., the best I could
manage.)

I had quite forgotten about it until the other day when I turned
up the notebook in one of those files I continue to carry about
the world with me to spare myself the expense of memory. And
there between a sketch of a fellow subway-rider and the formula
$sin^2A + cos^2A = 1$, in a scrawl jagged with the rhythms of a
bucketing train now thirty years gone into the dark, I read: "*Je
n'aime pas cette vie à demi-homme, il doit être plus dans l'école
que des bavards disciplinaires et des gentils distraits. Il faut
quelque chose ou quelqu'un à m'éveiller.*"

It was my other, my private rhetoric at seventeen or eighteen,
as false in its aspiration toward poetry and melancholy as was
my first, my public rhetoric in its yearning for political commitment and health: "We are now members of the Y.P.S.L. Fourth
International, fighting for the liberation of the oppressed masses
of the world through the world-wide Socialist revolution. We are
fortunate, in this day of many Marxists, to have discovered the
only movement perpetuating the traditions and ideals of the

Bolsheviks of October. We raise the slogan: Down with Stalin—
All Power to the Soviets. On with the October Revolution!"

Yet somehow out of a combination of the two I would have
to make whatever authentic voice I was destined to find—if,
indeed, I was to continue to cry out against those I felt to be the
world's enemies as well as mine; for the voice I had raised on
Bergen Street would no longer do, once I had worn out the uses
of being merely young and stupid and loud. Meanwhile, however, I had begun to redefine those enemies in terms of the life
I had chosen for myself, a life in universities, where the real en-
forcers were not cops at all. To be sure, even on the tiny campus
at University Heights there was a single college cop: old, kindly,
and more than a little comic as he walked his beat between
borders of violets, not even seeing the slogans whitewashed on
the concrete mall beneath his feet: HANDS OFF CHINA!
FREE TOM MOONEY AND THE SCOTTSBORO BOYS! And
on the vast acres of Wisconsin there were many more, but they
bugged no one except unwary lovers.

No, it was the Deans and Assistant Deans, University Presidents and Vice-Presidents and Chairmen of Scholarship Committees who came running in times of trouble, without sirens to
announce them or badges and tommy-guns to declare their
intent. And back of them—more dreamed than known, or rather
known only from tendentious plays and books—the shadowy
Boards of Trustees, looking for some new Thorstein Veblen to
break. Teachers were more equivocal, since they could even be
touched occasionally for good causes, or persuaded to sign
petitions; but none of us were surprised when they, too, played
the policeman. After all, we had been checked out for attendance
every day of our earlier school careers and were used to being
hounded down for smoking in toilets, cussing on playgrounds,
cheating at examinations. And we had not, therefore, expected
those who sat behind the master's desk in college to be less repressive, only somehow not quite so ridiculous.

It had struck us as rather unfair, but not shocking certainly,
when in high school our whole geometry class was given two
weeks' detention for having passed hand-to-hand under our
desks a copy of E. E. Cummings' translation of Louis Aragon's
Red Front, or when the editors of a mimeographed magazine

called *The New Student* were all publicly assured that they had
been blackballed forever in colleges all up and down the United
States. Perhaps the small bullies in the head office only bluffed
the threat that seemed to us the extinction of our only tolerable
future; but how were we to know, as we stood trembling beside
our open lockers—everyone in the school—and an inspection
team headed by the principal himself (with the Phys Ed teacher
in attendance as a sign of strength) searched through dirty
sneakers, old candy wrappers, and ink-stained books in search of
the forbidden publication—which contained the word "condom"
in addition to an article on Progressive Education by George S.
Counts.

But somehow I had not expected the continuation of such
silliness in the University. And I was shocked at accounts of
certain lengthy debates, leaked to me breathlessly, about whether
someone (me, to be precise) who refused to salute his country's
flag and advocated Communist candidates for national office deserved the honor of membership in Phi Beta Kappa; dismayed
at the final act of spite that in my Senior year took away from
me the scholarship which—along with the weekly torture of selling shoes to ladies—made possible my staying in school at all. I
was editor of the Yearbook and for a long time insisted that in
place of the customary dedication to a "beloved teacher" there
should be one to the "struggle for peace," illustrated by the
picture of a monstrous tank about to crush a miniature campus,
very fragile and fake-classical, under its great iron belly.

Somehow this seemed inappropriate (in the Spring of 1938)
and indecorous to those who policed us; and though finally I
compromised on a dedication to Abraham Lincoln, I was not
able to resist sending my version of the whole silly business to a
New York columnist who thought it as comic as I did and gave
it four or five lines—which, it turned out, my Dean considered
worth a hundred bucks apiece. Out of my pocket, naturally,
which seemed to me not quite so funny as the events that had
led up to it.

Actually, I suppose, I was lucky after such an incident to have
got into a graduate school at all, since that of my own university
would not have me, and my file contained not only an account
of the tank affair but also a letter from my Italian teacher, who

admired Mussolini (as he did not trouble to point out in that document) and felt that my "membership in an obscure Marxist sect precluded the objectivity of a true scholar."

True enough, by that time I had become a Trotskyite, i.e., sectarian and obscure enough in my politics to leave a lover of refurbished Rome as baffled as the Bergen Street cop about what I was really for and against. I tried hard, however, to make matters clear on that score once I had got to Wisconsin, not only speaking about my new position, but actually buying, with my first teaching salary, a mimeograph machine to publish it, and organizing in its name protests against protests, demonstrations beyond demonstrations, so that no one could be in doubt any longer about my hatred of the capitalist system *and* of those who did not oppose it purely and passionately enough.

That the Stalinists on campus understood me quite clearly became evident when they, my former comrades, joined forces with those who harassed us, in uniform and out. And I am sure that in short order they were informing on me as conscientiously as had the sole Liberty Leaguer, the lonely Right Wing Radical of my undergraduate days, who used solemnly to announce every Friday afternoon (I can call up yet his pale, mad face framed by sleek hair parted in the middle, more like some old photograph than anything living) that he had just sent to the F.B.I. his latest report on me and my friends. God knows into what file of nut mail his conscientious reports were thrown; certainly nothing ever happened, not even a visit from an investigator.

Nor did anything ever come of the Wisconsin Young Communists' informing, less frankly confessed; though when the War broke out and my own politics had dissolved into confusion, certain Trotskyite leaders of the Teamsters Union in Minneapolis, who used to come to address our anti-war rallies in Madison, were—at Stalinist instigation—thrown into the clink, where one of them died. But to me, nothing. Not a thing. Except a Ph.D., a marriage, a first child, a job, a new life—in the intervals of which I have continued to hunt down demonstrations, a frustrated vocation having become a sport and consequently unfrustratable.

No matter. For better or worse, and for whatever reasons, I found myself marching down the streets of Rome in the spring-

time of 1951, side by side with my Italian students, who should
have been listening to me talk about the White Whale but who
had been on strike for weeks. They were howling in unison as
they marched for Trieste, *"Italianissima Trieste,"* an odd slogan
for someone with my beginnings to echo, but I howled along
with the rest of them. And when the police cut us off just before
the American Embassy, toward which we were advancing, I almost hurled the cobblestone someone had thrust into my hand.
Almost. But then the *celere* were on us, the riot police "making
the carrousel" in customary fashion, which is to say, cutting the
crowd into smaller and smaller groups by making ever tighter
circles in their jeeps, from which they leaned out to thwack any
available heads. And finally the power hoses were turned on
against us, jetting *acqua rossa,* which dyed red anyone it
touched. So, as if it were still the spring of 1933, along with the
others, I ran.

Ten years later (my classes empty again, and I with unused
notes on *The Great Gatsby* before me) in the even fairer weather
of Greece, there I was once more—not on the dusty white roads
with the marchers this time, but on the sidewalks looking on, as
the cops with flailing clubs moved inexorably through the demon-
strators and tanks followed at their heels. The occasion was even
more trivial and foolish than the claim for Trieste (something
to do with more classes in religion in the high schools to insure
jobs for graduates in theology), but it had ended in broken heads
and the repeated cry of *"Demokrateia! Demokrateia!"* before
everyone fled for cover. In 1951 I had not really been one of the
howling crowd, but I could pass, since I had still looked young
enough to lose myself among them—indistinguishable, in my
belted black raincoat and my brand new beard, from my neo-
Fascist students. But in Greece and by 1961, I could wear no
other guise than that of a Visiting Professor, my beard grizzled
and my belly bulging: a tourist at someone else's war.

Nevertheless, both in Rome and Athens I had got certain
satisfactions beyond what I had ever managed to get when the
cause for which I marched was really my own; not yet the paddy
wagon or jail, but red water the first shot and tanks the second.
And at last in 1968, in the great student uprising for which all
the others had seemed only preparations and rehearsals, failing

to move fast enough on the Boulevard St. Michel, I got a whiff of tear gas: not enough to make my eyes stream, but quite enough to make my gorge rise.

It was Friday, May 11: springtime as always when cops and kids act out their bloody ritual of repression and revolt; but this time the University would be occupied and a government set rocking before the plainclothesmen, bourgeois and Stalinist, backed up a successful rally by the many-times-routed police.

And though I had not held a rock, much less thrown one, I had, on the previous day—in what I tease myself with believing was the very last lecture in the Sorbonne before violence closed it down—talked to an overflow crowd of French students, whose excitement seemed even at the moment all out of proportion to the event, about Thoreau: Thoreau, mind you, whom I had felt I had betrayed forever on Bergen Street back in 1933. Well, it's a way of keeping the faith, babies, a professor's way; but that is what, in the meantime, I have become.

Part Two

HIGGINS AVENUE: 1958

i

THAT THE MAIN DRAG of Missoula, Montana, was called Higgins
Avenue (and that the parallel streets between it and Mt. Sentinel
were named after Higgins's innumerable children) astonished me
especially. But then everything about that remote college town
in which I found my first job astonished me: the clean sawed-
pine smell of it, the hills hunched around it on all sides, the river
that ran through its center in the wrong direction—toward the
Pacific Ocean, which I had never seen. So dreamlike were my
days that it hardly seemed worth sleeping at night; and so I
would lie awake, listening to the long hoot of the Milwaukee
trains bouncing from side to side of Hellgate Canyon, the rumble
of the great lumber trucks that set my windowpanes to trembling.
And I would wonder was that really an Indian I had seen that
day pushing a cartful of peanut butter in the Safeway Store? Or
what do all those cowhands lined up in front of the ticket
window at the Rialto Theatre make of the images of themselves
projected on the screen inside? Or do those ladies in Pendleton
jackets and rimless glasses *ever* take their hair out of the curlers
they wear under kerchiefs, going to pick their kids up at school
and shopping up and down the aisles of the Missoula Mercantile?
    But chiefly I kept asking myself why it was here in Missoula
I had come to start my new life, to be a professor in earnest. I
knew, however, that insofar as any choice at all had been involved in the move, insofar as it had not just happened to
happen, I was *here* because it was clearly not *there,* because it
was, beyond any doubt, somewhere else—because quite simply
Higgins Avenue was not Bergen Street. In short I had rein-
vented the West, rediscovered Westering, since I had come like
all the others before me, peddlers and con men and pioneers, not

in pursuit of a vision or a manifest destiny, but only to get the hell out of where I had been.

Yet the mere fact of having made it, having stepped off the train and found myself in that other world—all the dazzle of black rock and blue sky, and evergreens dark almost as the rock itself—did not make me another Me, not at first, certainly. In those early Montana years, in fact, I found the role with which I began—professor, husband, father—an embarrassment and a minor hoax, like a fake I.D. Sometimes, I would think of it as a put-on of everybody else, a kind of comic disguise, which, to be sure, scarcely fooled the giggling girl students who seemed to know me for the boy I was. Entering each class, I would rush to take up my symbolic position behind the teacher's desk and hasten to write my name on the blackboard in my boldest, most illegible hand—before someone could slap me on the back and ask me to my beardless face (I shaved then once a week, whether I needed it or not) if I'd met the new Professor from the East.

Meanwhile, however, my graver colleagues and their wives (who, calling when we were out, would leave mysteriously *three* calling cards apiece) seemed completely taken in, as were my more serious students, especially freshman football stars eager to remain eligible: they called me Professor and Doctor—more often, actually, Prof and Doc—with no more irony than they directed at anyone else in my position. After a while, in fact, my confidence in myself was shaken, and I began to suspect that the real victim of the put-on might well be me, since my credentials seemed as valid as anyone else's. And yet—I assured myself—I could, if I would, unmask myself, prove myself a complete and utter fraud.

True, my Ph.D. was genuine enough; but all the courses I had taken (inscribed on the records as Anglo-Saxon, Poetry of Robert Burns, Lucretius, Old Icelandic, Contemporaries and Successors of Chaucer, etc., etc.) I had taken from the same beautiful old pest and nut: a kind of last Romantic poet, complete with flowing tie and long hair, who had made a sonnet sequence out of the suicide of his first wife, had been a conscientious objector to World War I, and had ended up incapable of moving more than six or seven blocks from his house without falling into abject terror. And from him, with whom I never agreed on anything more particular than this, I had learned that becoming such a pest and nut—and hopefully so beautiful—was the only subject worth studying.

My marriage was quite as genuine; but the J.P. who married me had been one of the leaders of the Farm Moritorium Movement, had been captured shotgun in hand when his ammunition ran out, and had become heavyweight wrestling champion of the Wisconsin State Reformatory during his stay there. He had long since shared all his political wisdom with me, over beers in the Campus Rathskeller; but after the ceremony he gave me a piece of premarital advice. "Be intimate with your wife," he admonished me, "but not familiar. When you have to fart in bed, lean your ass over the edge."

But I did not unmask myself, of course, since even when I told stories about my marriage and my Ph.D., they turned out to be —merely amusing. And so I had to content myself with dashing about to White Fish and Butte and God knows what other Montana places whose very names I could scarcely believe—organizing for the Teachers Union and talking to old-timers, pleased to have found a new ear, about the Wobblies and the Western Miners Union, and especially about "the Company" that controlled then not only the copper but all the radio and press in the State. It was a name that rang still with horrific magic in those days, "the Company," though its last flagrant brutality had been the lynching of a labor organizer in 1919, and the faculty of the University had won a victory over it just two years before, driving out of office the man its officials had presumably picked as University President. Still, the dirtiest thing one could say about a man (speaking, of course, from the Left) was that he "wore a copper collar"; and seeing the slag heaps and gaunt black scaffolding that rose on the flats and mountainsides of the company town of Butte, it was possible to believe politics and the class struggle something more real than abstractions in pamphlets.

What was left of Bergen Street in me had to believe itself political or confess itself dead; and so it survived oddly, dreaming before the derricks of a mountain town, remembering strikes and broken heads it had never seen, only read about. Actually,

s had become vestigial, nostalgic: little more than a
f my desire not to grow old, not to (how the phrase
ı my head) "sell out." Luckily for both of us, I found
-Stalinist on campus, a lonely old man who would
scream at me whenever I reminded him that I was an ex-
Trotskyite, as if I were his son and both of us still true believers.

But how hard it was finally to believe in the words invented
and wrangled over in cities, there in the shadow of a wooden
stadium where deer would venture on certain cold mornings to
nibble the grass; or at the foot of a mountain from whose bare
slopes we could hear coyote howling (were they? were they
really?) in the incredibly wide and starry nights. Politics—or at
least everything that Bergen Street had taught me politics might
be—was on the way to turning into something else: something I
would write about rather than live; a retreating past rather than
a future into which I, and the whole world with me, eternally
advanced; a subject for the ghostly voice of my first book, the
old soapbox voice become merely sounds inside my head, words
on the page.

But in 1941, 1942, I was not yet ready to confess that I was the
survivor rather than the heir of my own youth, somebody else.
No, it took a war to persuade me of that: the war I had long
screamed in easy prophecy from speakers' platforms, which had
already broken out in Europe before I ever crossed the Appa-
lachians, the Mississippi, and the Rockies and which would fall
on the United States, out of skies as far west of Missoula as
Missoula was of Newark, only a few months after I had made
that journey. Having prophesied it for so long, I was, in fact, no
longer waiting for it, no longer really interested; so that I did
not even know the bombs had dropped on Pearl Harbor until
nearly twelve hours after the event. I simply refused in those
days to listen to news on the radio and learn that history could
do no better than to confirm a decade later the prophesies I had
made at thirteen or fourteen, confirm what in fact *everybody* had
known the whole time.

Besides, I hated that War coming, or rather, disowned it. I
find it difficult now quite to remember how obdurately I refused
to grant that it might be in any sense my war; mine had happened long before in Spain and had been betrayed by everybody

on all sides, including me who did not go. Yet I volunteered to serve in that other War and wound up finally translating Japanese documents in Pearl Harbor itself, where, during coffee breaks, I would at last listen to the radio news, thrilling a little at the accounts of their victories, our defeats. It was not simple perversity, but retrospective sentimentality: all that was left of what had once stirred in me rising to take the Oxford Oath, or to explain to the uninitiate why the best of all possible events would be the defeat of the United States, the destruction of Our Side. Somewhere in my troubled head I could sense still the dying fall of a song I no longer sang:

> In 'seventeen we went to war,
> In 'seventeen we went to war,
> In 'seventeen we went to war,
> Didn't know what we were fighting for.
> Time to turn those guns the other way.

But all that was the middle of the journey, as it were, fourteen months after the beginning of my time in the Navy, though still two years before I was discharged and began my long trek home from China where, after Japan's defeat, I surprisingly found myself. What the War meant to me at first was quite the opposite of growing old or even up; once the doors of the Induction Center had slammed closed behind me, I seemed to have grown *down* for a while—demoted immediately from jacket and tie to a genuine sailor suit of a sort I had not worn since my head bobbed waist-high to my mother. Old ladies kept buying me comic books in stations and depots, and girl volunteers would hand me candy bars as I stepped aboard trains; while those who sat beside me in similar uniforms kept offering to swap, inviting me into a world of barter I thought I had graduated from forever, where one *Superman* was worth two *Captain Marvels*. And I would answer quite straight, "Sorry, I've already read it"—I, who just a couple of days before had been called "Doc" and "Prof" by aspiring all-Americans.

True, I acquired after a while a taste for comic books which has lasted me until now, and I had never lost my fondness for Baby Ruths and Milky Ways; but the sailor suit undid me, since once I had sealed myself off behind the thirteen buttons of its fly, I was hopelessly "Hey, Mac" or "Sailor, square your hat": a Yeoman Second Class, haircut to the raw, shut up for the night behind the clang of iron gates, and yelled awake in the morning to do someone else's chores with broom and swab.

Nor did it help much when, after a very few days, I was shipped off to Boulder, Colorado, where my wife waited for me with one child in her hand, one in her belly, and something of my old identity in her eyes. Because there I was back in school again, this time the Naval Japanese Language School, improvised within the shell of an almost deserted University of Colorado by cajoling, bullying, and tempting the draft-shy students out of all the graduate schools in the country—after certain government officials had discovered in horror that scarcely any Americans spoke the language of their enemy. And what kind of a war would that be!

So there we were, presumably the most eminently teachable group of overweight, under-height, anemic, walleyed, flatfooted neurotics in uniform anywhere in the world, but students at least, with classroom habits confirmed over eighteen or nineteen or twenty years and never broken for any of us except a stray accountant, steel products salesman, customs inspector—and me. For all the rest of those learning Japanese in sailor suits, nothing could have seemed more natural than to be boning up for and taking weekly exams or arguing about grades with those that marked them; and in free hours, walking the streets or riding the buses of that foothill city, flipping through flashcards inscribed with the characters which ages before the Japanese had misguidedly borrowed from China. Nor did they find it odd to be seated in wooden chairs with a single broad arm which defined their status as passive note-takers and repeaters by rote. *"Kore was hon des, kore was hon des,* this is a book, this is a book"; the childish chant went on class hour after class hour, and in between, at the signal of a bell, we poured out into the sunshine (I along with the rest) to play childish games with each other: arm-wrestling, palm-slapping, all somehow involving the boys' ritual infliction of small pain.

Well, they had never done anything else; but I had sat behind the other kind of a desk and had walked away from it to Com-

mittee Meetings and discussions of Freshmen Composition, all
somehow involving the grown man's ritual infliction of small
boredom. What I had to learn, therefore, was not Japanese (I
would slip off to the movies when I should have been reviewing)
but how to be a student—quite aware all the while of the other
half of the joke: namely, that those who taught us were busy
learning to be teachers. Like us they had been recruited hastily
from everywhere in the country, but in their case from a nonacademic everywhere, since Japanese had not yet made it as an
approved academic subject. It was therefore an odd assortment
of Japanese-American greengrocers, gardeners, optometrists,
typists, and car salesmen, plus a handful of pale-face mission-
aries from the East, temporarily out of work, who shouted at us,
"Kore was hon des, kore was hon des," and waited for the echo
to come back.

Fortunately, the possession of a wife and (by then) two children qualified me to live off campus, so that I was required to
be a child only four or six or eight hours a day, could sleep and
dream at least as an adult and ex-professor. And I was spared the
indignities of dormitory living with Navy trimmings: regulations
concerning all possible aspects of life posted on every available
space ("MEN WILL NOT USE THE URINALS WHEN FEMALE ATTEN-
DANTS ARE IN THE PROCESS OF CLEANING. THIS IS AN ORDER.");
required Japanese conversation at meals; and in the brief time
left unregulated, competition, envy, and the formation of rival
cliques based on earlier school affiliation or natural taste. I
would listen to anecdotes and reports about it all in the intervals
between classes, but it never seemed more real to me or much
funnier than a film heard about from someone else, however
enthusiastic and voluble: how the ex-Harvard boys hated the
ex-Berkeley gang; how the Yalies despised both; and how everyone joined together to snicker over the faggot circle that did
flower arrangements and squatted Japanese style on tasteful
mats, listening to homemade recordings of the *haiku* they had
written to each other. And how perhaps even they managed to
condescend to the *salami-gumi,* the wurst club that shared with
each other the weekly food packages sent by mothers in Brooklyn or the Bronx, goodies to sustain life in the Gentile hinterlands.

To make matters more complex, after about six months we

were put into officer's uniforms—*made* officers, I suppose I should say, though at first (our routine totally unaltered) we were aware only of a change in dress: the blue and gold garb proper not to a kid with a sandpail but to an enforcer with a club. To be sure, the physical misfits and rejects who made up the bulk of our group looked even less convincing as Lieutenants Junior Grade than as Yeomen Second Class; there was one particularly flimsy and swishy type who kept getting arrested throughout the rest of the war (naturally, he never had his I.D. card in his possession) for impersonating an officer. But we were all only impersonating officers, or at least most of us would have been more comfortable to believe so.

Certainly, none of us was ever asked to fire at anyone in anger —only to read and write and, especially, talk, talk, talk. At the war's end our only casualties turned out to be a suicide or two out of loneliness or despair, plus a couple of dishonorable discharges for incidents involving indiscreet newspaper boys; not a single death in combat, in any case, nor any serious wounds.

Yet back there in Boulder they kept assuring us that the whole thing was in deadly earnest, that we were not just run-of-the-mill officers and gentlemen, but trusted members of the Office of Naval Intelligence, which is to say, spies, secret agents by virtue of the classifications on file in the Bureau of Personnel. And to make sure we knew it, we were first of all locked into teacherless classrooms, where, sitting in silence between blank blackboards, we were required to fill in questionnaires which asked, romantically enough, whether we blabbed indiscreetly under the influence of drink or beautiful women, and whether we knew how to play polo!

Then, immediately after, came the Investigations, the security check of everyone. For a month, two months, the terror went on accumulating, unforeseen result of thirty, forty, fifty silly and trivial incidents, thirty, forty, fifty errors of judgment and understanding. During that absurd period, there would be a couple of victims packing up each evening and gone the next morning, found guilty by a court beyond our appeal of what no one had previously known to be a crime. One had given a radio address in praise of peace under Quaker auspices; a second had once had a college roommate who shortly thereafter married a known

Communist; a third had himself married a girl not quite white enough, a Ceylonese in fact. Naturally, the few card-holding, actively recruiting Communists among us were commissioned immediately, leaving the naifs and innocents to pound in vain on the Commanding Officer's Desk and cry what everyone knew to begin with: "Goddam it, anyone with brains and guts sympathized with the Communists in those days. That was 1933!"

And remembering '33, we were none of us children anymore; but for a second time adolescents: called to task for our past, and (when not tossed out as unworthy) declared O.K., full-grown, ready for what came next.

Finally, everyone in our group had been either sent off home or duly commissioned—except for me. And in that limbo of waiting and loneliness, appropriate enough to any adolescence, I decided it had all been a mistake from the first—my junket back toward childhood via the Navy, via the war. Was this trip necessary, I asked myself in the cant phrase of the moment, or, indeed, even possible? At age twenty-five, I should have known that no one can ever stay in childhood, even when the whole world is popping off guns; he can only light there for a moment, and then move on to that nightmarish in-between place where the Officials-in-Charge—principals, parents, C.O.'s, it makes no difference—threaten anyone who steps out of line with the canceling out of his whole planned future. I had already made it into such a future once, and I could go back to where I had left it in cold storage in Missoula, Montana, so to hell with them. "Pack up," I finally said to my wife one night, long after she had guessed my mood and was ready. "We're going home. To hell with them." And the next morning there was the letter from the Navy Department: I had been cleared and commissioned.

My first feeling was one of dismay, my next of astonishment, my third, and most lasting, of guilt. Now, I knew, there was no way out for me short of a court-martial; and it was as if another, a final door had clanged shut behind me—as if, at long last, I was really *in* the War that was not mine, in for keeps. Somehow, therefore, I must have been an accomplice in my own undoing, by secret wish if not by open deed; otherwise, why did I feel so self-condemned? Later, I tried to piece together the whole story of how I had been cleared, investigating my investigators, as it were, by following their trail back to New Jersey and Wisconsin and Montana; because I needed to know why I had been found, or—to say it as cruelly as possible—found *out*, all right.

What became clear immediately was that, in part anyhow, the Navy had been conned by a strange combination of Newark melodrama and Missoula irony. Investigator Number One seems to have encountered on the street where I grew up the sister of a childhood friend: a hysterical girl whom I remember chiefly as given to throwing kitchen utensils at both of us in her inscrutable rages, but who, confronted by a nosey outsider, drew back the lid of the pram in which her firstborn lay and screamed so all could hear, "You see this kid here. If he grows up to be one-half, one-tenth the man Leslie Fiedler is, I'll die happy!"

And Investigator Number Two, sitting across the desk from the quietly wicked occupant of the office next to the one I had occupied at the University of Montana, concluded his questions by asking, "And to the best of your knowledge, was Mr. Fiedler ever a Marxist?" To which the answer was, the words widely spaced, I know, and hardly audible, "Well, I couldn't rightly say, not knowing much about Marxism myself. But it seems to me that Mr. Fiedler may have been, just may, understand, I wouldn't want to commit myself, some sort of—Lovestonite."

I have no trouble at all imagining Number One flattened by that blast of shrill enthusiasm, at once so false and so true; and I can see Number Two carefully scratching his crewcut head, as he consulted first his memory, then some inadequate glossary of Left Wing Splinter Groups compiled by a W.P.A. project, until, baffled, he must have said, "What the hell. Lovestonite, Lovestonite, I probably got it wrong. Anyway, it's not here, so let's say it's O.K. and be done with it."

They explain a lot, those two encounters, but not enough. Two mistakes alone don't add up to a clearance (or at least I once thought not), but two mistakes plus a small truth do. And that small truth was that, in some fatal if still peripheral way, I had to be, I was O.K. Those bastards had me dead to rights.

I felt absolutely certain of it when, just after our War was over and the Chinese Communists were about to win theirs, I arrested my first and only "War Criminal" in the liberated city of Tientsin. I really wanted only to go home by that time, weary to my heart's core of interrogating the maimed and the dying, and of denying whenever and wherever I could what my uniform seemed so unequivocally to assert. "And how many women have you raped in the Great War?" the old Japanese lady asked me over the tea we drank out of rusty tin cans in the Detention Center on Saipan; and when I answered, "None, what do you think I am?" she took it for modesty or some strange kind of American joke. But what really unnerved me most was the prisoner about to be shaved of his pubic hair for hygienic reasons in a ship's sick bay off Iwo Jima, who, seeing my uniform over the doctor's shoulder, could only believe that the razor that fell toward his crotch threatened castration. And so he pissed all over himself in fright—afraid of *me!*

China, however, seemed at first nothing but fun and games in honor of us, the Deliverers, who were by virtue of that role guaranteed winners every time, awarded Samurai swords and silken kimonos, Ming vases and Japanese dolls. Small wonder, then, that in my euphoria and drunkenness (a drunkenness begun out of fear, when, quartered on Guam, we thought we were about to invade the main island of Japan) I took the arrest to be just one more game—or perhaps another performance, an entertainment like Chinese Opera or the Dance of the Young Lions as performed by *geisha* before their departure for Tokyo. Certainly the Nationalist Chinese Officers for whom I would interpret and who would formally make the arrest seemed toy soldiers fresh out of the box, so stiff and clean and sharply creased.

And the stories they told to justify the move seemed the stuff of melodrama, the background of something to be played before bed rather than lived in broad daylight. There was a certain Japanese mastermind, they assured us breathlessly, very rich, very powerful, who was presently holed up, disguised in Chinese clothing, in an abandoned factory. He had stolen a vast treasure which he then buried beneath a junk heap behind his hideout, where he kept by force a twelve-year-old Chinese girl with whom he whiled away his time in unspeakable pleasures; he had committed innumerable atrocities, the worst of them the deballing of a ricksha coolie who had offended him by dawdling in harness. It sounded ridiculous enough on the face of it by any standards I was aware of; but what did I know of War Criminals and China, except out of melodramas? It might well have been true, all of it; certainly, it had to be looked into.

But of course it was not true. The War Criminal turned out to be a plump, scared businessman in padded trousers and a stained skivvy shirt, whose only hoard was an accumulation of canned goods, chiefly fruit; and the twelve-year-old, whore or not, clung to him not like a prisoner but like a ward, though whether she thought of him as father, uncle, or lover was hard to tell. Certainly she wept bitterly and in terror as we led him toward the rickety back steps at the foot of which our jeep waited; and he turned back, again and again, to press small gifts on her and pat her head, at which the Nationalist Officer snickered and made remarks I needed no Chinese to understand. "The daughter of an old friend," he explained hopelessly. "I promised her mother I would look out for her when the troubles came." But when I translated, the Chinese officers only snickered louder.

And who could believe him, after all, on this score more than any other: a War Criminal, a hoarder of stolen gold, a killer and mutilator of coolies. When we dug for the gold next day, however, on the precise spot where our informants had located it, it was not there. And what about the coolie, then, and the other atrocities? Troubled and confused, I went, following the fiasco of the treasure-hunt, to the City Prison where my Nationalist confreres had presumably taken our Criminal. But the warden would not see me, and the underling who consented to talk to me after many delays and small lies consulted his records and assured me that no such person as I described was presently in prison, nor had anyone fitting his description ever been. It was all some sort of mistake. Very odd. Very unfortunate. Perhaps a language problem was involved.

It proved to be an effective charm, that very odd, very unfortunate mistake; for only a day or two later, my orders for home, which I had begun to despair of receiving, arrived and were delivered. And so there I was, strapped into a bucket seat in a plane heading eastward at long last, but with all remaining questions about my War Criminal forever unanswered. Of one thing I was sure, however, playing back in my mind as I jounced in and out of sleep over ten thousand miles the scene of the arrest in which I had been not victim but victimizer, not offended and on the run, but offender and on the prowl: that I, too (though only this once, I hoped), could play the cop. Did I remember really, or only dream afterward, that the little girl had clung weeping to the fat legs of her protector while I—like a Gestapo agent in a bad film—had dragged him heartlessly away?

ii

THERE I WAS—*out*, out of war and into peace, which is to say, nowhere. And appropriately enough I first found that new-old nowhere in the place where I began: not in Missoula, but back in Newark, where my two boys, who had been growing older all the time—not knowing any better—threatened to overtake me (one was by then four, the other two) as I prepared to grow young again by returning to school. This time, my third and last, it was going to be not just someplace that would have me, but the place I had read about in boy's books: alien, upper-class, unattainable Harvard. And why not?

Why not, indeed, since Harvard turned out to be, in fact, inhabited chiefly by veterans like me and their wives pushing baby carriages: an island of irrelevant grass constantly invaded by whooping kids on tricycles, pursued by whooping parents, who, drunk and after dark, took over those tricycles. It was, however, drunk and after dark most of the time, or at least so I recall it: someone always singing joyously off-key or playing the Poetry Game or falling out of a tree or being hypnotized or deciding he was in love with someone else. It was a prolonged recess in a surreal playground, debouching mysteriously in a Ph.D., the whole thing set up as if on purpose for those poor souls who had been deprived of their youth by the war, or those harder cases (like me!) for whom a second youth provided by the war had not seemed enough.

Needless to say, I loved it; and before the first month was out, my Navy experience had begun to grow as shadowy as it was presumably supposed to remain to everyone else, my Certificate of Discharge reading: "The individual was employed in a position of special trust and no further information regarding his duties in the Navy can be disclosed. He is under oath of secrecy, and all concerned are requested to refrain from efforts to extract more information from him." I would reread it occasionally (when two kids seemed too many for my tiny prefabricated house) to raise my spirits, or even occasionally show it to someone else to impress them with the glamor of what I had theoretically performed on their behalf. But most of what I could remember about my actual "duties" involved nothing more than sitting at a desk hunched over certain papers, in a circle of perhaps a hundred others similarly employed, and rising every once in a great while to make some perfectly reasonable request of the Commanding Officer, who never failed to answer, "Go shit up a rope!"

To be sure, I had also titillated an old lady on Saipan, scared a wounded enemy off Iwo Jima, and played the cop in China; but what I had done most of the time was described fairly enough, though with excessive discretion, by that same Certificate of Discharge: *Translation. Research. Analysis. Administration.* "Interpreting" or "interpretation" would have said it all in a single apposite word, since, indeed, "interpreter" was the name I had been officially called as I strove in a time of war to connect where everyone else divided, mediate where everyone else attacked. I have never forgotten a phrase of Lenin, who, asked what was the chief task of a revolutionary, had answered, "Patiently to explain"; but at that point in my life, I began to question whether the English rendering I knew might be inaccurate, whether "Patiently to interpret" or even "Patiently to translate" might not say it better.

At any rate, I retranslated my own revolutionary mission to myself during that recess of my life at Harvard, where I was in fact translating every day, as I learned Old Testament Hebrew in the Divinity School and worked in the library on an international anthology of verse—never, alas, published or even completed. I was, in short, still engaged in the two traditional modes of interpretation that I had practiced from the start, without, however, being quite aware of it. On the one hand, I kept trying to interpret what survived of the past to the present, i.e., to the young, including, at first, myself; and it was for this end that in graduate school I had studied Latin and Gothic, Anglo-Saxon and Old Provençal, Old Norse and Middle High German. On the other hand, I had begun even earlier trying to interpret the present to what survived of the past, i.e., to the old, who were to include, after a while, myself; and for this end, even as an undergraduate, I had introduced my teachers to Auden and Kafka, and had risen in the middle of Tennyson lectures to praise Gerard Manley Hopkins.

I had tended to underrate this double strategy a little, I think, before I had come fully to understand it, because it seemed to me too easy, too cheap. But the war had taught me how dangerous it was in fact to cross any battle lines, or to join in any way those pleased to think themselves irreconcilable enemies: not an evasion or a betrayal at all, but a fulfillment of myself, a way of keeping the faith. What had been partly concealed from me in the classroom and at academic committee meetings became sufficiently clear in combat.

"Don't kill those prisoners, I have to talk to them, learn from them what we need to know to survive," I would patiently explain to certain Marine officers, who would watch me hostilely, skeptically, their fingertips touching the butts of revolvers embossed with pictures of their girls and wives. Or "Cut it out! Stand back, for Christsake. What do you think you are, heroes?" I would yell at the sailors who crowded the rails of our ship, drawn knives in hand, every time we were about to take a prisoner-of-war aboard for questioning; and I would watch the rage and frustration on the faces that responded, "Aye, aye, Sir."

What remained to do in the playground of Harvard was only to work out the analogies in detail, to say it to myself the way it really was. Simply to learn to speak someone else's language is to seem a double agent to those who need to believe in clearly defined sides: the Past, the Present; Right, Left; America, Japan; Male, Female; Straight, Queer; Them, Us; You, Me. Dialogue is the opposite of war; and at least one party in every dialogue must be an interpreter, which is to say, a traitor to those for whom any peace is a betrayal. This I learned at Harvard, after I was all through with grades and degrees.

But to have learned so much was to have found for the first time the possibility of an authentic career, a way of leaving youth behind without seeming to despise or impugn it. And it was high time, since before I was ready to leave Harvard, I had already turned thirty. Thirty or not, however, it turned out to be impossible to do more in Cambridge than merely prepare for that career.

Part of my problem were the representatives of the Rockefeller Foundation, who were subsidizing my stay and would appear at odd moments to insist, with the greatest good will, that I remain faithful to the terms of our contract which pledged me to rest, refreshment, and research—certainly no real living until the terminal date. Another and perhaps more important part was the community itself: too close and cozy to encourage mediation at all. Who needed an interpreter where everyone spoke the same language and marched on the same side? In the end, I felt not merely unemployed but a little bored (as on a really successful vacation) by a world in which all bookcases held the same books and all readers the same opinions.

It was not merely that we had been cast up by the same war, but that most of us had been born in the same small area bounded on the one side by Boston and the other by New York, with outposts in Newark and Brooklyn; that we had made the same political commitments and undergone the same disillusionments at almost the same moment; and—worst of all—that we were headed for the same fate: i.e., success, primary or secondary, recognition and the big money—or a failure so interesting that somebody else would achieve fame and cash by turning it into a book or movie.

I never felt the whole exhilarating-melancholy weight of it more strongly than in the class in Modern American Poetry, to which we came faithfully three times a week during that Harvard year of 1946–1947, leaving our separate prefabs to rehearse, as it were, for the larger world to come. It seemed somehow the center of what we all had begun to suspect would one day be the center of everyone who read, the center of Us. There would be the little gray professor (dead by his own hand only a short while later) making silences into which we rushed, as he curled like a cat in his chair. And there at the very front of the room, the charming young man destined to be the most successful and elegant of the suburban poets of the fifties, talking and talking. Meanwhile, silent in a back row, the minimally articulate sobber, who would replace him in critical esteem when the fashion changed in the sixties, sat and bided his time, unheeded by everyone.

We were all of us writers, we knew, all of us destined to make ourselves heard, we were sure, whether as novelists, poets, or critics, so what did it matter who talked at any given moment; each represented all. And our faith in ourselves seemed to be confirmed by the literary agents, publishers' representatives, and editors of little magazines who swarmed into Cambridge, having got the word, and eager to be first to get this sector of the Future (Columbia already checked out, along with the America returners from Downing College) on their lists. Why then did I, when the excitement of it ebbed, dream of Missoula, Montana, where scarcely anyone was reading the few things I had published, and where almost as few read anything else I regarded with special affection: a closed world where the only word from the great outside was borne by salesmen peddling freshman texts and parents of young instructors looking out warily for Indians as they stepped off the Chicago Express.

It was not that nothing happened to me at Harvard, merely that it happened in silence, secretly even from myself sometimes, always from others, since if I was not quite voiceless, I was still in the process of finding a voice. In any case, the only polarities I found to mediate were in myself, the only interpreting I could do was between one side of my own head and the other. Therefore, I set about learning to read American Literature, on the one hand, thus making peace with Walt Whitman and Mark Twain, whom graduate school had convinced me were as dull as those who taught them. On the other, I worked on the Old Testament, thus making peace with my ancestors and their God, whom Hebrew School had persuaded me were as irrelevant as those who preached them. And slowly, slowly I began to become a writer, continuing to produce stories as I had for a long time and poems as I had for even longer—but also and even especially, as I wrestled with Isaiah and Huck Finn, essays —in which my street-corner voice learned to criticize my street-corner self.

Actually, my first book, *An End to Innocence,* was taking form, though I did not publish any of the thirteen (for the original states? the age of Bar Mitzvah? the divisions of the 1855 *Leaves*

of Grass? or the buttons on the fly of my old sailor suit?) essays
I included until I had returned to Missoula. No, I could not see
the shape of that book, out of which all my others were to come,
fiction and nonfiction alike, until I had got back to a place where
neither friends nor enemies made such books, or even talked
about them. I could not find the shape of myself until I was
back with those who—at home, or at the poker table, or before
the slot machines in the Press Club—knew that conversation dealt
properly with babies and heating plants and prices and other
people's adulteries and the weather; for art, like love or the good
green grass, grows not in the air, not on the wind, but from
deep beneath the weather, underground, in silence and the dark.

I do not mean that I ceased talking about other larger matters,
about politics and poetry and religion; but these I discussed not
as a comrade or friend or spokesman of a party, but as one
both amateur and professional, professionally amateur—as an
Interpreter, if you will, or to use the title by which I was introduced, a Professor. And those to whom I talked were neither
a clique nor a crowd, neither a party caucus nor a mass meeting;
they were, oddly enough, "organizations," those strange groups
who together (but they are precisely *not* together) constitute
the audience outside of large cities and great universities: the
Kiwanis Club, the American Association of University Women,
the Montana Institute of the Arts, the As You Like It Club.
Often they had not the faintest idea of what they were getting
when they got me, since more likely than not I would have been
called at the last minute by some "Program Chairman" at the
end of his (more usually her) tether.

But to all I patiently explained, translated, interpreted what
they neither knew, nor knew they did not know, nor cared they
that did not know they didn't know; interpreted me to them. I
suppose it was not much different teaching their children in class,
since the teacher teaches himself, diffidently at first, shamelessly
after a while. But in the University my context was always the
"Course,"—Freshman Composition, Lyric Poetry of the Renaissance, Shakespeare—a part of the compulsory boredom from
which students sought to escape; before "organizations" I represented an escape from what was boring and required in their
lives. Both were challenges, one to give freedom to structure, the

other to give structure to freedom; and I think I enjoyed the
second a little more.

I talked to my "organizations" about what was on my mind,
not theirs, what was fast becoming my first book: the ambiguity
of politics; the curse of innocence; the subversiveness of art. Or
more concretely, personally, the oddity of being an Easterner
in the West; a Jew in a Gentile world; an ex-Communist among
those to whom the very word with or without an ex- was a curse;
a liberal, which is to say an exponent of the third way, in a
time of right-wing repression and left-wing lies; a lover of courage
in a time of no heroes at all. I did not give them (but saved
for publication in metropolitan journals which turned out later
to have been subsidized by the C.I.A.) accounts of my special
distress over the cases of Hiss and Chambers, of the Rosenbergs
and of Joe McCarthy, in which over and over and again those
who might have shouted in the faces of their accusers that in
the thirties they had spied for the Soviet Union chose instead
to cry, "Innocent, innocent, innocent," and so were jailed or even
died for a mere equivocation, for nothing at all. What cheer
this gave the C.I.A. they are welcome to; for me, it was the
occasion only of grief.

Nonetheless, sparing them the details meaningful only to those
who felt themselves in the dock with Hiss or Ethel Rosenberg,
I tried to make clear to my Montana listeners the sense in which
the old distinctions of Right and Left, American and anti-
American, were a delusion and a trap for them in all their
Western purity, as well as for the apologists of the Soviet Union
in all their Eastern duplicity. And lest they think I scourged
only myself and the world I had left behind, I spoke to them
of the poverty of spirit betrayed by their own wooden faces;
and the absurdity of their acting out, for the sake of tourism
and the lying pieties with which they protected their parents,
some Chamber of Commerce version of "going Western"; and
the panic which lay behind their reactions to Jews and fairies
and Indians. Occasionally they would make noises of protest
back at me, or meet some sally with disapproving silence; but
chiefly they would laugh and applaud or, pressing up to me
afterward, take me by the hand to say how interesting it had
all been.

But then, on the verge of forty, I made my book at last, my not-young man's book out of what I had told them, plus what I had saved for readers much more like myself, which is to say, more victimized by left-wing illusions than by right-wing self-deceits. It was a much more *American* (as well as somewhat more Jewish) collection of essays than I might have made earlier or was to make later, because two confrontations had helped confirm for me in the meanwhile the identity I had discovered rereading *Huckleberry Finn:* my encounter with the Italians on my first trip abroad in the early fifties, and my dealings with the Indians in Montana just before and after. To both I had talked as I had been learning to talk to the Book Club ladies of Montana, using what Italian I had for the former, and for the latter, what lay behind all language, the sound of my voice and the swing of my body.

Face to face with the Italians, I knew myself to be an American simply because, compared to them, I was something else; and what other name is there for the European's Other, than that title I had long regarded as more than a little comic? Face to face with the Indians, however, my American-ness seemed called into question once more—rooted as it was not in the land their ancestors had hunted for thousands of years, but only in a language which even my grandparents hardly knew. But they resolved my doubts by adopting me into the Blackfoot Tribe, facing me West, and shoving me from behind so that I stumbled into rebirth as an imaginary Indian: at once the absolute American and the nightmare terror of those paleface invaders who had invented the name.

Between them, the Italians and the Indians managed to convince me of the truth of what Mark Twain had first suggested to me: that no one was born an American even in America, only adopted or reborn as one; since America was a myth created in the dialogue between those who at any point inhabited our land and those who remained outside. And understanding this, I understood that to keep on being an American—or more properly, to keep on becoming one—required not a pledge of allegiance to some definition given once and for all but a resolution to change that definition, whatever it might be, to suit oneself, one's history, and one's fate.

This, then, is what I thought I was announcing in my book: the news that Redskin, Paleface, Negro, and Jew—we were all of us each other's invention, no one of us more real than another, and none of us as real as Huck, who invented us first. This truly subversive notion disturbed no one, however, perhaps because no one noticed it. What did bug certain of my old political friends in the East was what they chose to call my "Red-baiting": i.e., my assertion that Alger Hiss play-acted and lied; that the Rosenbergs should have been spared not because they were innocent, but because of the triviality of their guilt; that "left" did not automatically equal "good" or "true."

What troubled my new political enemies in the West, on the other hand, was what they did not yet bother to call "Montana-baiting": i.e., my unkind remarks about the immobility of their faces and the inanity of their ideas about Indians. My attitude toward "Reds" they thought they approved of, understanding it as little as those who disapproved. Meanwhile, my colleagues in the academic world were concentrating on the single essay, "Come Back to the Raft, Ag'in, Huck Honey," convinced that it asserted Mark Twain was a faggot and that I was, therefore, guilty of slander, fatuity, and, in general, behavior unbecoming my station in life.

Only the Indians themselves continued to dig me, because they did not read; and besides, the man who wrote those essays signed himself with a name that belonged to a man from Newark, New Jersey, rather than one who had been reborn as Heavy Runner. No, it was in response to pre-Indian exigencies that I wrote *An End to Innocence,* whatever role the Indians had played in helping me discover who I was. What did they have to do with my conviction that since no one would ever again stand up in court to justify seeming treason in the name of ultimate justice, it was incumbent on those who would be beautiful traitors to bear witness henceforth in books? It was an obligation to revenge that the Indians had laid upon me when they re-named me Heavy Runner: an honorable name which I shared with a mountain in Glacier Park as well as a great Chief who, they assured me, "had gone East and come back with the weapons of his enemy."

Shortly thereafter I went East in fact, to spend a year at Princeton; but when I returned, I bore no trophy of victory except for the beginnings of a vast horrific-comic overview of American fiction which I would call finally *Love and Death in the American Novel,* and of which a disturbed critic was to remark, "Wherever anti-Americanism is at home, this book will be welcomed."

I enjoyed Princeton well enough, as I have enjoyed all the parenthetical episodes of my life (being, if anything, overfond of parentheses); but I had the sense somehow that failing my Indians, I was failing my essential, which is to say, my Montana self. And that suspicion seemed confirmed, when, being so close for once, I revisited N.Y.U., my undergraduate university, only to be told by a former teacher that I had been—long, long ago— "a very difficult young man." Watching him watching me, I could see that he felt at ease with me at last, sure that, quite like him now, I was no longer "young" or "difficult," perhaps not even quite a "man." Certainly not "very" anything.

Maybe it was no more than I deserved, having returned to the place I'd left as an untidy Red from Newark in the guise of a Visiting Professor and Christian Gauss Lecturer from Princeton: that clean old town, whose very A & P storefronts declared, in their fake colonial austerity, how many millions of light-years they were from Bergen Street, which lay, in actuality, only about forty miles north down the pike. My writing students, certainly, well-tended, well-heeled Preppies all of them, understood that cultural distance and were given to handing in stories about how, feeling desperate, they had gone off to *Newark* to get laid —but encountering some sodden old Princeton alumnus at a bar, had been persuaded while there was yet time to return intact to their artificial paradise.

In all ways they increased my sense of alienation from my past, most simply by calling me "Sir" at the end of every sentence (the rudeness of Montana students had protected me till then) so that I felt myself become grayer and more reverend moment by moment, but especially by the anecdotes they would tell me in perfect trust. There was the boy, for instance, who boasted of how well he had got along that past summer with his fellow workers in a factory (whose superintendent, he explained, was an old friend of the family), because "My motto is, sir, *everybody* is human."

And then there was the young man who came one day to tell me that his mother had been accosted on her way back from the New York Public Library to her Park Avenue apartment by "this ragged old beggar or something" (it was the year everyone talked like Holden Caulfield) who, after staring long in her face, said, "Shit on you, you rich bitch."

"Now why did he say that, sir?" my student asked; and of course I found no answer for him, as I found no answers for anyone that year—until I managed to write "Nude Croquet" and "Dumb Dick": a dirty story and a dirty poem, variations both of them on what seemed to me the dirtiest of all themes, growing old and going away.

Returning to Missoula, at any rate, I told the story of my disconcerting visit to New York University the first chance I got. I was speaking to a student group which called itself the Friday Club, since—they used to boast in the lovely Missoula way—it met on every other day of the week; and I could not resist talking about "the problem of the younger generation," for the first time in my life, though I was uncomfortably aware of how standard a subject it was for forty, like Today-I-am-a-Man for thirteen.

I can no longer quite recall what I said on that occasion; but looking over an obviously garbled account of the talk in a campus newspaper for November 1, 1957, I learn that I was moved to cry out: "There aren't even cops on the New York campuses anymore. They don't need them," stirred by a wonder nobody not a survivor of the thirties would have understood. Then I apparently went on, "presently everybody is writing to let everybody else believe anything he wishes, because nobody really believes anything," which seems a little silly in the light of what was to come. And in conclusion, if the student reporter can be trusted, I seem to have insisted that "the thing to do is keep your neighbors disturbed. While they are in pain, they know they are alive."

Judging by the response in the letters columns of the following days, my listeners must have been taken in by the pretense that I was talking about them; it was a time when young people

in the universities spent most of their energy blaming themselves
for not having enough energy to do anything else, though, in
fact, Allen Ginsberg's *Howl* had already appeared, preparing for
them quite another kind of voice. Whatever may have been happening in California, however, in a thousand Missoulas, students
still thought of themselves as the "silent generation," cripplingly
aware that they had been born too late for one youth revolution
and not yet able to perceive that they lived on the verge of
another. It was a lack of vocabulary they felt most of all, being
moved as the young are always, to abuse, but finding words to
abuse only themselves and their age.

In any case, I had not been talking about them really, certainly not *to* them, whose attention I felt only as the occasion
for a soliloquy. In the presence of the young, I have long believed, one should talk only to and about himself; since nothing
is more vain (how I wish those who have over and over charged
me with corrupting the youth knew this as well as I do) than an
old man trying to whip up the young—no matter how honorable
his motives. On the other hand, I find it endlessly fascinating to
tell the young how it is with me, just as I did to inform the old
about my own state when young. And I have always found my
auditors, old and young, equally interested.

Even more, however, I like disturbing the peace, whenever
that peace seems to me the product not of mediation but of
torpor and fear. And to do this, one must talk to his peers, which
I did one day in April, 1958, when—as every year in that cold
climate—we were all taut with the pent-up fury of an apparently
endless winter, convinced that the release of spring would never
come without some act of political madness or sympathetic magic
on our part to break the spell. Oddly enough, in Montana it had
traditionally been the faculty which went thus publicly mad at
the vernal equinox, our kind of student being then incapable
of anything more political or magical than a panty-raid.

In the springtime of 1958—seventeen years after my first arrival in Montana and some five after having become a full
professor—I arose before an audience of faculty and students to
demand the removal of the President of the University. "I would
strongly urge a declaration of No Confidence in the present
administration," I said, summing up. "I myself (and I speak, I

repeat, only for myself) can see no prospect for decent teaching conditions or for the good will that makes education possible so long as the present administration stands." It was mild enough, close to what I remember as one of those lovely speeches in which for once the words seem not invented but found, what one is really after rather than some imperfect indication of it; and the rhythm of one's voice is like the shape of the truth one sees, one's tone the true color of the passion one feels.

If it had been an Indian meeting I was addressing, where the first real roar of assent ends all legislative deliberation, becoming action before it dies, it would have been all over that very afternoon. But the world out of which I and my listeners came, and to which we would return, was a world not of immediacy, but of newspaper reports and second thoughts, further consideration by committees, parliamentary procedures, and a series of inconclusive votes up an inadequately defined chain of command; far from anything being over, it had all just begun. But I had already had what the part of me wanted that had been properly renamed Heavy Runner: the moment of saying how it is, of making it how it is by saying it; and I had, therefore, had all the response that Heavy Runner could dream—not majority subscription by a show of hands or a counting of secret ballots, but the creation of a consensus that asserted itself in a simultaneous release of breath and a synchronized leaping of the heart.

It was Leslie Fiedler, Leslie A. Fiedler, as I still made a point of signing myself, who would have to live through what followed, as, indeed, he—I—had surmised beforehand, with a sick heaving over of the stomach. The deposition of a leader in a bureaucratic, parliamentary community means either a true revolution, a kind of reversion to tribal life which obviously our minor power-struggle could never become, or else it is a headache, a long pain in the ass—with the possibility of someone's being defeated in the end, but no hope of a victor. All this I knew at forty, having lost the immunity of ignorance along with the stable inner chemistry of youth. I had survived the collapse of my liver in Italy, the melancholy of hepatitis; now I was about to live out in America events that would justify that pointless depression.

Why, then, had I started it all, knowing what must come, especially since some seventy per cent of the faculty had already voted (in my absence) confidence in the President? There are ways enough to be difficult, if that only is the point—some quiet and sneaky and satisfactory, as any imaginary Indian knows. Why *this* way?

The text of my ten-year-old speech is before me, and it opens with the answer I was prepared to give then to these questions. "I should like," I began, "to make clear *why* I am speaking to you; though it would be easier, more comfortable, to remain silent. Some of my colleagues, I know, will resent what I am saying, will think me a disturber of the peace. The issue seems to be settled; the faculty has voted. So let's settle back into the old routine under the old regime, which is not really so bad. In return for eating crow occasionally we are given pay raises and the privilege of watching such fellow faculty members as will not eat crow get themselves fired. Even many who agree with me would hesitate to wash dirty linen in public. My own conviction is that it is better to wash it in public once and for all than to continue to wear it in private. When it gets dirty enough, it can no longer be kept secret. . . ." Etc. Etc.

The immediate occasion for this onslaught will not repay rehearsal; like most squabbles that move academics deeply enough for action, it was at once quite mad, quite banal, and quite irrelevant both to fundamental issues of education and to what was really bugging those concerned. Suffice it to say that it involved such classically unresolvable questions as "standards," distinctions between in-state and out-of-state students, pay raises for present staff versus expansion. The whole issue had, by the time I spoke, almost disappeared behind just such a haze of ennui and paranoia as makes most novels about university life at once quite convincing to those who know it from inside and completely uninteresting to all readers, no matter what they know. Unlike such novels, however, our case of an unloved President and a faculty revolt was quite unredeemed by the conventional touch of sex, at least at levels available to casual scrutiny.

In any event, the immediate occasion was quite inessential as far as I was concerned, except as it revealed the bureaucratic rigidity, lack of candor, and—especially—the perilous emotional balance of the man at its center. Unfortunately for all of us, he had been a student at Montana State University many years before becoming its President: a particularly unhappy student, it would appear, under quite another name than he now bore. It had been, in fact, an embarrassingly *Jewish* name, which at one point he is alleged to have tried secretly to expunge from the school records; though whether it was properly his or belonged only to foster parents remained to the end unclear. Whichever it was, he seems to have believed that it not merely handicapped but misrepresented him utterly; and his lifelong hatred of it fed the unconfessed anti-Semitism which, in him and others who were to join him, constituted a secret motive of much that was to follow.

Moreover, the President, it turned out, hated not merely that lost name, but all of those—especially his former professors— who had known him under it, poor and excluded and bitter as he had then been. Many of those professors, however, were still alive and powerful in university councils when he returned to us from the bureaus of Washington, where, in the interim, he had learned like a good civil servant to consider forms and memoranda more important than the mere people who filled them out or forwarded them. They had, in fact, managed to remove from office another hostile president in the years between, and must have seemed to him at this moment of assuming that office unforgivably sassy and full of life.

He apparently regarded with special disfavor the tough uncompromising man who had been Chairman of the English Department for thirty-odd years, and whose firing had started the fracas which led to the removal of the earlier president. When I succeeded to that chairmanship, at any rate, he called me into his office and—blowing a screen of cigar smoke between us— invited me to join with him in condemning my predecessor, as a warrant of my loyalty to the new regime. Even if I had hated that ornery beautiful old man, as I did not, I could not possibly have declared it under such circumstances; so I coughed, flapped a hand vainly before me to restore visibility, and changed the subject.

I had as a matter of fact returned to Montana for the third time precisely because I was proud of the department the old chairman had built, though I knew the sense in which he had made it too good for the total institution, and therefore a constant offense to some of my colleagues who only waited a chance to attack. That chance the President, in need of allies and indifferent to their motives, gave them. But not until I had made a mistake, two really: the first an error in strategy, and the second a lapse in self-control.

I had begun soft and easy by appointing new staff members with degrees from Harvard, Yale, and Princeton, figuring that their Ivy League associations would appeal especially to that hunger for and innocence about the traditional which I knew our new President must surely share with all other Montanans. Actually, our students offered each year a ten-dollar prize to the one of their fellows who suggested the "best new tradition," and no administration, including this one, had failed to approve. What had been odd about my first choices (two of them were Jewish, one had a permanent writing block, all were more than normally prickly) had passed unnoticed; what counted with our administrators was the tone of the public notice anything got; which turned out to be, in these cases, quite favorable. It was just the same with the pair of distinguished visitors whom I invited to lecture at almost the same moment: one an alcoholic and inaudible novelist, the other a homosexual and incomprehensible poet.

Nevertheless, hundreds of people swarmed in on us from all over the state, even pitching tents in the fields around campus, for the privilege of not hearing or not understanding them; the newspapers, impressed by the numbers who came, gave our visitors a good press. True, there was one bad moment when the poet, taken like all visitors some five miles east down Route 10 to the Club Chateau for a steak, had cried aloud among real estate agents and lawyers—perhaps genuinely moved at the sight of a bevy of college girls in formals, perhaps only bored enough to feel naughty—"My dears, I know *exactly* how they feel. I used to be a *mad* queen myself." But no one reported it, and no one complained, not even anonymously. And so he, like my first three appointments, passed muster; since—I was about to learn—the only unforgivable thing in the university or the state was to be "controversial."

Meanwhile, however, I had become convinced that it was precisely "controversial" people we needed to recruit into our

Department (and this was, of course, my first mistake): known
eccentrics and misfits, which is to say, those who had already
got into trouble elsewhere by professing the wrong religion or
not professing the right one; by assigning the wrong textbooks
or failing to list the right ones; or by having been born the wrong
color or not being proud enough of having been born the right
one. Otherwise, it seemed to me, we could expect to attract in
a university short on funds and remote from all cultural centers
only the other kind of misfit: the inoffensive and quiet ones who
had failed to make it in the rich and lively world outside, not
because they had in some way challenged the smug mediocrity
of their colleagues, but because they had not been able to com-
pete even on that level. Such men invariably love fishing, and
the fishing was very good indeed in Montana.

And so I began to make offers to young instructors who had
quarreled with their administators, or had asked their students
to read *Catcher in the Rye*, or had themselves written poetry
containing dirty words, or were flagrantly Jewish or simply Black
—and had not, to redeem any or all of these faults, gone to
Harvard or Yale or Princeton.

This decision to proceed imaginatively and without due discretion was taken as a declaration of war by the President, which
it was not; since I thought I had decided to ignore rather than
fight him. And, in fact, he might well never have found out about
it, except that two or three scared White Anglo-Saxon everybody-
else-haters in our department (including a Southern Lady in
whom malice and Christian Science were locked in destructive
combat) began to gossip about our new policy over tea, cock-
tails, games of Hearts in the Student Union, and on hiking trips
into the hills. But this constituted, of course, *controversy*—meaning that we, I, the Department, having become "controversial,"
were now fair game.

Worst of all was the case of the single Negro I tried to hire,
thought I had indeed hired, after he had been cleared by a vote
of the Department itself and approved by all the duly constituted
University Committees. I had actually written him a letter con-
gratulating him on his appointment—and (I'm afraid) myself
a little for having swung it, since we had not yet reached the
time when every campus was hastening to enroll a token Black

on its staff; certainly our University had never done so before. The self-righteousness of administrators worked quite the other way still—in favor of resisting such appointments as provocations, thus protecting the sensibilities of the most self-consciously White members of the faculty and the larger community.

In this instance, the nasty whispers were whispered; a second *ad hoc* Committee was chosen from the slate of Methodist Youth counselors, Air Force Reserve officers and run-of-the-mill toadies, with our own Department represented solely by the Southern Lady; the Negro candidate was rejected on reconsideration and I enjoined to write him a second letter telling him so.

No matter what I wrote in the black lines of that letter, I knew that he would read the same familiar and disheartening message in the white spaces between; and though perhaps *I* deserved the indignity of it all, surely he did not. And so, at my next meeting with the President, I lost my temper, utterly blew my cool, crying that the fight had just begun, that we were not yet through with each other by any means. It was the only time that I have ever blown up on such an occasion, knowing very well that rage is a passion as irrelevant to committee meetings and campus politics as love itself. *Mistake number two.*

I had a year to cool down, however, since I was already scheduled to take off for Princeton shortly thereafter; and despite the fact that my temporary replacement as Head of the Department was (on the teeth of an overwhelming vote against her) the Southern Lady, it was hard—even when sober—to nurse a grudge among magnolias and at a distance of three thousand miles. Besides, neither Princeton nor turning forty proved to be very conducive to sobriety.

I sobered up fast enough, however, when I returned to Montana to discover my colleagues wrangling with each other. Injustice had made them feisty; apparently discretion had suggested that while taking out their grievances on the President might be rather expensive, working it off on each other would cost them neither promotions nor raises.

My choice was clear: to join one or another of the existing factions and settle down to the pleasures of impotent self-contempt; or to speak for myself alone by launching, coolly and on the far side of anger, my promised attack on the President. The

worst that could happen to me would be, I reckoned, total isola-
tion; but loneliness, I reassured myself, offers at least the opportunity for meditation. And so I said aloud—for the benefit of the
students, who, it occurred to me, might as well learn something
from our pain, and more especially of the new faculty (the
turnover in the time of troubles had been, of course, large)—
what I considered my best wisdom on the subject. "The moral
is clear," I told them, after detailing a bill of particulars. "To
know the President is to lack confidence in him."

I must have realized by then that it is both stupid and unfair
to expect anyone to profit by another's experience; and I was
sufficiently aware that even among those who knew the President
as well as I, most would be too circumspect to admit that they
shared my sentiments, much less to do anything rash about it.
It seemed probable that not he but I would, in the end, go down,
have to go away.

Maybe it was time. Seventeen years had passed since I had
first entered Hell Gate to see the mountains beyond; each year
I had assured myself would certainly be the last, since I had
never intended to do more than try it out for a while, surely
not spend my whole life in Missoula. But looking up nearly two
decades later, it seemed clear enough that I was on the verge
of doing precisely that: first, because I had come to love that
absurd place ("where culture and rugged wilderness meet," the
radio announcers told us every day), which was O.K. if disconcerting; and second, because I had become habituate to it, which
was really troubling.

Something like this was no doubt on my mind when I insisted
in my talk that "my conclusions here today are my own. I accept
for them full responsibility. . . ." Or maybe what moved me even
more deeply was my old desire, which had survived my old
politics, to play the part of society's victim at long last, to take
on the role that Sacco and Vanzetti had accepted (or so at least
I still believed in 1958), but Alger Hiss and Julius Rosenberg
had refused. Some sense of just how old-fashioned my stance
really was seems to have possessed my first hostile critics—one
young instructor from the Forestry School (moved by quite other
nostalgias, obviously, than my urban ones) describing it as "a

remnant of the 1920-ish school . . . of debunk," which did not
quite hit the mark.

He was seconded, however, by a member of the Journalism
School, who came much closer, perhaps by virtue of his profession, perhaps because he was another Jew in flight from metropolitan beginnings, he did not ordinarily admit, though he would
give me a smile of tired complicity whenever I would meet him
Sunday mornings taking his little girls to the Baptist Church.

It was the thirties that he called up, returning to what he
knew of my past (obviously he had read *An End to Innocence*)
in an effort to impugn what he called a "shocking diatribe" and
a "vitriolic harangue" which gave "aid and comfort to the enemies
of the university." Nor did he stop short of saying the dread
word "Communist," which, oddly enough, had not been evoked
in Montana even during the just-passed time of Joe McCarthy—
because the Company had a favorable contract with a Communist controlled union and could not afford to rock our boat lest
its own be swamped.

Our irate journalist had no sense, I think, of the frustrated
rage which waited to be released in small-town lunatics and
back-country Right radicals, frustrated by the discretion of Big
Business, whom they expected always to stand by their side. It
was not even rage which moved him, as he claimed afterward,
becoming aware of what he had started and hastening to apologize: "These remarks were uncalled for . . . and made in haste
. . . Leslie, I am sorry." No, he had been a Rhodes Scholar, and
had learned at the Oxford Union the debater's strategy of simu-
lating rage to excuse malice and slander.

But Montana was not Oxford, where games are played by
gentlemen for points; those who listened to and remembered his
initial remarks, but not his retraction, were no gentlemen, and
they played for keeps. What he had said, the following day,
was: "I was reminded Wednesday of the student political meetings of the thirties and forties—when the young Communists
moved in. The tactics, the ad hominem attacks, the labor lyceum
delivery, the so-called facts—all were the same. Dr. Fiedler
loves causes—an admirable trait—just as he loved causes in the
thirties." And before the long hassle that followed was over,

there were to be anonymous postcards directed to me and my supporters inscribed JEW COMMIE GO HOME; in the paranoid fantasies of the Rightist Westerner, Jew and Red and Eastener blend into a single image of fear, all being equally "controversial."

It would not have been so bad, however, had things stayed as simple as that: all the right-wing Enemies of Progress on the side of the President and my traducers, all the Defenders of Trade Unionism and Public Power and officially approved Causes of the Left on mine. And for a while it looked as if it might work that way, quite like a boy's dream of the ideal case, a wicked Them versus a righteous Us. Even the most hard-bitten local Stalinists (inclined to believe any contributor to the *Partisan Review* a Red-baiter and social fascist) rallied to my side, along with the veterans of Populist dissent and the struggle against the Company.

The Company itself, disappointingly, refused to take sides, being—though those who had defined themselves fighting it refused to grant the fact—through with all Montana problems. It was currently in the midst of a process of disengagement, selling its newspapers and radio stations and abandoning its interest in the University, as its major operations were being moved to South America.

I had never quite believed in the legend of the Company to begin with, having discovered that most of those who claimed they had been silenced by its power had been born without voices. What did dismay and pain me, however, was the discovery that the issues seemed much less clear to the right-wing enemy than they did to me; that as a matter of fact, the more naive among them had great trouble in deciding just which side they were opposed to in the fight down there in Missoula. After all, the President was a Jew, too, was he not—a *secret* one, which everybody knows is the worst kind. Besides, he had left Montana to follow the New Deal to Washington, and had even allowed a Negro or two to speak on the campus during his administration. So was not anyone who called for his dismissal all right?

How my heart would drop when, opening the sort of letter whose very handwriting declared it the product of ignorance and malice, I would find vilification not of myself but of *him*.

It happened only twice in the course of our troubles, but that was enough to shake my faith, temporarily yet deeply, in the justice of my cause, the justice of *any* cause, whose final meaning is the sum total of all perceptions of it. "I am glad someone is moving in on the president," one such nut wrote," whose bosom friend is Bayard Rustin, the nigger jailbird. . . . It makes you weep we have sunk so low." Another anonymously confided of my opponent: "he is a man who has a big head so bad . . . that you can't reach him with a ten-foot Pole. . . . He was Roosevelt's lawyer—that is enough said. . . ."

In any case, there was never a face-to-face confrontation with the President, nor even a chance for another direct onslaught; having declared war, we became immediately unavailable, invisible to each other. A fight was what I had longed for, real contact between real men over real issues; what I got instead was an endless series of meetings and caucuses, varying in size and degree of secrecy, and usually concerned with the question of when and where to hold the next meeting. These meetings were, of course, attended only by Our Side, and so we spoke, of necessity, to each other. That their side was also caucusing about when they should caucus again, we surmised, because what else was there for them to do? Besides, we had spies who checked out the houses of known sympathizers with the President, counting the cars that gathered along the curb and attempting to identify their owners; and we could observe, playing the counterspy with an eye to the crack between someone's living-room drapes, their spies counting ours.

But only rumor ever told us what they were planning, who they were contacting, how many votes they had lined up in the main faculty committees and on the State Board of Education. Rumor, however, proved whimsical and unreliable, for them presumably as for us; so what we both knew consisted entirely of what we read in the newspapers, to which both sides talked. It was there, for instance, that we learned that the President, feeling, we guessed, both impatient and confident, had submitted his resignation to the Board to force a decision quickly. In effect, this meant that the vote of non-confidence which I had originally asked of students and faculty no longer depended on anyone in the University, much less in the large community outside, but only on the ten or eleven (depending on whether the Governor cast his vote) members of the Board.

It was to these that all interested parties had now to address themselves, bullying or cajoling, calling up old obligations, family ties, or lifelong political associations. The President and I had become irrelevant except as targets for abuse and harassment; this should have been a relief, but somehow was not. I cannot speak for him, since I never talked to him again and only saw him occasionally strolling at nightfall across the campus toward Mount Sentinel, quite as I liked to do. He walked very slowly always, his head down and his body hitched a little by the not-quite-limp which made him easily recognizable; he would pause every once in a while to touch the back of a stone bench, the trunk of an elm, or the brick side of a building. Perhaps he was only resting, but I had the sense that he was trying to reassure himself that there were actual things out there beyond the limits of his troubled head. We were obviously all a bit mad in those days, but he seemed somehow the most disoriented of us all, the most—untouchable.

Certainly I never heard anyone hail him, nor saw anyone approach him, much less take his hand or slap him on the shoulder; and maybe the whole affair came finally to mean for him the loneliness which, in the beginning, I had feared for myself, which is to say, maybe it was he who became the real "victim" instead of, or at least along with, me. In actuality, my case was quite the opposite of his; I could not walk down the street without being buttonholed by friends, acquaintances, utter strangers. True, a very few people in whose houses I had drunk and played cards ostentatiously avoided me—especially one colleague in psychology who had for years oddly wooed me with huge hunks of venison he had shot and bushels of Swiss chard out of his garden. But even he, though he turned his head away as we passed, muttered loudly enough for me to hear the insults that would have been pointless spoken outside my range.

Most people, on the contrary, seemed to feel that, acting as I had, I had given them a warrant for greater intimacy than they would otherwise have claimed. They plied me with questions, sometimes sympathetically, sometimes hostilely; but it was clearly *me*, the feel and sight, the mere presence of me, that they were curious about, rather than my answers to their questions, to which they never appeared to listen. It was as if, becoming an issue, I had ceased being a person and was quite unentitled henceforth to opinions of my own, being now what others had opinions about.

Those opinions they sent me by mail, five-page harangues or two scrawled lines of obscenity; they shouted at me across streets; they wrote in newspaper columns and by-lined articles; they woke me at two in the morning—leaning on my bell until I staggered downstairs—to shout at me drunkenly in my own living room; they confided to my students or my oldest friends, sure that they would be carried to me forthwith. And when toward dawn I had found refuge in sleep from anything that anyone, including me, thought of Leslie Fiedler, the telephone would ring, and I would hear not silence but breath without speech, the music of the long day's hostility without the words.

Worst of all, however, was the press, which hounded me even when my political friends and enemies gave me a little peace. There they would be at my doorstep, or in my office, or on the phone to ask what did I think of so and so, had I yet heard about this and that; and always I was aware of the notebook and the poised pencil ready to misquote whatever I said. I chose silence as the lesser evil, but it did me no good; it whipped them on rather than discouraged them, until I had the sense of an endless pursuit quite unlike any I had imagined on Bergen Street, since the pursuers were not cops but reporters, and the pursued not a victim but a "story." And there was no way out in that little town; even in the darkness of a movie theater, half asleep before the screen that seemed a better guarantee of privacy than my own bed, a voice from the rear would rouse me, drowning out the clatter of imaginary hooves and the shouts of the actors: "Is Dr. Fiedler in the house? Telephone call for Dr. Fiedler." And I would brush past the protesting knees between me and the aisle, hoping they thought me a real doctor called to some emergency, rather than a fool going to talk to the A.P.

But I did not even talk really, except to say, "No comment, no comment." I made no big statements throughout, issued no explanations or apologies; only waited for the vote of the Board that would settle things once and for all, and—whichever way it went—release me from my own harassment, as well as the harassment of others for my sake which I could no longer bear. I had said my piece, delivered myself of the pressures built up during the years I had seemed to suffer injustice; and I began to be overtaken by a feeling I had never experienced before. I was tempted to call it "resignation" or "sweet reasonableness," for it resembled what I had read of such things, and I had been hoping that the end of youth might bestow such blessings on me; but perhaps it was only simple exhaustion. On May 2, 1958, I wrote in this mood what I intended as a final word on the subject.

A particularly troubled young instructor, too fond of both the President and me for his own peace of mind, had posed publicly some thirty questions—all quite beside the point by then—which earlier he had sent me by mail. And in a letter to the student newspaper, I tried to explain why, for all of our sakes, I was taking the trouble to answer only one of them, which asked what I "would consider to be my moral obligation if the decision of the Board went against my view and the majority of the faculty continued to support them."

"I would do what I always have done," I answered, "when a faculty vote has gone against what I consider to be desirable policy: accept that opinion and work inside of it as best I can for the goals we commonly desire. I am never convinced by a majority vote that an idea of mine is wrong; nevertheless I accept it, sustained by a faith in the democratic process. Similarly I shall accept the decision of the Board whichever way it goes; and I shall (for a while at least) hold my peace."

Peace! It seemed the only apt word to close on—though it was, in fact, as inappropriate to what lay ahead as the phrase "moral obligation" was to the horse-trading and low comedy which were actually going on in the Board of Education. The original issues of freedom and integrity had long since been translated down out of the moral realm into that of politics, understood not as I had when I'd first mounted the horseshit box on Bergen Street, but as when, on second thought, I'd called the ward leader to help out in court. In this instance, it was at least Democratic Labor rather than a Republican lawyer who came to the rescue.

Rumors had reached us in the days just before the final vote that the Board was split right down the middle; and so we dispatched one of our more articulate supporters to present our case to a member we'd heard was wavering. "And so you *must* vote to accept the President's resignation," our friend reportedly said at the end of a long, passionate speech; to which the Board Member allegedly responded with the single word, "Why?"

"Why?" our advocate repeated, nonplussed. "My God, I've just finished telling you, for the Good of the University, the Good of your Children, the Good of the—"

But the Board Member cut him off at this point. "Fuck the Good of the University," it is claimed he said, "that's like Home and Mother. Who's on your side?"

"The Secretary of the Mine Mill and Smelters Workers Union," our friend answered, and pointed to where that labor leader sat behind him. And the argument was over, the case won.

The vote was taken on May 6: seven to two in favor of accepting, with one member absent and the Governor spared the necessity of going on record. I had been called immediately after the balloting; but by morning I must have believed it a dream (no one I knew ever won anything, not even a lottery), because I was surprised by the headlines in the newspaper I picked up on my front porch, wincing in anticipation as I had learned to do over the months before. RESIGNATION ACCEPTED, they screamed in red ink, which I had seen used before only for the attack on Pearl Harbor and the end of the War. Why, then, did my heart drop? And why was I oppressed by feelings of guilt?

Simply to have been victorious was, I suppose, enough to depress one whose whole mythology identified virtue with the loser, whose models from childhood on had been Vanzetti and Tom Mooney and Veblen and Dreyfus. But to have won by the same manipulation of power that might, that *should* (if I had been brave enough and true) have crushed me, by strategem against strategem rather than truth against lies, was to have deserved the comic ending at which I somehow could not laugh.

"Fuck the Good of the University," I would say over and over, telling the anecdote as if it were a joke on somebody else, "that's like Home and Mother. Who's on your side?" I knew the joke was on me.

To make matters worse, I had won nothing at all really. True, the frightened and unjust President whose dismissal I had demanded at the start was gone, but his mere absence did not make room for courage and justice. Like some stupid peasant in a fairy tale I had got only what I was dumb enough to ask for. Not a bit more. Besides, all the world turned out to hate a regicide, as I soon learned, seeing some of my more sympathetic colleagues regarding me with a horror whose cause they did not understand, while the man-in-the-street stopped yelling at me to my face and began whispering about me behind my back. And now the writers of anonymous letters were no longer confused; there was just one Jew enemy, not two, only a single man left whose head was so big he couldn't be touched with a ten-foot pole.

Therefore, when they were not busy protesting against Federal irrigation projects, the United Nations, or laws regulating guns, they were writing their legislators about me. In fact, some of the wildest of them were State Legislators, who would rise to ask why a "controversial" figure should get a two-hundred-buck raise *this* year. And one was a Board Member—a loudmouth dentist, as it happened, who considered that his profession qualified him to find hidden decay everywhere.

He had plenty of competition at that game, however, since even storekeepers and housewives felt capable of spotting conspiracy and corruption—which they did practically daily. Did someone articulate and honest run for the local High School Board; the "Fiedler Faction" was at work. Had not my wife signed, along with two hundred others, the nominating petition? Did an Episcopal youth group play in church a disturbing drama by Christopher Fry; the "Fiedler Faction" again. Had not my sons, hiding behind four hundred others, attended the performance? Maybe, indeed, I had written the play myself. Was not "Christopher Fry" clearly a pen name?

Nor had the internal caucusing ceased, since there was now a new University President to be chosen. In fact, there were to be three acting and "permanent" Presidents over the following five years—making eight, or was it nine, for my entire stay: twice the normal rate for state universities, in any event, where Presidents last on the average five and a half years. And how mad-

ness, always at home in universities and never more than at
times of turnover, flourished now; since every paranoic on the
staff had found to his delight a publicly recognized name for the
mysterious "They" who had pursued him all his life long: the
"Fiedler Faction."

No one any longer had to confess that his being fired or given
an inadequate raise might be due to normal bureaucratic incom-
petence or some fault of his own. It was, in each case, the "Fiedler Faction" once more, which is to say, a conspiracy organized
by the President-killers still hungry for blood. And in order to
fight so insidious a foe parliamentary means would not do; what
was needed instead were secret communications to the Board,
unsigned mimeographed manifestos slipped under office doors
during the night—maybe even guns. For two weeks, one particularly disturbed member of our own department stalked the nearest hillside carrying a rifle with telescopic sights; or so at least
he let it be known, in his madness, and so we believed, in ours.

Blessedly, summer vacation came quickly; and the enemies of
the "Fiedler Faction," lovers of the outdoors every one of them,
duly headed for the hills and the lakes—where, alas, they seem
to have renewed themselves for combat (did they hold caucuses
over campfires?), since the fall saw the climax of their attack
in the form of a fifteen-page pamphlet called *Is This Your University?* No one in the university itself assumed any responsibility
for it; indeed, only one man on the entire faculty—the lapsed
provider of venison and swiss chard—would even say a kind word
for it, though some must have smirked in secret satisfaction.
Signed by an alumnus who, after selling off an inherited sawmill,
was living in Missoula with nothing better to do than kibbitz, it
purported to be an exposé of the "minority dissident group"
which "controls the university."

Actually, twelve of its fifteen pages were devoted to a much
narrower set of questions than it promised to confront: namely,
"Who is Fiedler? . . . What does Fiedler teach? Does it parallel
what he writes? What more should we know about him? . . .
What must be done?" A couple of the pages devoted to me
treated my conflict with the President; one dealt with my exchange with the ex-Jewish journalism professor, quoting his
diatribe against me but not his retraction; a couple discussed my

relations with my disturbed colleague with the telescopic rifle;
and the rest offered a detailed analysis of my printed work—
literary criticism, in short, written presumably by and for Montanans, to whom I had first fled precisely because they did *not*
read what I wrote.

Actually, I suppose, the literary-critical passages must have
been provided by the unfortunate with the gun, since he was,
I regret to say, a writer, which means inevitably, a *rival* writer;
the pamphlet itself reported that before his resignation (he had
followed the President out and away) he had done his best to
make the State Board of Education "aware of many of Fiedler's
writings and activities. . . . His material contained many of the
Fiedler quotations quoted here."

What he had put together and turned over to the heir to the
sawmill constitutes a little anthology of snippets from my works,
chiefly *An End to Innocence,* plus a story or two and one satisfactorily pornographic poem. Nothing, however, except the poem
is reproduced complete; and even eked out by occasional unfavor-
able critical comments, the whole remains quite incomprehensible. There was, I suspect, little if any deliberate misrepresentation of the sort I had expected, only a general misunderstanding
on the part of the compilers (quite as dumb as their intended
audience), especially of my tone. Such incomprehension I had
anticipated from the Left, looking only for distortion from the
Right, since despite my boasting about a lost innocence, I
really still believed liberals more honest than conservatives, and
both smarter than anyone committed to politics can afford to be.

In any case (I know now at long last), it didn't matter in the
least if in most of the passages they adduced I was actually
disapproving rather than approving of the leftist tradition with
which they sought to identify me. Negatively or positively, I was
criticizing from *within,* and even at my most negative, with
tenderness and regret. This they perceived more correctly than
my liberal reviewers, some of whom seem to have taken me for
an agent of black reaction; for the latter attended to the sentiments which divided us rather than the vocabulary we shared.
But the former knew that it is words which count, the language
a man speaks, whatever he may think he is saying in it.

Certainly, it was the words to which most of the seven thousand readers (legislators, members of the Board of Education, school superintendents, Kiwanians, directors of Chambers of Commerce) to whom the authors had sent copies would respond, detaching them even from the inadequate contexts provided in the section of the pamphlet called "Writings of Leslie Fiedler— Political." At the head of that section they had set, as a kind of control, the oath I had signed many times along with my yearly contract as a teacher at Montana State University: ". . . support the Constitution of the United States of America and the State of . . . by precept and example, promote respect for the flag . . . reverence for law and order and undivided allegiance to the Government of. . . ."

Coming across it in the pamphlet, I read it through, with some astonishment, for the first time. And turning to my own words, I could see how alien a world they evoked to those who really lived in that presumed by the oath: ". . . myself as a liberal, intellectual, writer, American, Jew . . . influence of Marxist ideas, Communist and Trotskyist . . . sons of the original Jewish immigrants . . . a marriage of Greenwich Village and Marxism . . . from Bohemianism to radicalism . . . *avant garde* aesthetic ideals and radical politics . . . struggle for a revolutionary politics and the highest literary standards. . . ."

Never mind what I was trying to *say;* every word of it must have struck many of those who thought of themselves as paying my salary not only as foreign but as almost dirty. And there were downright vulgarities, scatological as well as political, in the quotation from a review I had written for the *New Republic* (itself suspect), with which the section ended:

> But the phrase 'God's Country' . . . is the hackneyed boast of the insular and idolatrous at home, the sigh of the man to whom the gurgle of the flush toilet under him is the running over of his cup before the Lord.

What better transition could there be to the following series of sections labeled: "Writings of Leslie Fiedler–Dirty," "Fiedler's Stand on Dirty Writing," "Writings of Leslie Fiedler—On Sex," and "Opinion on Aberrant Sexual Literature."

The last turned out to be a lengthy citation from an obscure

book review by a certain professor of psychology from Smith,
which maundered on about the "minority group" of "sexual
aberrants" who "praise one another's work . . . represent themselves as most enlightened . . . decry normal sexual love," and
cause "many sophisticated people" to think of serious art as
inseparable from "sexual perversion." Having quoted it almost
in full, the editor of the pamphlet then asserted—presumably on
his lawyer's advice—"This is not intended to imply anything
about Leslie Fiedler." Yet just a page or so earlier, he had quoted
me on the subject of "chaste male love" as the *leit-motif* of
classic American fiction, ending with my reference to "Huck's
feeling for Nigger Jim"—which he apparently hoped would titil-
late his readers by adding a fillip of miscegenation to simple
homosexuality. The implication is clear, despite the perfunctory
legal disclaimer: I was not merely an expositor and defender of
"sexual aberrants," but, though perhaps not a card-carrying homosexual, a dangerous fellow-traveler.

It all amounted to a flimsy enough case, to be sure, but rested
on an earlier demonstration that I was, in any case, a self-
confessed pornographer as well as a Jew and an intellectual, and
therefore capable of almost anything. As in the case of my
politics, the proof offered for this was the vocabulary of certain
selected passages from my fiction and verse: "pale flagrant breasts
. . . thought seriously of making her . . . rested one hand gently
on her ass . . . she wore nothing underneath, no girdle, no pants
. . . a little tuft of hair where the buttocks . . . can't even remember to button our flies . . . nipples, not brownish or purple but
really pink. . . ."

"Dumb Dick," a phallic poem of considerable tenderness which
had first appeared in *Partisan Review,* was quoted in full—
thus becoming by all odds the most widely circulated of my
almost secret poems, though what corruption might be wrought
by its melancholy music was hard to see:

> Love seethes to suds, seed runs
> Like whey in the raveled vein.
> Dumb Dick stands alone, or shrunken
> Sleeps. No matter. More than the stunned
> Wonder matters; more counts than who comes. . . .

But it was a story called "Nude Croquet" which must have seemed to my detractors the real clincher, not only because it provided frequent passages larded with Jewish allusions and other dirty words, but because the issue of *Esquire* in which it was published had been banned in Knoxville, Tennessee; and I had written in response what I thought a troubled apology for my art, as well as an ironic attack on the very notion of dirtiness in literature. I had, however, called it "On Becoming a Dirty Writer," and those immune to irony could presumably read it as self-condemnation, a confession of sin. Why else would the authors of the pamphlet have reprinted its last paragraph?

The authorities in Knoxville are apparently afraid that the game I describe might become a fad—doubtless among those juvenile delinquents about whom it is fashionable to be concerned these days. But they have clearly not read beyond my title, since my point is precisely how hard it is to strip naked—and how terrible! I had written a story, I thought, about youth and age, husbands and wives, success and failure, accommodation and revolt—and especially about the indignity of the failing flesh—all of which is, it seems to me, a dirty enough story, the dirty story we all live.

Even this, however, was not quite the last word, since the final heresy, the unforgivable sin for Montanans is not to betray decency or to impugn "God's Country," but to prove false to Montana itself and, especially to criticize it to Easterners, outsiders, dudes. Had I not done precisely that, however, in an article originally entitled "Montana: or the End of Jean-Jacques Rousseau"—invariably referred to by natives of the state as "The Montana Face." The article appeared in *Partisan Review,* as well as in a short-lived local magazine called *Montana Opinion* and in a book widely circulated under the auspices of the Unitarian Church; it had been quoted approvingly—in an editorial deploring the resistance of the West to the regulation of guns—by the *Washington Post.*

Oddly enough, Montanans are not really provincial; they only choose to appear so for reasons nostalgic and commercial, which right-wing politicians know how to exploit. At worst, they tend to be decadents playing a canny pastoral game, as I had tried to make clear in a passage of my offending article actually quoted in the pamphlet: ". . . the West is strictly business. There is scarcely a Montanan who does not at one remove or another share in the hoax and the take; who has not like the night club Negro or the stage Irishman become the pimp of his own particularity, an exploiter of the landscape and legend of his state."

At best, they are genuinely sophisticated (this I realized most vividly confronting the naiveté of my Princeton students), as befits the inhabitants of a state which was urban before it was rural, and where, even three generations ago, a lonely horseman crossing its plains was more likely to be recruited for a polo game than for a sheriff's posse.

Perhaps it is the sheer mobility of Montanans that has kept them so little provincial; they seem to have shifted from the horse to the automobile to the airplane without once slowing up or touching the ground. Simply to look at a cowboy's high-heeled boots is to know how far even the most mythical and authentic Montanan is from the dull earthbound plod of the peasant. And in this sense, F. Scott Fitzgerald's story "A Diamond as Big as the Ritz" tells a deeper truth about the quality of life in the state than most of the "Westerns" written by its native authors.

A few Montanans, as a matter of fact, proved to be not only aware but proud of their heritage of sophistication. One such family, in fact, owners of a large ranch near Two Dot, invited me down for a weekend at a time when the yahoos were in full pursuit and I had nearly panicked. Quite correctly they had figured that it would lift my spirits to be reminded of what, under pressure, I was tending to forget: that somewhere in the shadow of the Crazy Mountains there might be a house in which I could drink myself to sleep in the company of civilized men and women and wake to find a pile of old *Partisan Reviews* on the table beside my bed. Most of my fellow-Montanans outside of the University, however, apparently preferred to play the Know-Nothing game of the pamphleteer, echoing the tone with which he introduced an excerpt from my essay "The Face": "Leslie Fiedler, hired by Montanans, paid by Montanans, and teaching Montanans, has this to say of Montanans."

And maybe they were really offended, after all, even the most sophisticated among them; for they are a people physically vain, as they may well be, having produced in their own image Gary Cooper, most enduring of screen idols. Yet it was of his face that I was thinking in particular when I wrote in general about ". . . a face developed not for sociability or feeling, but for facing into the weather. It said friendly things to be sure, and meant them; but it had no adequate physical expressions even for friendliness, and the muscles around the mouth and eyes were obviously unprepared to cope with the demands of any more complicated emotion . . . the poverty of experience had left the possibilities of the human face in them incompletely realized."

Between November of 1958, when the first pamphlet appeared, and February of 1959, when a second effort called "Reasons for Investigation of the University System" was published, the campaign of vilification continued in print and in whispers, becoming even more obscene and comic. Yet I could not laugh, though the second pamphlet (identifying this time *twenty-five* members of the "small, dissident minority") was not even distributed on campus; presumably most faculty and students had decided by then that the whole thing was a joke, and their scorn served to keep even their most bigoted colleagues silent. Theirs was a judgment, in fact, in which even the Associated Press had come to concur—reporting the new publication not, as they had the first, in all seriousness but with tongue in cheek. Once more, it was *language* which divided the college community from the world of downtown, since to the former the rhetoric of the latter, especially under stress, seemed disconcertingly like the sort of parody they had been accustomed to laugh at ever since *Babbitt*.

Only lady preachers in storefront churches, crank editors of small-town papers, and a frantic student or two (rightists were in those days, it is difficult to remember, the most radical and articulate kids on campus) kept up the clamor—timing their attacks to coincide with the appearance of the new pamphlet. On February 20, 1959, for instance, the *Lewistown Daily News* in an editorial headed "WHO IS THE MORE DISPENSABLE?" took issue with another speech I had recently given, in which I had attempted to define an ideal college President. I had suggested, among a long list of other qualifications, that such a president ought to realize how dispensable he in fact is; this

moved the Lewistown editor to write: "Professor Fiedler is a man
who practices what he preaches. He has already demonstrated
how dispensable he thinks college presidents are. . . . Upon what
does this Caesar feed? Our definition of an ideal college president is exactly opposite to Professor Fiedler's. We yearn for a
new President at MSU who will regard some faculty members
as being dispensable."

It was the clearest call yet spoken aloud for my removal (the
pamphlets had depended on inference to do the job) and was,
in effect, seconded by a long communication from a freshman
out of Melville, Montana, who had been attending some of my
lectures and who confided his reactions first to *The Big Timber
Press*, then a couple of weeks later to *The Daily Interlake*.
Anyone enrolled in the University, the irate freshman revealed,
is being taught, by one or another member of the "faction"
which controls it, "existentialism, atheism, agnosticism, debauch-
ery, filth. . . ." And though he names no names, he describes
three corrupters in detail, beginning with me:

> The man who heads this faction is a Jew who came from
> the east coast to escape typical eastern prejudices, and I
> suspect, because at this school he appears to be a "bigger"
> man than he would at Yale or Harvard.
>
> This man writes material for magazines that is no better
> than the rawest "stories" that are passed furtively from
> hand to hand among men in military service. . . .
>
> He intimates that faith is blind; it has no place in an
> intellectual's life. His ideas on sex are not those which
> normal children accept. The man is brilliant and very articu-
> late, which makes it doubly hard for 17- and 18-year-olds
> to distinguish right from wrong.

He follows with an exposure of "a husband-wife team that is
pretty choice, too" (both, by the way, now professors in distinguished European universities), reporting that the wife "told
one boy in class that he couldn't know how to 'make' a girl. A
fine sort of instructor for pliable young minds!" The "husband of
this team" had asked his class to analyze a couple of stories out
of *Playboy*, one of them "so filthy as to cause the post office

department to stop the mailing of that issue." And he concludes: "If we don't change the present situation, the university will in 10 years be teaching something similar to Marxist doctrines, and will be attracting only 'young workers.'"

But the State Board could not ever, despite the prejudices it shared with the Lewistown editor and the Melville freshman, quite bring itself to fire a tenured professor (or professors) simply for being Jewish and/or using "dirty" words. How they would have loved really to have had just such a full-scale "Investigation" as they had somehow missed, when every other school board in the nation was having itself a field day finding "Marxists" and "perverts" in the classroom; what better way to exorcise that baffled rage that mounted and mounted in the World War II veteran (some of them had served, too), watching his Peace turn into somebody else's Cold War?

Finally, however, they were as much afraid of the American Association of University Professors and perhaps even of the big mouths of twenty-five dissident teachers as they were of editorials in the Big Timber and Lewistown papers; so they settled for denying pay raises to academic disturbers of the peace, and bugging the one group of people in the State more frightened than they: the poor administrators of all six units of the University system, who—in order to get the Board off their backs —went about for the next few years hushing any of their faculty who spoke above a whisper. A finger laid permanently to their lips, they kept hissing "shhh!" to everything, being, of course, especially tough with any young instructor who *before* he had tenure, dared say unkind things of the Power Company, or the Alumni Association, or the R.O.T.C., or the Football Team—or, God, forbid, the Board itself. Actually, they whimpered more often than they bullied, the Deans and Presidents, urging the eccentrics in their charge, whom they had never really understood to begin with, not to rock the boat, not to disturb the peace, and, above all, not to be *controversial*. Otherwise, what would happen to next year's budget? the new dormitories? the Foundation Funds for scholarships?

There was even one very little "Investigation" of the English Department on our campus, conducted behind closed doors by an aging dean from elsewhere imported for that purpose and

guaranteed in advance to discover nothing that would upset anybody, but only to produce a "Report" that cleared no one and
condemned no one—and was, in any case, to be seen by no one
except the then president (second after the one who had so
stupidly offered to resign), who, I was tempted to believe, probably did not even read it himself, lest it affect his tender nerves.
In the end, of course, none of the interested parties was satisfied;
certainly not those who had sympathized with the plea of the
Daily Interlake: "But we do feel it is about time the board of
education realized that . . . it is time to do something about the
situation, either by getting rid of him and his kind, or by publicly exonerating him (or them)." Nor were "him and his kind"
any happier, being granted neither the recognition of a public
condemnation, nor a license to speak without being apologized
for or explained away or, worst of all, banned at the last minute,
for reasons which theoretically had nothing to do with the controversial nature of the views expressed, but were invariably
logistical: a sudden lack of space, too great a demand in a short
period on the students' time, etc., etc.

The last episode in my own *comédie larmoyante* (all the more
funny and tearful because, from time to time, I was tempted to
take it as a tragedy or at least spectacular melodrama) involved
the President of Montana State College, our sister institution in
Bozeman, an Agriculture and Engineering School typically lust-
ing for cultural respectability and the right to bestow Ph.D.'s in
the Humanities—both of which depended, of course, on the good
will of the Board. I had been invited to its campus by the local
chapter of the Teachers Union, a tiny organization which had
been ineffectually but annoyingly challenging their President's
paternal tyranny. A liberal in politics, especially on questions of
Public Power, he therefore felt his authoritarianism beyond reproach, from the Left at any rate; and besides, he was as interested in budgets as the next fellow—which made me an undesirable guest, though he never quite said so.

Perhaps he feared that I would launch some sort of direct
attack on him, though I had intended to stick to sympathetic
commonplaces, figuring that what the Union wanted of me was
chiefly my mere presence: a real live flesh-and-blood teacher
who had won his fight with a University President. But there

was mayhem in the air even without me. As a matter of fact, the very week I was originally scheduled to appear, quite another sort of fight was due to occur—a less, as they say, symbolic one, that is, one fought for hard cash rather than the elusive "Good of the University": ten rounds for the Middleweight Championship of the World between Gene Fullmer and Joey Giardello.

It was, indeed, the first championship match at any weight which Montana had seen since Tex Rickard conned the cattlemen of Shelby into putting up the money for the Dempsey-Gibbons fight way back in whenever the hell it was. And, to tell the truth, I was eager to see it myself, though, to maintain the proper professorial detachment, I had offered my hosts some alternative dates, both before and after the great event. One of my staunchest and sweetest-tempered supporters on my own campus in Missoula had once got annoyed enough to suggest that my taste for boxing, combined with my contempt for team sports, betrayed an archaic mind which thought all conflicts should be settled by a duel of champions.

What really pleased me about prizefights, however, was that —unlike, say, college football—it involved no cheerleaders, no marching bands, no pennants: only the spotlighted ring and the darkness around it, a kind of theater in which the bleeding actors and the yelling audience are equally isolated, only the referee a mediator, dancing his detachment from the kill.

Or maybe it is a lot simpler than that, a minor vice learned, like any, from someone especially loved. Certainly it was my grandmother who initiated me into a lifelong fascination with the sport, though to her fights happened in her living room, in words, over the radio. Still, she cheered as wildly as anyone at the ringside over the victories of her favorites—especially Max Schmeling, whom she insisted on calling "Shmelnik," doubtless so that she would not have to confess he was a Kraut.

It turned out, moreover, that not only were Fullmer, Giardello, and I to be in Bozeman during the same week (we are now in April, 1960), but our own college President was due to visit the campus as well. And, indeed, *he* may have initiated my banning, arguing that it would be indiscreet for him to appear in tandem with so controversial a figure as I. In any event, I was canceled out at the last minute, barred from campus on the grounds that "three cultural events" in a period of a couple of days might overextend the already heavily burdened students; I was then invited to speak instead at the Methodist Church, which, under considerable pressure, canceled me out, too. In the end, despite student protests, petitions, and leaflets, along with some jocular criticism in the local press, I did not officially appear at Montana State College at all.

To be sure, I went to Bozeman anyhow, incognito as it were, attending an afternoon coffee hour in a fraternity house and a largish faculty party in someone's private home during the evening; at both places I spoke my piece in an atmosphere of excitement and conspiracy which would otherwise have been lacking. Yet *for the record,* I was not there, and so M.S.C. and its President stayed clean—as, indeed, I did too, indulging a petty vice in the guise of doing my duty against great odds, which is to say, I remained for the fight. It was all very Western, with young ladies in cowgirl outfits as ushers and parking lot attendants all looking like extras in a Gary Cooper movie; and besides it was, in quite unforeseen ways, amusing. Not the fighters, however, who hit each other chiefly with their heads, apparently out of a common conviction that butting drew blood quicker than padded punches, and blood was what the crowd wanted. Joey Giardello crossed himself, at least, a religious gesture that made him a favorite with the crowd, while Fullmer, who began with the disadvantage of being a Mormon, contented himself with glowering.

Actually, the real attraction of the evening was the joker in the house who yelled, just as Fullmer climbed into the ring, "Jee-*sus,* he's a white man. I thought he was a Mormon." But the college President was something of a star, too, taking the mike briefly to assure the crowd of his "extreme gratitude for all the wonderful things that were happening to his campus, including the visitors from far and near. . . ." The summary of his remarks is not mine, since I was too tickled at his performance really to listen; I dug it up later out of the sports pages of the *Arizona Republic.* The man from the Teachers Union who sat beside me insisted afterward that the President had meant to include me among "the visitors," and I should prefer to believe it, but I fear he was referring only to the noncontroversial ones.

Still, you can't win in Montana, no matter how careful you are—not outside the prize ring, anyhow; for despite his valiant efforts to keep clean, the President from Bozeman eventually got into trouble, too. Almost a year later, after I had escaped temporarily to Athens, I was sent through the mail a newspaper clipping headed MSC PRESIDENT URGED TO RESIGN; reading further, I discovered that a luncheon speaker at the Yellowstone County Woman's Republican Club had "declared the MSC head has become 'too controversial to serve the people of Montana.'"

Still later—as he tried, I suppose, to move up rather than simply go out—that same M.S.C. head was defeated for the governorship of the State by a particularly vicious Bircher. I should like to think that his defeat was due not only to the tens of thousands of voters on the Right, who remembered he had been called "controversial" and voted for his opponent, but also to a few score on the other side, who remembered that he had thought me so and failed to vote at all. It was a very close race, I was told, though by the time the count was in I had departed the State forever—why, I'm not precisely sure. Perhaps it was because, despite my comic misadventure in Bozeman, I'd really won my long, loving battle with Montana; and there was, therefore, no longer anything to stay for. It is not as perverse a reason as it sounds, for if true, it meant that my double commitment to fight and to explain was henceforth elsewhere: with the people who pretended to have read my actual books, rather than with those content just to have read—or even heard about—the reviews.

By 1960, Montanans were at least reading reviews of my works in *Time* and the national Sunday Book Reviews, rather than in locally produced pamphlets, since I was, in fact, being more generally noticed; and they had been convinced by those pamphlets that literary criticism, even of other literary criticism, can be in some cases as titillating as politics and gossip. Moreover, the publication date of *Love and Death in the American Novel* coincided almost exactly with the Fullmer-Giardello fight, so that the sports reporters covering the bout could scarcely avoid making connections between that event and my exclusion from the college which sponsored it. One such reporter observed that

my book had been "the subject of lead reviews in major publications the past few weeks . . ."; another commented: "*Time* magazine thought enough of the man's ability to utilize more than a
full page . . . reviewing Fiedler's book . . ."; still another observed that ". . . indications are that it will be a best seller."

True, the U.P.I. correspondent was still sufficiently victimized
by old habits to add that "Dr. Fiedler . . . has been a controversial figure in Montana education for many years." But his observation was already out of date (though in fact his "many
years" had been only two), since my fattest and most ambitious
book had shifted my critics' attention away from my role as a
Montanan and educator. It was my fellow professors from the
East who now took up the hue and cry; one of the most favor-
ably disposed of them (another, less kind, had called me "The
Dead End Kid of American Literature") remarked that I had
"consolidated" my standing as "the most controversial professor
of literature in America since Irving Babbitt." Yet though he dug
a good deal of what I was saying, it was precisely the "controversial" aspect of my work which he found inessential and
annoying, doubly annoying because inessential. To me, however,
what struck him as pointless bad manners, pretentious anti-
academic posturing, and fake heroism was all part of a resolve to
be as passionate and gross about our great flawed books as other
men were about our petty flawed politics—knowing full well
what it cost.

That cost he, of course, was quite unaware of, not knowing
Montana; and so, after granting with a certain qualifying irony
that I had not yet been "called to any of the genuinely voluptu-
ous chairs of American Literature," he went on to remind his
readers and mine of my many fellowships and rewards. And he
concluded a little sternly that my tone everywhere was unfortunate,
"more appropriate to a half-starved young writer on 4th Street
than a man making good money in Missoula."

It was a little hard to take, since the State Board had at that
very moment chopped two hundred bucks off a seven-hundred-
dollars a year raise for me—precisely on the grounds, I suppose,
that my prose style smacked more of 4th Street, New York, than
South 4th Street East, Missoula. "Good money in Missoula. . . ."
"Goes to extreme lengths to demonstrate his courage. . . ." I did

not feel either a pauper or a hero, but reading those phrases I was aware of being once more at the center of a joke—I hoped on their author, but I suspected on me.

The reviews of *Love and Death in the American Novel* served, in any case, to shock me into an awareness of how ignorant the big outside world was of our little inside one, and how abjectly I had allowed myself to be lost in its parochial concerns. I had become, in fact, the Montanans' Leslie Fiedler rather than my own, thus turning what had been at the start an escape from the prison of my old self into just another cell, though this time a mountain madhouse rather than an urban jail. If for half a million Americans Montana is total reality, for another one hundred ninety-nine and a half millions it is total fantasy; to leave it is not so much to leave home as to abandon paranoia, recover from a breakdown. So, at least, I told myself at a point when, after a leave-year of Greek sunshine (three local Greek-American merchants of one thing or another had protested my unworthiness to the State Department, but I had gone to Greece all the same), then two more back in Missoula, I decided to take off for Buffalo—to depart Montana forever.

It was not easy to pull up stakes after twenty-three restless but rooted years in which I had come and gone, come and gone —to Cambridge and Newark, Rome and Bologna, New York and Vermont and Athens, yet always back to what I never ceased thinking of as home: the home I had not been condemned to by birth but had chosen for myself, my wife, for all of us, including the three of my children born there. I had begun with few illusions about the place and left with fewer because I knew—by heart, as they say—all the things that had gone wrong with Missoula since I had first stepped off the train, weary and dazzled and scared, and younger than I knew then how to suspect. The trains themselves had gone to begin with; the last steam engine was preserved in a tiny park framed by a turnabout at the north end of Higgins Avenue. And even the Diesels that hooted rather than snorted in Hell Gate Canyon, setting no lovely lonely echoes going, had grown less and less frequent. No railroad any longer took you to Paradise, next stop after Missoula on the old Milwaukee Line; you had to go by bus or not make it at all.

Even the skies were no longer quite so astonishingly clear, since a thin pall of smoke now hovered permanently over the valley, fed by the Pulp Mill whose managers rose each year before the Chamber of Commerce to promise "real abatement" this time. And when the wind blew from a certain quarter, a smell of decay, of trees dead and gone wrong, swept down on us from that same Mill—which, after all, employed a lot of men who would otherwise have been jobless, since the sawmill had been automated.

Meanwhile, out of the ugly expensive sprawl of new houses that had crept up both banks of Rattlesnake Creek and the near slope of Mount Sentinel, earnest ladies drove weekly to meetings of the League of Woman Voters, where they reminded each other ritually that the Clark Fork was growing ever more polluted with their own garbage and detergents, plus industrial wastes; that local government had fallen, apparently forever, to the most mindless of the Birchers; that the school system tended to grow less efficient and more irrelevant year by year; that yet another Indian tribe had been screwed by some new Power Company deal.

Yet the litany of small disasters, all quite real, was easy to forget in a world still largely as virgin green as the day the old lake dried up in the cup of the hills: a world whose frost-pitted roads led in every direction toward vast stretches still populated chiefly by gophers and magpies, still smelling only of sage and pine.

Nonetheless, there in Missoula on the corner of Higgins and McLeod we had quite human neighbors to contend with, and they were the final small horror. Not so much on Higgins, of course, a main thoroughfare where the great logging trucks rolled once the sun was down, and the kids cruised the drag north to downtown, south to the A & W Root Beer Stand, while the shopkeepers who served us kept an eye on each other all day long through their plateglass display windows.

It was McLeod that was the problem: a streetful of own-your-own homes—the newer ones California-style in contempt of the actual weather, quite like the rows of red maples which had been planted in place of the native cottonwoods, both representing that dream of Somewhere Else which possessed the doctors and lawyers and owners of shoestores and lumberyards, who polished their cars with endless patience or cleaned their shotguns against the hunting season, while their wives tried—with Vigoro and constant watering—to extort gardens out of the porous soil.

As much as they longed for Somewhere Else, however, my neighbors feared and hated Somebody Else; but that was what we were, hopelessly and forever, no matter how long I stayed or how my public fortunes went up or down. Warning their children against playing with my youngest daughter, they would cry, "Don't you know her father's a Communist and her brothers are beatniks!" For the second generation had got into the act by now, and sometimes the anonymous voice over the phone would say, instead of "Red" or "Jew," "D—O—P—E—." But what seems really to have bugged them out of their minds was not so much my sons' long hair or the drugs they inferred from it as the totem those boys had painted on our fence: a four-toed foot, very red against the white planks.

It must have seemed to them the ultimate offense, a symbolic flaunting of all that was most "controversial" about us, and that we didn't even have the good sense to keep concealed.

And so nights they would come and paint it out; and in broad daylight we would paint it back, only to have it painted out again; and so on, round and round. It seemed if not a losing game exactly, a damned silly and monotonous one— quite a come-down after the excitement of the times in which my future, my whole life, seemed at stake; and after a while I could not abide the parody of twenty-three years implicit in that petty struggle. Besides, real job offers were coming in, as they had not at all in the bad period (except for a warm-hearted Dean from just across the border, who kept offering me exile in Canada). At long last, staying seemed more pointless and dull than going.

At any rate, I went, driving the whole breadth of the State, as I had so many times before and perhaps would not again, avoiding where possible the new four-lane interstate so that I could go through Fishtail and Two Dot and Lame Deer, savoring the very names in which I knew it would get harder and harder to believe. It was a satisfactorily undramatic trip. In

Fishtail, we heard a myna bird who had been taught to whistle at girls passing the café where he perched above the sizzling grill. In Two Dot, we screamed at and were screamed at by our rancher friends who were all hot for Goldwater—though an ikon of F.D.R. still hung above the cookstove in the original kitchen, preserved because grandma felt at home nowhere else in the grand new house. In Lame Deer, we stopped to look at the beautiful little Catholic Church, almost abandoned now that the Northern Cheyenne had adopted the peyote cult, and explained to my small daughter that, alas, there was no synagogue in that tiny Reservation town.

And when I got to Buffalo, there was a letter waiting to tell me that an "an old Indian fighter," learning that this time I had gone East for good, spat and said, "That goddam Fielder [*sic*]. I always knew he would run out on us some day."

Part Three

JUST OFF MAIN: 1967

i

Strange, though, to have ended up in Buffalo, where my grandfather, a leather-worker, had gone briefly in 1904 to find a job;
where my mother, as a girl of ten or twelve, had given pet
names to the rats who shared their crummy flat on William
Street; where, when I arrived in 1964, I discovered a long-lost
uncle running the cigar stand in the Erie Bank, and some
cousins living on an oat farm just outside of town in Lockport.
It was a little like going back to Newark: memories, relatives,
and the place itself quite as unspectacularly ugly, and just about
the same middling size as the city in which I was born.

The only difference was that I had not quite made it all the
way East; for the Atlantic lay a couple of hundred miles or
more ahead of me still, in the same direction I had been heading
since leaving Missoula. In a certain sense, indeed, Buffalo
seemed neither an Eastern or a Western, but an *ex*-Western,
city: a seedy memorial to a dream of expansion into the wilderness long since outlived, though the Chamber of Commerce
kept on talking about the "Niagara Frontier." Between us and
the real west of Montana, however, what dreary stretches of
asphalt and abandoned car-tracks; what a conglomeration of
indistinguishable cities: Erie, Cleveland, Detroit, Chicago, Milwaukee—their black hearts destined to burn now with the coming of each summer.

But Buffalo was not finally home, of course, since I had never
lived there, never even seen it before, except out of the corner of
one eye as I had watched out for the bypasses to Niagara Falls.
And it was for the Falls I headed this time, too, even before
I was unpacked; for I needed to convince myself once more
that they were always even more splendid than I, perhaps than
anyone, could remember: a major miracle in a minor river

running between two lakes about to give up and die—licked by oil slick and dead fish and the shit of all those unlivable cities.

But the dying lakes do not matter, finally, any more than the junk shops and pizza palaces and wax museums and hot dog stands on both sides of "the friendliest border in the world," where the guards bug teen-agers for long hair, but the Mafia manages to keep its heroin supply lines open.

Nothing matters, really, when you lean over the protective railing and see that endless hump and heave of green water breaking to white, that relentless soft power grinding a cliff to boulders, boulders to pebbles, pebbles to sand—all in its own sweet time. And you can understand why men are moved by the mere sight of it to do damfool things like riding bikes over it on high wires, or walking those wires with long balancing poles, or going down with the falling water in barrels—or even living in Buffalo. But leaving the Falls via the Victory Bridge, you find yourself in short order on Main Street.

And the melancholy of Main Street, my God, with the broken sidewalks and the wind-gathered rubble in the railroad underpasses; the uncountable Funeral Parlors and the Helpee Selfee automatic laundries; the intolerably dark and dirty bars, and the unbearably bright and clean cafeterias; the porky, punchy men, and the women too busy or up-tight to be beautiful; and the Spade kids just standing there daring the White kids to do something and vice versa, while the cops get jittery enough to kill somebody. To be sure, after a while, you begin to notice what flanks and mitigates Main Street: a lovely Sullivan building hidden away in the by-streets of downtown, and the quite elegant library which houses all that's left of the manuscript of *Huckleberry Finn;* an occasional store window which picks up the heart, full of imported cigars or secondhand instruments or hand-me-down dresses; the front of the abandoned Burlesque House.

There are also a few fine old church steeples, an aging deserted mausoleum of a railroad station, a couple of brand new banks which seem satisfactorily handsome tributes to what the town's leading citizens have really believed in at one time or another; but your initial impression is not wholly false. True, at first glance, you think that something quite terrible must already

have happened, though Buffalo has only been waiting over the
past half-century or so for some catastrophe to justify its desola-
tion. Or maybe, after all, the urban renewal that everyone talks
about all the time will really work, but it will require a miracle
—another miracle beside the Falls. And the rule seems to be:
only one to a customer.

In any case, Buffalo is a disaster area without having had a
disaster. Not war or fire, plague or earthquake has afflicted it,
only history: the history of a WASP ruling class that abdicated
control, no longer willing to pay the price of proximity to the
mills that produced its wealth and the system of courts and cops
that protected it. Retired to the suburbs and beyond, that class
has concentrated ever since on good works, chiefly subsidies for
the arts, and on sports, chiefly squash, while maintaining that
happy combination of anti-Semitism and anglophilia which in-
dicates the life-style it despises and the one to which it aspires—
despite the handicap of money.

In the meantime, the city itself has been up for ethnic grabs:
looted for a while by the Italians, then by the Poles, then the
Italians again, and so on round and round, though all pretty
much White and Roman Catholic. The Jews have been largely
shunted off into making money as storekeepers, lawyers, doctors,
professors, and shrinks; and though they, too, are headed for
the suburbs these days and support the arts, they have got there
without ever having held political power. And the Negroes have
been sealed off in their ghettos with neither power nor money—
except in the form of weekly wages, the form that buys nothing
except what is consumed on the spot. As quick consumers, they
are as necessary to the material well-being of Buffalo as the quick
absolvers, those innumerable priests and nuns, are to its spiritual
health; but no one seems much interested in delivering them
from impotence. The Poles especially appear bent on keeping
the blacks perpetually without power, perhaps out of some sense
that they themselves are regarded as "niggers" by too many of
their neighbors, who put them down with friendly condescension
or standard "Polack jokes."

It is hard, in any case, to be eternally second; and Buffalonians
cannot forget that they are, in fact, second in the State, and a
poor second at that, to New York City. Nor is there much

comfort in reminding themselves that at least they are ahead of
Syracuse and Rochester and Albany, much less in reflecting on
their clear superiority to Schenectady and Utica and Troy. Yet
Buffalo has certain real advantages even as compared with New
York, advantages which go beyond those ambiguous ones associated with mere smallness of scale. One of these, the University,
brought me to Buffalo in the first place; another, the unsuspected
presence of green oases in its gray wastes, pleasant neighbor-
hoods for those who can afford them, I was shown almost immediately by one of those lady real estate agents who await new
arrivals to the "Queen City," eager and numerous as the taxi
drivers in Naples or the shoeshine boys in Istanbul.

They are a terrifying crew of dislocated females—widowed,
divorced, or simply burdened with some loser of a husband—
who seem to find as much pleasure in doing each other down
as in talking about their town or making a fast buck. Though
a little uneasy about my status as a professor, indeed about the
status of professors in general, they were just beginning to understand that a teacher at what they still called "U.B." was not
necessarily a *shnorrer* looking for a bargain but might end up
buying a place that paid the sort of commission they were used
to getting only out of sales to Managers of Electronic Plants or
Cancer Researchers at Roswell Clinic. Poor things, when my arrest hit the headlines, they grew confused all over again and
now, I am told, approach new members of the University staff
with even greater wariness, especially if they are bearded or
confess to teaching literature or, worst of all, to writing books.

In any case, it was from these garrulous ladies—though not
so much from what their words said as what their tone betrayed—that I began to learn what the old University of Buffalo
must have meant to the city, and why not only they but trades-
men everywhere seemed astonishingly unimpressed to learn
my new affiliation. In Montana anyone associated with the University grew accustomed to being greeted sometimes with a
certain amount of admiration, more often with a good deal of
horror, most commonly with a mixture of both—but never,
certainly, with indifference. And this was due, I suppose, to the
fact that anyone who went on past the twelfth grade was likely
to go into the State University system, guaranteed by statute to

be "forever free" (we cheated on this a little), as well as forever
open to any graduate of any high school in the State.

But New York, like much of the East, had never had a proper
State system of higher education at all until a couple of years
before my arrival, when the University of Buffalo, along with
several other established schools, was taken over from private
control. Before that, U.B. had been attended, by and large, by
students who represented neither the most powerful nor the most
numerous part of the local population. The sons and daughters
of the old ruling class had gone, as inevitably as their parents
had headed for the suburbs, to Ivy League colleges if they were
boys, or to one of the "Seven Sisters" if they were girls—in
order, as a very expensive study, mounted by sociologists and
psychologists, later discovered to no one's surprise, to "reinforce
the values of the peer group." So reinforced, their deepest senti-
mental allegiances were forever after directed away from Buffalo
in terms of space, as well as back from the present in terms of
time. And they lived those allegiances, having sufficient leisure
to really function as alumni, a privilege denied the poor. When
they were not interviewing the latest candidates for admission
to Harvard and Yale, they were likely to be raising funds by
selling pecans for Vassar, or organizing reunions to turn nostalgia
into cash for Dartmouth and Mount Holyoke.

From time to time, to be sure, some such alumnus or alumna,
out of a sense of obligation to less fortunate fellow-citizens,
would divert money from his own University to set up a Special
Chair in This or That, or to enrich the limited culture available
on a campus only a streetcar ride from home, by endowing a
String Quartet in Residence or a Series of Poetry Readings.
Actually, concerts and readings were more desirable than Chairs,
since they could be attended by their donors when they happened to be in town, thus providing them the special satisfaction
of being entertained along with the very people their generosity
had benefited.

But the working class, I surmise, did not go to the old U.B.
either; since most of the Negroes, plus a substantial number of
Poles and Italians, were sorted out early into technical high
schools or the nonacademic "tracks" in more comprehensive ones
—when they did not simply abandon the pointless boredom of

the classroom for the sort of "real life" they could wait no longer to begin living: "dropping out," as the process came to be called invidiously by the anxious petty-bourgeoisie who stayed on and on and on.

It was, in fact, from this class that U.B.'s students were chiefly recruited, White Protestants and Jews on their way to becoming dentists, pharmacists, accountants, teachers, technicians, insurance agents, and real estate lawyers. What Roman Catholics made it this far went to Catholic schools, where they were sorted out by sex and given required courses in theology; or if they could not qualify for these, there was always the local Teachers College ready to certify them for grade-school teaching. But wherever they went in town, they endured the indignity, which they thought of as an opportunity enjoyed, of acting out the all-American charade called "Bound to Win," "Onward and Upward," "Getting Ahead," with the promise of a degree and a job at the end.

I can see them in my mind's eye, having been in a similar spot myself: the young men especially, clean and spruce in their jackets and ties, or sometimes the more casual garb suggested for the "college man" in the back pages of *Esquire,* textbooks in hand and their heels hitting the pavement hard as they hurry to class. To an outside observer, particularly one whose son (he has just learned over the telephone) is sobering up from the Big Drunk after the Big Game, or is waiting to be tapped for Skull and Bones, even the palest Protestants in their ranks must have seemed earnest and sober and grubby enough to be Jews. At any rate, their University came to be called, more jocularly than viciously perhaps, "Jew B" for some such reason; though also because many of the faculty—quite conspicuously in a time when most American colleges still resisted the hordes of Jews clamoring for professorial rank—were Jewish, too.

It was not a great University, old U.B.-Jew B., but it performed its intended functions in a way that kept the community around it happy. My own college was quite like it, though even more overwhelmingly Jewish: a middling school for the moderately gifted and ambitious, who would have been embarrassed to be part of an enterprise that was either a challenge to those in it or a pain in the ass to everyone around it, or both. I do not mean to suggest that teachers of truly outstanding talent were not attracted to Buffalo from time to time (as they are to every sort of school everywhere); and a few of them, I know from firsthand experience, actually stayed on till retirement, for reasons they would have found it hard to explain even to themselves, but which were doubtless no worse than those which keep people at much more eminent institutions.

A considerable portion of the faculty, however, seems to have been made up, on the one hand, of types who longed to break into Buffalo society, and who could, if they were simultaneously witty and noncontroversial enough, that is, believed nothing they said, make it to the larger dinners and cocktail parties of the first families. On the other hand, it included those who, though sometimes brilliant enough in the classroom, publish little or nothing and only really come into their own at faculty meetings or on committees; these dream as their ultimate reward of the Chairmanship of a Department or an appointment as Assistant Dean.

The former are useful only for "making contacts" or attracting endowments, and develop skills which tend to destroy character; but the latter are likely to be straightforward and affable, even honest and lovable men—at their best when it comes to protecting the rights of their underpaid and overworked fellows: lifelong libertarians and staunch supporters of the A.A.U.P. It was their heritage, indeed, which made Buffalo, after it had gone State, the only school out of some hundred-odd in the enlarged and revitalized system in which faculty members (five of them —four, naturally, connected with the English Department) refused at the risk of their jobs to subscribe to the Feinberg Oath: a declaration that the signer had never been a member of the Communist Party, or if so, had informed the proper administrative officials when and under what circumstances. Their case was, in fact, finally fought all the way to the Supreme Court, their colleagues standing by them, and the same firm of lawyers which was later to defend me pleading their case and winning it.

What seemed strange to me when I first arrived in Buffalo, however, was the absence of any kind of activity which would, to the most panicky enemy of Communism, seem an occasion

for such an oath. It was just there, on the books, a certificate
to be signed and filed: part of the price one paid presumably
for the expansion and higher salaries that State support brought.
To be sure, somewhat earlier, Congressional Investigating Committees had come to campus, as they had come everywhere; but
only with the greatest difficulty could they unearth a staff member or two who were by their lights Red enough to justify publicity, much less genuine alarm; and, I gather, they turned with
relief to some of the local unions where they did a bit better.

In any case, the handful of super-discreet Socialists and weary
ex-Stalinists whom I encountered in Buffalo were quite over-
balanced by certain extreme patriots: an odd departmental chairman or two, for instance, who gave required Fourth of July
parties for their junior staff and mourned the splendid times
during the War, when students had marched to and from class
in orderly ranks, counting cadence.

What chiefly reassured the surrounding community, however,
was the prevailing sense of a school which knew and accepted
its predetermined place, and whose students only sought to
move up to the predetermined slot next above the one into
which they were born. Permitting the system thus to limit the
range of their discontent, they certified rather than called it into
question; and in so doing, they defined the university, as it had
always been natively defined in the heartland of America, as an
institution which taught, under the thousand rubrics from
Agronomy to Zoology, the simple science of making it. But the
very "it" so long taken for granted in a world concerned only
with the techniques of making was already being challenged
elsewhere, in colleges and universities eager to redefine themselves lest they perish—by violence or inanition—along with
the society that they had so long and (it appeared all at once)
so ignobly served.

When, therefore, a governor of New York decided in the early
sixties to create at last a university system worthy of a state
so populous and rich, and to depend no longer on private institutions for first-class higher education, the movement of challenge and redefinition was beginning to crest everywhere. What
else then for Buffalo—chosen along with Stony Brook, Harpur,
and Albany to be one of the four major university centers—but

to turn away from old modes in quest of distinction. Everyone understood that it could not stay as it was and simply grow larger; but few realized that neither could it emulate Harvard or Columbia or Johns Hopkins, or even the University of California.

Conventional academic patterns had ceased to be viable in a time when, quite abruptly and terrifyingly, everything else— everything hitherto untried or thought absurd—had come to seem worth trying. The leaders of the community, however, perhaps even the governor himself, when they dreamed a great university for Buffalo, had in mind as a model some long-established school they themselves had attended, or one to which they were sending their children. And their vision was apparently shared by the rest of the community who had gone to the old U.B. or the State College or Canisius or D'Youville or even nothing beyond high school, but who had assimilated notions of Ivy League style from boys' books, the screen, and fashion magazines.

It was a Harvard-in-Buffalo or a Princeton-on-the-Erie which they seem to have imagined, an institution born hoary, frequented by young ladies and gentlemen of perfect manners though of local origin; and presided over by kindly, white-haired eccentrics from rural New England who were given to extravagant talk in the lecture hall but always pulled the Republican lever in the voting booth.

And here is the crux of the matter: the clue to all that has vexed and continues to vex the relationship of the community-at-large and the new U.B., renamed the State University of New York at Buffalo, or SUNYAB for short. It is the key, as well, to much that motivated the events leading to my arrest. For SUNYAB came into existence, loaded with dough and flushed with the enthusiasm of an institution all of whose mistakes lie ahead of it, at the very moment when even the most ancient schools were being challenged to change or die, yet no one knew for sure how to change, or even if change was possible.

In light of all this, it was appropriate enough that our current President, our first *new* President, appointed in 1966, emerge from the then much publicized though still little understood upheavals at Berkeley: the first failed manifestation of what has come to seem more and more clearly a real, though perhaps abortive revolution. At a particularly critical moment, he had served as acting President there; and throughout, he seems to have behaved better (so at least reports from all quarters agreed) than most of his administrative colleagues, who, calling in the cops presumably to restore order, discovered that they had in fact marshalled them against the future, thus starting a battle which no one could stop, much less win.

Though I myself had been a member of the staff at Buffalo for two years by then, I was not a member of any faculty committee involved; and, indeed, I had vowed after my experiences in Montana to know as little as possible about the President of any institution in which I found myself. In truth, however, no matter what one resolves, it is impossible really to learn about college Presidents except after the fact, since, inevitably, they come from someplace else, which they have left under circumstances that no one is ever willing to talk about with absolute candor. So I suspect that none of the bodies concerned, neither the lay Board who legally appointed him nor the advisory committee of the faculty who pored over his dossier, knew the whole record of the man we finally invited to preside over us.

And I am sure they would have been reluctant to look too closely in any case, since the development of the student movement at Berkeley had been particularly vexed and complex— improvised from moment to moment, at a point when there were still no useful precedents. Beginning with a demand for the freedom to talk, it had moved on to an assumption of the freedom to act; just as starting out by insisting on the traditional privilege of protest over Civil Rights and Vietnam, it had passed to the subversive call for the right to utter obscenity.

And few of us on the new faculty were quite certain how we stood on the problems this posed. We were divided not only among ourselves, but even, from moment to moment, inside our individual heads. So that, finally, all we could offer against the traditionalists' advocacy of condemnation and restraint was a plea for resiliency. "Be faithful to your ambivalence," I remember advising myself, "when the crisis comes here, too, as it must. And whatever happens, don't make up your mind too soon."

I suppose this is why I hoped much from the new President (more, perhaps, than I should have known any President can deliver), since even his hesitancies, which annoyed some of my colleagues, his very uncertainty of manner, seemed to me guarantees of the openness indicated by what I had learned of his record. And an open university, I was convinced, was what we must become, what we must remain if we were not to be stillborn or an infant casualty: open to students, Black and White and no particular color, from sections of society we had not reached before, as well as to those whom earlier we would have rejected; open to the unbuttoned as well as the buttoned-up, the non-matriculated as well as the duly enrolled, the short-time "drop-in" as well as the degree-bent long-termer; open to new subject matters, even those which verged on the trivial and mad, and to new techniques for teaching them, including backtalk and silence; open to the establishment of new forms of authority and control, and to the development of new modes of challenging them; open to everything I myself could imagine, and more beyond—up to the point where I would no longer be able to endure it and would be driven out of teaching to meditate or brood or just watch television.

In his first months, indeed, the new President seemed to be interested in moving in such new directions: organizing a symposium, for instance—at a place happily named Kissing Bridge —in which representatives of the faculty, including me, were joined by an advisor on education to the British Labor Party, his clichés uncustomarily accented at least; a sociologist, eminent and unorthodox enough so that his University had had to hire him outside and over the opposition of his proper department; a psychiatrist who had been reflecting on the "protean" image held by themselves of the young in the United States and Japan, and in particular on their resolve to work temporary "gigs" rather than full-time jobs, when they worked at all; and one of those then still startlingly unconventional nuns in short skirts who had just dropped theology as a required subject in the college of which she was the head.

She was, in fact, the only one of the invited experts naïve enough to realize and relaxed enough not to resent the fact that ours was a ritual session rather than a working one. Indeed, some of the faculty, especially among those who had not been present, had as much difficulty as the experts themselves in evaluating a session more interested in discovering new commonplaces of commitment than in formulating new plans. I, however, was reasonably content; for the real point seemed to me to set goals worthy of being failed, rather than more "realistic and workable," that is, somewhat ignoble ones, which anyone long connected with universities knows will be failed, too. But perhaps I was reassured, as others in other departments could not be, by the considerable progress we had already made, under the leadership of a Chairman who proceeded on the basis of energy and intuition and a contempt for over-all plans, meanwhile baffling administrative interference by his refusal to learn good academic manners or proper bureaucratic procedure.

In our Department, that is to say, we had already been changing things for some three or four years, varying our mix of students, for instance, so that—first on the graduate level, then hopefully among the undergraduates—the standard aspirants to respectability could confront in the same class the newly conventional seekers for disreputability; and thus, at the very least, their hypocrisies could illuminate each other, or, at the best, both could be illuminated by books immune to all hypocrisy which they were asked to read together.

And those who taught those books were, after a while, as likely to be men currently trying to write similar ones as bibliographers and editors and commentators upon them. Live writers, in short, moved up and down our corridors, as in many other universities; but they were not, as in most other places, defined as not-quite-colleagues of the scholars, destined only to be "in residence" or to teach "creative writing." Instead, they taught books, quite as if having written a novel or collected a volume of poems was as good a qualification for saying useful and interesting things about literature as a Ph.D., the standard degree earned by following certain academic regulations in which no one any longer quite believes, and meeting certain scholarly standards which no one has yet managed quite to define.

I am not trying to say, of course, that our situation had become utopian, or even that an overwhelming majority of our students believed it so, which would be, I suppose, much the

same thing. Students have always griped, since their discontent is
functional, like that of G.I.'s and Blacks; and they will continue
to gripe until their lot is radically altered, which is to say, until
they are not in any ordinary sense "students" at all. But in our
case, the grounds of their discontent were unusual at least.
Some, to be sure, cried still that we paid only perfunctory attention to what was truly advanced in the arts, that our hearts
really belonged still to "the Tradition"; but more typical was
the young man who confided in me once, after I myself had
spoken publicly about bypassing certain standard authors in the
curriculum, "I am altogether dismayed at our department, this
easy playing with the avant garde. It is disgraceful. It lacks
humility. It lacks seriousness."

However stuffily expressed, this represents a genuine response
to a real breakthrough on our part, which may not have made
our graduate students happy, but has at least raised the level of
their misery, transforming the dullest of aches into a pain almost
fascinating. In any case, word seems to have got around in fairly
short order that we are somehow different, perhaps actually
interesting; and we have, therefore, over the past couple of years
been overwhelmed by thousands of applications for the handful
of slots which open up annually in our graduate program. In
part, I suppose, this pressure reflects a nationwide flight to
graduate school based on the fact that for young men such appointments carried, until quite recently, automatic exemption
from the draft; but we have profited all out of proportion to the
national average.

No, our students have come chiefly to find each other, as well
as those of us on the faculty whose names they may have heard,
or whose works they have read. And though, not infrequently,
they decide quite quickly to take off again for someplace else
even more mythical, most often they remain, and remaining,
begin to create for themselves the kind of community they had
come expecting to find ready-made. It does not even matter if
that community soon fragments, broken into factions based on
differing tastes, divergent life-styles, and sometimes, alas, con-
flicting estimates of and allegiances to one or another of us.
Their conflicts aspire at least to principle, quite like our own
high-toned squabbles over new faculty appointments, which

more unite than divide us with the bond of passionate debate.

In diversity there is the possibility of future change and the actuality of present richness. We could not, for instance, have one official journal to speak for all of us, or even a quite non-existent consensus; yet we are all agreed that it is good there be ten or twelve or fifteen (no one knows for sure, being too busy at the mimeograph machine and the typewriter to count) little magazines, called *Intrepid, Presence, Mother, Paunch, Incense, Free Poems,* etc., etc., in which such students and younger faculty as have no access to more "established" publications can achieve print and, hopefully, a public. And between issues, the same writers, usually poets these days when it is once more easier to write verse than prose, chant their latest efforts at each other, in Readings organized in honor of some large cause, or in support of someone just busted for that cause, or just for the hell of it.

Most of the poetry is *à la mode,* which is to say, fashionably the same, so that it is tempting to believe that any poem picked at random could be cut into snippets and interspersed between the lines of any other poem, without anyone's being the wiser, except, possibly the two authors. But this seems fair enough, since to be young means, nine times out of ten, to want to be a writer rather than to have the need to write a poem; and to want to be a writer is to suffer the dictates of fashion in diction, cadence, tone, and subject matter. By the same token, however, to be old means, nine times out of ten, to have written poetry rather than to be writing it; and to be thus out of it means to be able to see through it—a poor pleasure. And in any case, whenever I feel sure that I cannot bear even one more series of pious banalities in verse against the War in Vietnam, or in praise of Ché Guevara or somebody's cunt, miraculously a genuine voice is heard, an authentic word spoken.

Moreover, I believe (only I wish sometimes that all bad poets under 25 would go away) that any writing is better than dumbness, any movement better than paralysis. And that the young *move* there is no denying; but where they are moving or why remains quite unclear even to them until some visiting poet, the model whom they had been imitating at a second or third remove, arrives in the flesh to perform what they had only surmised.

On such occasions I find us most ourselves, whether we are two thousand rocking the rafters of the gym in response to an extravagantly admired poet not quite heard over the blurred P.A., or whether we are only seven or eight gathered for the kill of somebody else's favorite, his every word falling clear and dead among the rows of empty seats.

Moreover, we are visited not only by poets but by successful Jewish novelists and lost Gentile ones, absurdist playwrights, underground film-makers, stand-up comedians, folk singers, mime troops, rock guitarists, electronic musicians, designers of geodesic domes, structural linguists, pop artists, puppeteers, defenders of mass culture or polymorphous perverse love, Zen Buddhists, Russians on good will tours, jazz flutists, nude dancers, Black Power organizers, pianists who play with their feet as well as their hands, and pianists who sit motionless over the keyboard, daring the audience to laugh. And before each event, there is a reception, after each a party; sometimes, when visitors overlap, two or three parties combined into one: all in all a nonstop festival, a continuous ball—as the All-American Cultural Road-show rolls into Buffalo for a one-night stand between Albany and Ann Arbor, New Paltz and Chicago.

What football was once for colleges everywhere—and remains still at cultural backwaters like Notre Dame or Michigan State— the endless Happening of What's New is for the reborn university: entertainment, business, but even more, the ritual celebration of what we otherwise would not know we believed. Like football, however, the Cultural Jamboree represents only that over which we yell the loudest, not that in which we invest most of our time. After the freedom of my first months at Buffalo, I found myself involved, as I have been all my adult life, in the routines of academia: sitting on committees to choose a new Chairman for Drama, a new Provost, a new head of the English Department; preparing reports on the desirability of a Program in American Studies, and the proper function of a College of Arts and Sciences—about to be eliminated, alas, but never mind about that!

Meanwhile, I was teaching Shakespeare, the Nineteenth-Century American Novel, Poetry of the English Renaissance, the Literary Criticism of Aristotle and Longinus; for I do not enjoy talking in class about topics on which I am currently writing, fearful of boring myself or going stale. And I tend to resist assigning and formally discussing contemporary works, out of a sense that something first-rate should be left for whim and casual conversation. Besides, I have come more and more, as I have moved further and further away from my own grim university training, to dream aloud in class, rather than do anything like what my own teachers would have called "teaching"; and it is the old ones, the long-time survivors I find I love to dream over, as I come closer and closer to seeming a survivor myself: Shakespeare or Dante or, at the very latest, Melville and Dickens.

Needless to say, my colleagues are engaged in precisely such routines, too—not just the traditional scholars, but the rest of us as well, even those who look to the outsider more like Martians or solitaries or mad Heads than like Mr. Chips. But of all of this our hostile critics out in the community remain necessarily unaware. They know about the continuing Festival, since many of its events are open to them, indeed depend for survival on their patronage. And they take note when those who perform at the Festival, or those students in attendance who clearly regard them as interlopers, get involved in scandal: some kid, who looked to them dirty and shaggy enough for anything, picked up on the way home, stoned out of his mind; or a performance which shocked them in Buffalo banned elsewhere; or a performer they found pointlessly obscene busted for pot a month later.

Such incidents are duly reported in the papers and magazines they read, as are campus demonstrations and protests and teach-ins and clashes with the police—all complete with pictures, and quite out of context. When I was young enough to think all error and malice the result of conspiracy, I used to believe journalistic distortion venal and deliberate. Now I am convinced that newspapers do not choose to distort; they simply do not know how *not* to.

It is tempting to believe that their ignorance on this score is accidental, the result of a failure on the part of the university itself in what administrators like to call "public relations" and teachers prefer to think of as "education": the education of the whole community in the meaning and purpose of the university. From time to time, some enterprising college president, convinced of this, organizes a briefing session for his local press, at which he tries to tell them certain basic truths: that the university exists not primarily to train technicians, for instance, or to indoctrinate the young with the values of the old, but to free the mind. Such sessions, however, are usually not convened until some notorious "Case" has already made the headlines, involving a professor or student who has challenged those values—which is to say, until it is too late.

But it is really always too late, for there is no way to communicate in the daily press the daily concerns of the university: the inscrutable ordinary business in committee room and class which, despite a thousand betrayals, somehow furthers its ends. Even when an occasional article on curriculum reform or a change in administrative structure appears, it is bound to be garbled and to seem, in any case, irrelevant to everything that surrounds it, other news stories, ads, comics, whatever; for to tell what the university is at any point really up to involves the use of a kind of language quite alien to the popular press and its readers, whether they subscribe to *The Amherst Bee* or *Time* and *Life*. Besides, *they do not care.*

In the past, it has been chiefly the language of professors which has baffled and bored the average reader of newspapers, except when he has taken it to be concealing some heresy or blasphemy: such phrases as "general education," "academic freedom," "the liberal tradition," "the heritage of humanism," "avant-garde art." Certainly this was true in Montana in 1958, as I learned with some small pain; and to a certain extent it remains true everywhere to this very day, as the falling out over Vietnam between the academic community and those who subsidize it has testified.

More recently, however, it has been the language of students which has particularly bugged the lay community; over the past ten or fifteen years that language has altered so rapidly that communication even between them and the professors they talk to every day has grown more and more difficult. Professors,

understandably enough, expect to be the language teachers of
their students; and, indeed, the traditional function of the Freshman English course, once universally required, was to drill them
in the dialect of their seniors and convince them to use it on
all academic occasions forever after.

In many places, this situation has changed radically; more and
more students (largely but not exclusively, and not originally,
Black) have been insisting that the language they bring to the
university rather than the one they find there be the academic
lingua franca. In reaction to this, more and more faculty members (there have always been some, in my lifetime at least, who
have sought to mingle unnoticed at the Kiwanis Club) have
chosen to abuse those students in the language of the larger
adult community and its press. Chiefly, however, teachers, young
and old, have felt it incumbent on them precisely at this moment
to act as interpreters—translating, mediating—though they have
suspected that in the end they would appear to both sides to
be speaking somebody else's language: the nonacademic community taking them for secret allies of the students when they
explain rather than condemn; the students finding them finks and
agents of established Power when they refuse to disengage completely from the world of business and government. And perhaps
there is truth in both charges, since a true interpreter is in some
sense a double agent. And why not?

Meanwhile, the spokesmen for town and campus confront each
other in mutual bafflement, mutual incomprehension; they cannot even abuse one another properly, for what seems to one an
insult is for the other an honorific. I do not mean to suggest
that there are no genuine issues which separate them, but surely
there are none which could not be—granted a common language
—arbitrated. The boy who smokes grass and the man who smokes
Camels, like the girl on LSD and the lady on Librium are, after
all, not that far apart, if only they could share a few clichés,
or at least realize that even saying the same words they mean
quite different things.

It is not a matter of one group learning the *argot* of the other;
since any young man not an orphan has learned his father's
slang along with his favorite jokes, and television has been teach-

ing his father his. Even family magazines and Sunday supplements are useful in this regard, providing "Hippy Glossaries" for those over thirty, no matter what and how poorly they read. If there is anyone left in America who has not been told a score of times what "hip" and "busted" and "drop-out" and "psychedelic" mean, he will be told so before he has a chance to complain.

No, the rub comes with words apparently shared but responded to so differently that their dictionary meanings no longer matter: "Revolution," for instance, and "dope" and "fuck." The last word illustrates better than either of the others—more vividly at least—the real crux: for in discussing "obscenity" both sides are forced to confess what may well remain forever concealed in debates about "revolution" and "dope," that what is at issue is in fact language itself, the most fundamental of all our conventions.

For the young in general, perhaps, and for students certainly, the word "fuck" is a customary and important part of their speech, the only word which describes properly what they think they are doing in bed, though their parents, they know, call a similar experience "copulating" or "having relations." It is hard for them even to remember sometimes that there are others who find it shocking; for it is written into their history and inscribed not only in the text but even on the bannerheads of what they read. After all, it was blazoned on the banners of the "dirty-speechers" in the last stages of the demonstrations at Berkeley; and one of their poetry journals, important enough so that no reputable library can refuse to stock it, is called *Fuck You.*

Yet the aging and sympathetic but genteel lady who presides over the Poetry Room in our own library feels obliged to refer to it as *F. You;* and so far as I know, no widely circulated newspaper in the United States has ever printed the word in any context, preferring evasion, circumlocution, or a blank. To be sure, the parochial papers of the young—college newspapers in many cases, as well as the "underground" press—use words like it casually enough, but they are talking to an in-group in its own language. Most members of the adult community are scarcely aware of the existence of such papers, and when they try to read them are likely to be put off not so much by "obscenity" as by the absence of anything which seems to them proper style or proper news.

But there are certain representatives of that community *required* by their role to glance through the journals of the young —faculty advisors, for instance, and printers. The latter, in particular, tend to be disturbed by what they find, for as a class they are apparently conscientious and even censorious men. Twice in my own experience, printers scrutinizing student galleys in the course of proofreading or making up a page have been so offended by the language that they have stopped publication and run off to the appropriate administrative officials to demand sanctions.

But college presidents, too, however liberal they may be politically, seem to be tender on this score; and though they seldom act on their own, stirred up by pious printers they turn pious and tough as well. So at least our own President behaved, losing his temper and his nerve for the first time, when an irate printer waved under his nose copy for the campus paper which sought to report faithfully the lyrics sung by an East Village rock-and-roll group and the lines spoken by the performers in a kind of anti-Minstrel Show: both events in our Continuing Festival.

In the end, however, the President had to back down, because in America these days it has become a little comic, certainly on campuses, to object to the word "fuck." Moreover, the law has grown more and more permissive in this regard. The irate citizen unable to press charges against perpetrators of "obscenity" must content himself with writing letters to the gripe column of some newspaper which he knows agrees with him, whatever the Supreme Court may say, or else he must find something else legally actionable (usually the possession of narcotics) by which the pornographer can be, if not silenced, put temporarily out of sight.

And yet the situation in this country is relatively favorable, as I learned spending a year recently in England, where it is still possible to settle such matters by calling a cop: to arrest someone reading aloud a poem, say, containing one such offensive word; or to confiscate off a bookseller's shelves magazines containing many.

I myself appeared in a Magistrate's Court, shortly after my arrival in Brighton in 1968, as a witness on behalf of a young man charged with "obscenity" for having read on the beach Allen Ginsberg's comic-pathetic poem "America." One line in particular was at issue, "America go fuck yourself with your atom bomb," and the prosecutor eventually asked me—more plain- tively than in anger—if I did not think the poet might equally well have said, thus risking no offense, "America go rape your- self with your Atom Bomb." And when I responded, "No, because that *would* be obscene," everyone laughed, including the judge; at which point, the tide turned and the case was won, the English if not dearly loving a joke, having a need to appear to.

But I had not meant a joke at all, wanting quite seriously to kidnap from that Other Side the word "obscenity" which they had taken for their own.

In America, too, this is the advantage the readers of the *Courier-Express* and the *Buffalo Evening News* have over the subscribers to the *Berkeley Barb* or the *East Village Other*. When in rage or anguish one of the latter cries, "Shit!" or "Go fuck yourself!" he is called "obscene," and no matter what happens in the courts, everyone on both sides knows what is meant.

But then a correspondent in the *Buffalo Evening News* writes of the student followers of Eugene McCarthy: "About the only conspicuously special thing about the convention city is the pres- ence of a great many roughly dressed young people with beards and long stringy hair. They swarm the headquarters hotel and indulge in their special brand of monotonous chanting to the strum of out-of-tune guitars." And when some truly sweet singer to a well-tuned guitar shouts back "Obscenity!" this is under- stood as metaphor only, or hyperbole, or crude student humor.

Similarly, there are standard epithets a shocked father can use (some of which still possess legal meaning), when, flipping open one of our ten or twelve or fifteen mimeographed mags, he comes across a poem by his daughter, ending:

> how carelessly   they form
> the round
>   of the dream.

                    their cocks
                    are heavy   dark.

But no words are sanctioned, by custom or law, to express what
that daughter feels reading the poems her father makes or loves,
not even realizing they are poems, but inscribing them over the
front of his office, or pasting them as bumper stickers on the
back of his car:

                    I will   insure any-
                                        body
                    but a draft-
                                card burner

                    If guns   are outlawed
                    Only outlaws
                                will have
                                guns

    Clearly, however, the difference in language which separates
the celebrator of heavy cocks from the execrator of draft-card
burners is basically *not* a difference between those in the university and those outside. Despite my present anomalous position as an aging professor caught between two warring sides,
and despite similar attempts at mediation by other faculty members of equal age and rank, the current confusion of tongues
represents quite simply a difference of generations. Those good
citizens of Buffalo who insist otherwise, identifying the University as a whole with the Enemy, have been misled by the
accident of history which transformed U.B. into SUNYAB at the
very moment when the war of the old against the young—which
had started sometime just after the end of World War II—had
reached the peak of its fury and the young were about to mount
their counteroffensive.
    Actually, even the scare stories in their own newspapers suf-
fice to tell them that student protest and provocation and revolt
is part of a larger cultural revolution in Buffalo: young nuns hiking up their skirts, and young priests forsaking their vows to get
married; young Blacks, in jeans and knotted bandanas, running

like crazy cowboys down ghetto streets to smash store windows and steal T.V. sets; young draft-resisters, as likely to be cab drivers as students, slugging it out with Federal Marshals before the altar of the Unitarian Church; the Road Vultures, in black leather jackets and swastikas, so filling the night with the roar of their bikes that waking, honest householders cannot tell whether their nightmares have ceased or only just begun.

Essentially, however, it is their own kids, of course, with whom the writers of anonymous letters to the newspapers and the makers of anonymous phone calls to dissidents are fighting the vainest of fights: each side shouting in a language the other cannot understand, and the parents, at least, pretending they are shouting at somebody else.

Not that they weren't expecting some trouble, understand, having given *their* parents trouble when they were young, as presumably, those parents had given theirs; and so on back to the Garden of Eden. But nothing had happened in quite the way they had expected and prepared for, vowing not to be this time the damn fools their old men and ladies had proved earlier. That their sons would figure out some new way to cut their hair and wear their clothes, they had foreseen; but not that they would be coiffed and draped so you couldn't tell them from the girls—and not even faggots, to make it worse. Similarly they had anticipated those boys hitting the booze at one point or another, getting drunk enough to fight or maybe even to smash a car up around them; but drugs were something else, their effects inscrutable and terrifying to one who had got his kicks on beer and bourbon: the giggling highs, the trips through love into terror—with chromosome damage at the end of the line, if the scientists could be believed!

As for the girls, Christ, even nice girls had got knocked up before, no use kidding about that—but not with *Black* babies. And even worse were the ones who didn't get knocked up ever, buying their ration of pills at the drugstore as regular as Kotex, and consequently without even the fear of pregnancy left to tamp them down a little. Not that anything would make any difference once they were out of their heads with marijuana or LSD.

Worst of all, though, was the madness that seemed to dog

them all, boys and girls alike, as common as acne used to be in the old days—somebody always flipping, or psyching, or spacing out, or whatever the current term for going nuts was. True, adolescence had always been a favorite time for psychological troubles, ever since it and they were invented at about the same time, when society got rich enough for two such luxuries. But things had seemed better in those tough times when repression bred the sort of neurosis everyone was used to, or the kind of occasional impotence that didn't even show or matter a hell of a lot. Sick or well, in those days at least the "I" that had been the child and was going to be the mature man was always *there*— scared maybe, but fighting to assert itself against all the others fighting it.

But these kids lived a life of total surrender, all flow and impulse and letting go, in which they didn't seem to know or care whether they had a self or not. When they suspected they might, they tried to blur it out with chemical compounds and the juices of magic mushrooms or poison cactuses. Looking into their burnt-out eyes, you could see no core at all behind, nothing looking back, only blackness inside the skull. So how could you tell the sane from the mad anyhow—being brought up to make that distinction, and what's more, believing in it—when all of them were lost in a world of sound magnified beyond real hearing, their heads full of wild images and ideas out of comic books and science fiction and fairy tales, *I Ching* and *The Tibetan Book of the Dead* and *The Book of Judgment*.

God knows such notions have not been absent from my own head as I have watched over the last decade or so six children of my own grow up—or down or out or in, whatever the proper directional term is these days; and part of my problem, as is true I suspect of my neighbors as well, is that we cannot tell even in which direction our kids are going, and are not sure whether we or they are disoriented. In any case, the dismay I share with my neighbors, watching them go, constitutes the dark side of that ambivalence toward Right Now which I try so hard to balance and protect, aware that both sides of it are authentic responses to what is really happening, though either alone falsi- fies the way things are, for us as well as for them. If I were not so scared at how far the young are willing to travel and the price they must pay, I could not feel in the face of their courage the sympathy, wonder, and admiration I do; and I am further aware that neither my fright nor my affection matters to them nearly as much as it does to me.

But there are no surprises here, since this is precisely what we have always been told it should mean to be old and just what we remember from our own experience it does mean to be young: to prize ambivalence and to despise it. The young seem to have little choice in the matter, but the old can, and in many cases do, refuse their option. Yet to deny either side of our earned ambivalence is to turn ourselves into caricatures: Falstaff on the one hand, the Lord Chief Justice on the other—the comic falsifier or the absurd represser—and thus to betray the only real good bought with the expenditure of years, "wisdom," as it is customarily called, though that sounds more like a boast than a description.

From the point of view of too many of my Buffalo neighbors, however, the refusal to abandon ambivalence, the resolve eternally to have it both ways, seems exactly what has turned the University into a source of corruption rather than salvation for the young. It is the characteristic vice of academic liberals— "damned wishy-washy eggheads," as they would say in their own language, or "pathologically permissive neurotics," borrowing that of their doctors. The real point is that they had expected more and better of us, though they will never quite say so, only abuse us for having failed their unexpressed wish, maybe even their unconfessed faith in us, and especially in our institutions.

More perhaps than any people in the world, middle-class Americans have traditionally expected the school system from kindergarten on to do for their children what their homes and the churches of their fathers have conspicuously failed to do: to make them "well-rounded" and "responsible" and "godfearing" men and women. And college is, or should be at least, the climax of it all. Certainly it represents a last chance, after opportunities fumbled or utterly missed in grade and high school, to go forward by seeming to go backward, to insure ultimate maturity by prolonging adolescence just a little longer for an ever larger elite: an elite which theoretically (it is a lovely American ideal) could become a majority without losing its exclusive status. But this gift of four extra years in which play is granted equal time with work is not a free gift; those who subsidize it with endowments or annual giving or taxes expect such "higher education" to pay off.

And so it has in the past, guaranteeing to the reasonably diligent young man who survives and gets his degree a better job, a longer car, a bigger house, and a chic-er wife than his father had before him; while the reasonably charming young lady who lasts all the way is guaranteed marriage to precisely such a young man. But above and beyond this, the university has traditionally taught such young Americans, male and female, to desire precisely what they were going to get, and to relish it once gotten. All at once, however, things seem to have changed. Not that colleges have altered radically over night, merely that what has been happening for years has passed a critical point and become highly visible, apparent even to the producers of mass entertainment, so that now in commercially successful books, plays, films, and T.V. scripts, universities begin to be portrayed as having betrayed their traditional function.

No reader of the popular press, at any rate, can doubt that these days universities encourage young men not to make it but to drop out, and to despise the modest jobs, medium-length cars, moderately large houses, and adequately rewarded jobs of their fathers—not because they are no grander, but because they are (misguidedly, pointlessly, offensively, it would appear) as grand as they are. Similarly, readers of Sunday supplements are told, higher education downgrades marriage in the eyes of young women, who before their college careers are over are likely to have had, unmarried, all the pleasures of sexual companionship—not just furtive one-night stands on car seats or in the grass, but public long-term affairs in apartments, paid for by pooling the allowances from home of both partners. And there is a considerable amount of truth in these accounts—not in terms of their diagnosis of causes, perhaps, but certainly in their description of behavior.

Not all students in the university by a long shot learn thus to despise marriage and worldly goods; but those who strike the large public as the most obnoxious and big-mouthed (which is to say, the brightest and most articulate) tend to, even if to begin with—properly brainwashed and lock-stepped into the world of total education from the age of two and a half or three on past their majority—they were vocation-oriented, course-happy degree-pursuers. And even that large, less conspicuous majority which does not, those who go on in increasing numbers every year to get final degrees, marry, and buy according to expectation, spend a hell of a lot of their time *talking* against the values of their parents' world, screaming arguments (ironically the occasion will sometimes be borrowing the family car) against it, which they may later betray in action, but can never manage to controvert in theory.

And how else can their heartsick parents explain them, these spoiled kids who were "given everything" and ended not merely failing to appreciate it (ingratitude is only to be expected), but by sneering at it (heresy is quite uncalled for)? The university is the simple-minded explanation, meaning dope and the professors: dope which "weakens the mind," and the professors who then warp it.

It is, in fact, true that many university students—more and more of them each year, quite regardless of what sort of homes they come from, or where they go to school—smoke marijuana, and that a smaller but still considerable number experiment with LSD and other psychedelics, as well as with "speed," which is to say, the amphetamines (though heroin, special terror of writers for the popular press, is seldom used). For better or for worse, as is already known both to those who accept it and those who deplore it, a large proportion of the people now in college (along with their somewhat older brothers and sisters, plus God knows how many generations to come) will smoke grass with as little stress of conscience and as little harm to themselves as their parents taking a drink. The patterns for doing it, social and psychological, are set; and the law, chief source of difficulty and danger at present, will doubtless be changed before very long.

And this shift in taste, habit, convention will occur, has already occurred even for the straightest kids of all: the crewcuts as well as the long-hairs, the joiners and voters and go-getters as well as the protesters and sit-downers and get-losters. The world, I suspect, will probably not be a much better place when the changeover from a whiskey culture to a drug culture is rec-

ognized by courts and cops and priests and parents, as it is now
by kids. But it will not be worse, either, only different—which,
considering the present shape of things, may *just* be an improvement, after all. At least it will be an improvement not to send
young people to jail for anticipating the habits of the immediate future; and perhaps professors and others willing "patiently
to explain" can be of some help in this regard.

What they cannot influence, what they have not influenced, is
the shift itself; nor can they exploit it, even if they would, in
order to persuade the young to despise what their parents claim
most to believe—except insofar as the professors are parents
themselves, as dishearteningly conditioned as a car salesman or
a surgeon to the world of work and consumption. It is not those
who challenge, but those who accept the values of our society
who teach the young to reject them. And they learn not in the
classroom but at home, where by and large the marriages that
produced them seem to work no better after a year or two than
the shiny cars that took them to Cub Scouts and Little League;
while the psychiatrists who tinker with the former produce results as expensive and unsatisfactory as the mechanics who work
on the latter. Their instructors in Sociology or Literature perhaps help the young to see all this—or rather, remove certain
obstacles between them and seeing. In the end, however, it is
not the man who points, but what he points to, what is really
there, that makes the difference.

Nonetheless, we are not entirely innocent, we professors,
though not guilty as charged. What should irk our neighbors,
who ordinarily do not appear to notice it, is the fact that like
them we, too, these days (gone the times when we were vir-
tuously underpaid) flourish in an ambience of good jobs, long
cars, big houses, and well-turned-out wives; and yet we will not
pretend to the young that what we relish is truly worthy. But
this is a kind of hypocrisy, is it not, as well as a legitimate cause
for complaint, this willingness to live high on the hog at the
same moment we are writing on blackboards all that is wrong
with the world which sustains us, and assigning great books
which reveal the horror at its heart. Nor is this mitigated by the
fact that our neighbors are also guilty of their own sort of
hypocrisy, by living in that horror and claiming to their children

not merely that they do not know it, but that it is not even present.

We need each other to illuminate our complementary self-deceits, difficult as this is for both of us to admit; though I suppose I did admit it in a way, moving into Central Park, one of the greenest oases left behind by the movement of Buffalo's first masters out toward the periphery, and touted to newcomers ever since by the real estate sales ladies. Or maybe it was a kind of *hubris* that took me to that formerly forbidden place, into which not only my working-class grandfather but no Jew could have moved in the days before Saul Bellow and Harry Golden and Isaac Bashevis Singer had become best sellers. Maybe I deserved what I got when my troubles came, for behind them some place surely was the neighborhood taking its revenge; maybe it was a mistake to think that my grandfather had paid *his* dues and so *I* had a right.

At first, however, I worried about none of this, believing simply that I had fallen in love with the place, its well-tended cushiness, its fat-cat air of peace; because, to tell the truth, I was ready for peace, and to find it just off Main seemed a double blessing. I should have been warned, though, by the evidence of the price paid for that peace, put off a little by the signs of how insecurely it was based, after all: floodlights burned all night, illuminating the yards of my neighbors, and I would wake sometimes in the darkness just before morning to see the prowl cars of private police agencies stopped just across the street, so that the guards could try the doors and check the windows of a house whose owners were in Palm Beach for the winter, or off to spend a weekend at the Lake. Protection and exclusion were only vestigial, perhaps, by the time I came, but they had been built into the neighborhood from the very beginning.

Those great stone houses, as old as the century, staunch as battlements and crenelated like castles, had been constructed to protect the verdure in whose midst they rose and the peace their WASP owners sought against all ethnic interlopers, all who had come too late to our shores or had gotten rich after the proper moment. But they had long since departed, those original builders, along with the immigrant girls who had

polished their silver and scrubbed their floors; and the cruel gray
of the stones they had had set, grim as a prison or a Florentine
palazzo, had softened toward green under the moss, and the
foliage of the great elms lining the streets had lifted and spread
till the light that filtered through made the playing children
beneath them seem like dim figures at the bottom of a lake. And
there were plenty of children now, for the second wave of householders were largely Roman Catholics: Irish and Slavs grown
wealthy, but pious or punctilious enough still to have all the kids
they could afford.

But no one any more, certainly not families so large, could
afford the live-in help that had tended the houses and gardens
so long. Now it was mother who oiled the mahogany woodwork
and grandmother who pushed the dustmop or dipped the lustres
from the crystal chandeliers one by one in vinegar, while father
guided the power mower, and his older boys clipped the hedges
or pruned the trees. To be sure, once or twice or three times a
week some cleaning lady or yard man would appear to lend a
hand; but they came and went in weeks, not a lifetime. And
they were almost invariably Negroes, who would walk from the
Main Street bus stop in the morning, toward it in the evening—
their faces and bodies stiff, uncertain, their eyes studiously
blank, for they were far from their own turf, strangers in a
strange land. And as the times changed and they became more
and more visible, their white employers, watching them leave
through the parted living-room drapes, began themselves to feel
strangers on their own street, in their own homes, as if no one
was on his own turf anymore, not even in Central Park.

Meanwhile, however, the kids kept whooping it up: little
girls riding the velvet-smooth banisters from second floor to
entrance hall, with a whoop and a shriek; little boys tearing the
green plush covers of the immovable billiard tables with some
wild, show-off thrust of the cue; both taking off for their
parochial school classrooms hung with ikons and dark with
bustling nuns. The coach-houses had long since been converted
to garages and the back gardens dug out for swimming pools,
so that swerving up the circular drive through the lilacs, drunk
as a coot, papa could now end up in the drink, Buick and all.

But nothing fundamental had departed, had only somehow shrunk and withdrawn as the city closed in around Central Park, its shifting population pressing and pressing: lower-middle-class Jews buying pastrami and bagels on Hertel Avenue; the Negroes flooding into the nearest high school on Main Street, from whose open windows passers-by can now hear the "soul-music" fight songs of the basketball team.

Still, in the declining summer squirrels ran the high tension wires that separated the backyards; and in the fall, ducks heading south would light briefly on the surfaces of the pools, camouflaged by the dazzling play of light and dark under the half-stripped branches. And at noon on Sundays, the old Methodist Church huger than any of the huge houses around it but hewn at the same moment out of the same stone, would ring its customary chimes. And who cared, dreaming in their gardens, the funnies fallen to the grass at their feet, if fewer now came to its call than responded to the musical bells of Mr. Softy, the ice-cream man? A few old ladies, maybe, aging survivors who on their good days might go still to arrange the altar flowers, and who visited each other, their chauffeurs driving them up on the lawns so that they would not have too far to walk.

The pillared housefronts were painted and unpeeling still; the lawns remained cropped to green trimness, as the war against dandelions continued unabated. Even the price of property, therefore, stayed up or mounted; so that the third wave moving in, which consisted largely of professors—I among them—had to have it made already in order to afford the mortgages and the taxes. But we had not made it in the same old American way as our predecessors, by learning to believe in the "it" on the road to attaining it. And this, I suppose, is what really bugged the survivors of the first and second waves, among whom we came to live: the old peekers and peerers, as well as the middle-aged starers and doubtful wavers.

It was not that we latest migrants did not tend our grass quite so lovingly, nor polish our cars quite so hard, nor hover over our garbage cans quite so diligently to repair the ravages of dogs; nor even that, making no secret of it, we did not go to the Church of Our Choice, or ride herd on our children in conventional ways: none of these lapses were what made us seem unredeemable strangers.

No, it was that we had come with reservations and ironies, with tongue in cheek, *camping* rather than living our bourgeois lives. But how did our neighbors know, really? Maybe by checking out our odd furniture, the weird pictures on our walls, the eccentric ornaments in our gardens—like the cockeyed pot thrown in Montana which I had put in a niche just outside my study window, where formerly a stone Virgin had stood. Certainly, I could see those neighbors casing the changes we had made, when we had them over for tea or drinks and they sat, glass or cup in hand, a little puzzled, more than a little uneasy.

But especially, I think, it was our kids who gave us away: their bare feet, their uncut hair, their Salvation Army dresses, their *lumpen* friends—Black as often as not. Our three sons, it happened, were together and with the rest of us for the first time in many months, even years: the youngest, who had graduated from high school in Italy and had lived for a short time in New York, back to organize a rock group with some old Montana friends; the second, who had worked on a Kibbutz in Israel, dubbed films into English in Paris, and served as secretary and companion to the only U.S. Representative to have voted against both World Wars, home to draw breath; and the oldest—with his wife—visiting briefly, after having farmed outside of Florence, not liked Tokyo, and settled into Fiji, where both of them had taught school for a year.

Everything about them, and my three girls as well, seemed to declare that they would neither stay on in Central Park nor strike out for the next fashionable suburb, like all the second generations before them, but would head out as soon as they could for ghettos old and new: Drop City, or the Haight-Ashbury, or Death City itself—the lower East Side of New York, where their grandparents had started life in America, just off the immigrant ships.

I do not mean to suggest that our neighbors were not cordial enough at first, delighted even, as they kept saying, to have a "writer" close by; to which I kept wanting to respond, adapting the old anti-Hungarian joke: "Who needs an enemy, when he has a writer for a friend?" I figured, however, that they'd change their minds soon enough; but they appeared to bear up quite well even after other writers came to call in uniforms and with attendant publicity which made it quite clear who they were: a Russian Communist on tour, complete with translator and C.I.A. agent in tow; a notorious "Beatnik," bearded and balding, with an incredible entourage including one certifiable psychotic; various wandering "hippie" poets with guitars, obviously convinced that dirtiness is next to Godliness; queers, Black and White, swishy and non-swishy, middle-aged and adolescent; one or two old-fashioned Hemingway-era drunks, etc., etc.

It was a standard enough selection; and our neighbors must have been sure of their unsavory habits and beliefs on sight, having read about them—or others much like them—every other week in their favorite journals. Yet for a long time I heard not a word of complaint, even when we would celebrate the arrival or departure of one or another of them with a party: a gathering together of their admirers and detractors, plus the just plain curious, to shout at and kiss each other, and sometimes to dance until three or four in the morning to music whose emphatic beat almost buckled the stout old beams of the house, and must have come close to jouncing some of our nearer neighbors out of bed.

For a short while, in fact, I deceived myself completely on the basis of this evidence, knowing full well that a similar scene in a working-class neighborhood would have stirred instant cries of rage, much pounding on ceilings and doors, maybe even a fist-fight before it was over, and at last the cops; while on a tight petty-bourgeois street, there would have been a hushed phone call or two, and then the squad cars. Well, I thought, this is how it is when you're really *in*—the police called only against outsiders, unidentified trespassers after dark; professor or not, disturber of the peace or not, having become a Central Park householder, I was immune to such harassment: by geographical definition, all right.

It was a notion that made me uneasy, though I had no crimes on my conscience and no desire certainly to tangle with the cops just for the hell of it at fifty and just off Main; that possibility had been used up once and for all at seventeen and on Bergen Street. Still it left me feeling somehow unmanned to think that I had lost forever so old an enemy, and must now, as if I had turned child again, look to my local policeman only to shoo off bad boys and to help in crossing streets.

But waking on the morning of April 29, 1967, I read in the *Courier Express: Western New York's Greatest Newspaper* the story which assured me that I had not been dreaming in some troubled sleep the events of the night before. UB PROFESSOR, WIFE, SON ARRESTED ON DOPE CHARGES, the headlines declared, over the standard newspaper pictures of us all, whose point seems to be to blur identity in favor of making clear that before the law all men look like criminals.

And reading on, I knew that I was in the process of becoming (unless I managed quickly to find my own version and voice) a character in someone else's fiction, as false to the core as those photographs themselves, but perhaps for that very reason a potential best seller: "Dr. Leslie A. Fiedler, a University of Buffalo English professor and novelist, his wife, their son and daughter-in-law were among six persons arrested on narcotics charges Friday night in the Fiedler home. . . . Dr. Fiedler, 50, author of four novels and faculty adviser to LEMAR, a U.B. student organization which advocates legislation [*sic*] of marijuana, was charged with maintaining premises where narcotics are used . . . police had kept the Fiedler residence under 24-hour surveillance for the last 10 days . . . they saw marijuana users enter and leave the house. Police undercover agents had been in the Fiedler house on numerous occasions . . . agents had observed members of the Fiedler family and visitors smoking marijuana and hashish."

ii

WHATEVER MISLEADING emphases there were in the first news-paper accounts of my arrest, they were at least faithful to the only facts which interested the reporters, i.e., what the police actually said and did. Any falsifications present were attribut-able to the cops themselves and their "undercover agents"—a single teen-age agent, as it turned out, whom they perhaps hoped to dignify with the not-quite-accurate plural. But the tone and selection of details were enough to cue further distortions in the minds of unwary or hostile readers. On April 30, for example, the President of the University, distressed, under pressure and presumably informed only by such accounts (he had not yet talked to me at all), issued a statement which read in part: "I have made it clear that this administration will not tolerate students who are found trafficking in illegal drugs. We will not tolerate faculty colleagues similarly involved."

The implication that I was—or, at any, rate, that I had been accused of—"trafficking in drugs" may well have been only an inadvertence. There was, however, nothing inadvertent about the Letter to the Editor which appeared in the *Courier Express* on May 7. Its author, a fellow-Buffalonian, indignant enough to rush into print (or are such communications produced on order by the staff?) but cautious enough to sign himself only "Con-cerned Citizen," began by referring to "The arrest of a college professor in our city for the illegal use of a drug . . . ," though the original charge had read quite clearly, "maintaining premises where narcotics are used."

And on May 19, *Time* compounded the error for the benefit of its national circulation of millions, by tacking on to the end of a somewhat flippant piece on students and drugs, headed "Potted Ivy," the Rogues Gallery pictures of four Fiedlers out

of the *Courier Express*, and a reference to our case, which—
in the context of the not-really-appropriate article, ran as follows:
"When it comes to drugs, though, the ironic fact is that often
adults with whom alienated students do establish contact are
themselves narcotics users. Example: last month Yale's popular
Art History Instructor . . . was arrested by New Haven police
for possessing marijuana. At the State University of New York
at Buffalo, Critic-Novelist Leslie Fiedler, 50, was arrested in his
home during a pot-and-hashish party. . . . *Time*'s only improvement on the original in the direction of accuracy was to get
the name of my university right, whereas the Buffalo paper had
preferred as always to use the good old name, U.B., presumably
in honor of the good old days before pot and disruptive professors. On the other hand, the notion that the bust had occurred
during a "pot-and-hashish party," along with the suggestion that
I was, like the popular Yale instructor, a "narcotics user," and the
implication that students from the college were present in our
home when the police arrived are all that magazine's own invention: there were no college students on hand at all, and
actually no party in progress—only one of my sons taking a
bath, while two friends waited for him, and another son and
daughter-in-law preparing to leave for a movie with me and
my wife.

"Concerned Citizen," if, indeed, he existed at all, was safely
beyond my reach; and for coming to terms with the President,
there were regular channels and established procedures, all of
them properly private and discreet. *Time*'s misrepresentations,
however, had been made in public—by an anonymous editor to
be sure, but beneath the *Time-Life Inc.* masthead; and so I decided (foolishly I now think) to set the record straight in public,
which is to say, beneath that masthead but under my own
name: to write a Letter to the Editor, in short, a chump's
game if there ever was one. For when, after phone calls and
telegrams and pointless annoyance on both sides (I should
simply have sued, or forgotten it), the letter appeared, it had
had all the point and passion cut out of it, with no indication
of how much had been excised where.

In the end, however, it was not just waste effort, since I
had learned in the course of it that the letter I really wanted

to write had to be written in my own time, on my own terms, and to the world—not to meet deadlines and space requirements, and, above all, not to any Editor. I had known all along that I must eventually write something, resolved that this time I would not make the mistake—so it seemed anyhow in retrospect—which I had made in Montana in 1958, when I had chosen to keep silence and trust that somehow the truth would emerge.

But where to speak my piece was the problem. At first, I considered *Playboy* and *Ramparts*, the two magazines I had come to find the most pleasure in writing for in 1967, feeling somehow less falsified on their pages than elsewhere—as had been the case with the *New Leader* and *Partisan Review* around 1947, and with *Commentary* and *Encounter* around 1957. The readers of *Playboy,* however (at least the ones who actually read it, rather than thumb through for the foldout), and of *Ramparts* were, being largely young, committed to the Pop libertarianism characteristic of their time, quite as the readers of *Partisan* were to the literary Trotskyism and of *Commentary* to the Cold War skepticism characteristic of theirs. They therefore could be expected to be, instintctively and by definition, on my side in any case involving drugs and cops and improper surveillance, whatever its merits. What I wanted, though—and not just in terms of strategy, but in response to some deeper need I have not yet quite explained to myself—was to convince those of my own age and historical experience: the more enlightened members of what the young call (because that's what it *is*, I suppose) "the Establishment," both in the university and in the larger world of arts and letters.

Such aging and established liberal humanists had gone back Left with the times; but longing, in their second leftist period, for the words of dissent spoken in the voice of sweet reason, and not finding them anywhere—certainly not in *Ramparts* or *Playboy*—they had joined together to create a journal in which they could communicate with each other in the tone and vocabulary (and at the inordinate length) of the sort they looked for in vain elsewhere. That journal is, of course, *The New York Review of Books,* which began and remains their house organ. I do not mean to put it down; for that would be in one way too easy and in another, quite unfair—especially since it stood by me in the time of my troubles, generously providing me with a forum, as it has to other dissenters, some of them temperamentally quite alien to its editors: critics of Vietnam, draft-resisters, student activists, champions of Civil Rights and Black Power, critics of the Warren Report, etc., etc.

It would be less than candid, however, not to confess that I find it generally a bore, since I do not especially enjoy overhearing a small circle of friends and former friends admiring or castigating each other at merciless length. Having been a Trotskyite once gave me quite all I could stand of living and wrangling in a self-enclosed intellectual province; ever since, any hint of it makes me a little claustrophobic. Moreover, the *NYRB* seldom has a good word to say for the kinds of current fiction and verse I find most moving, including my own; but that is another story for another day.

Our dealings about the article itself were peaceful enough, except for some minor arguments with copy editors over style and syntax; and though I shall probably not write for the *NYRB* again, just as I had not written for it before—not having been invited, as a matter of fact—what I feel chiefly is gratitude.

The article itself, however, troubles me as I suspect it may have troubled some of my readers, who perhaps found it more apology than confession, more special plea than total self-revelation. And, indeed, though what I wrote is nothing but the truth, it is not quite the whole truth—not even in the approximate sense in which that phrase is used in courtrooms. It is, however, as much of the truth as I could then and can now tell without endangering other people whose lives and fates are inextricably bound up with my own. I might have said a little more without my lawyer looking over my shoulder; but I am not finally unhappy that the account I give is incomplete and must remain so forever. A parable should be a never-quite-told-tale; and this is a parable on its interminable way to the Supreme Court of the United States.

I hope only that its incompleteness does not seem evasion or subterfuge, or, worst of all, self-deceit. I have kept in mind throughout Nathaniel Hawthorne's admonition to the writers who came after him to tell of themselves if not the worst, something by which the worst might be inferred; and I have tried not to forget what I first surmised reflecting on the trials of others, then learned fully in my own difficulties with the law: that guilt and innocence are not polar opposites, but merely the obverse and reverse of the common coin with which we buy and sell the necessities of life—and with which, at desperate moments, we gamble.

I trust that, in any case, the following account makes clear to the jury of my peers—which is to say, all who shall ever read this book—precisely how I am innocent and of what, precisely how I am guilty and of what. Rereading the first account of my bust as objectively as possible (quite as I tried to read the cases of Alger Hiss and the Rosenbergs), I have found myself guiltless of the charges brought against me in court, but guilty of some self-pity and more than a little rhetorical self-indulgence. Yet I reprint that original article uncut and unrevised and uninterrupted (what additions I could not resist making, I have appended to it) out of a sense that it has now become, for better or worse, a fact of my life, as well as a document entered in evidence. Let us, therefore, label it:

Exhibit A: On Being Busted at Fifty *

"*Az m'lebt, m' lebt alles*," my grandfather began telling me when *he* was fifty and presumably thought me old enough to understand, "if you live long enough, you live through everything." And, I suppose, justice being as imperfectly practiced as it is in our world, one could consider getting arrested as inevitable a function of aging as getting cancer. But some people I know would have to reach 150 at least before falling afoul of the law, and others have sat in their first cell by sixteen or seventeen: so there must be some other, more specific reason why I find myself charged with a misdemeanor just past the half-century mark of my life.

Where did it all begin, I keep asking myself, where did it really start—back beyond the moment those six or eight

* From *The New York Review of Books*, July, 1967.

or ten improbable cops came charging into my house, without
having knocked, of course, but screaming as they came (for
the record, the first of their endless lies), "We knocked! We
knocked!"; and producing only five minutes later, after considerable altercation, the warrant sworn out by a homeless,
lost girl on whom my wife and daughter had been wasting
concern and advice for over a year. It seems to me that the
actual beginning must have been, *was* the moment I got up
before the Women's Club (an organization of faculty wives
and other females variously connected with the State University of New York at Buffalo) to speak to them of the freedom
and responsibility of the teacher.

I have no record of the occasion (was it a year ago, two?),
can remember no precise dates or names or faces—but I do
recall the horrified hush with which my not very daring
but, I hope, elegantly turned commonplaces were received.
I spoke of the ironies of our current situation in which a
broad range of political dissent is tolerated from teachers,
but in which no similar latitude is granted them in expressing
opinions about changing standards in respect to sex and
drugs. I invoked, I think, the names of Leo Koch (fired out
of the University of Illinois) and Timothy Leary (dropped
from the faculty at Harvard, I reminded my ladies) and ended
by insisting that the primary responsibility of the teacher is
to be free, to provide a model of freedom for the young.

Needless to say, tea and cakes were served afterward, and
one or two members of the Program Committee tried hard
to make conversation with me as I gallantly sipped at the
former and politely refused the latter. But there was a growing
space around me no matter how hard they tried, a kind of
opening *cordon sanitaire*, that kept reminding me of a picture
which used to hang in my grade-school classrooms, of Cataline
left alone on the benches of the Roman Senate after his exposure by Cicero. That evening there were phone calls rather
drastically reinterpreting my remarks (I had, it was asserted
by one especially agitated source, advocated free love and
"pot" for fourteen-year-olds), as well as—for the very first
time—voices suggesting that maybe there was something

anomalous about permitting one with my opinions to teach in the State University.

It was then, I suspect, that my departmental chairman as well as some officials in the loftier reaches of Administration began receiving hostile letters about me—not many in number, I would judge, but impassioned in tone. Still, though this constituted a kind of prelude, it all might have come to nothing had I not then accepted an invitation to speak to the High School Teachers of English in Arlington, Virginia, at the end of January of this year. It was an intelligent and responsive group to whom I tried to talk as candidly as I could about the absurdity of teaching literature, i.e., teaching a special kind of pleasure under conditions of mutual distrust and according to an outmoded curriculum.

I said many things both in my initial presentation and in response to a considerable stack of written questions about what students should be asked to read in high school (essentially, I said, mythological material from Homer to Shakespeare, and similar stuff from the twentieth century, which they themselves prefer, e.g., J. R. R. Tolkien's *Fellowship of the Ring*); what they should *not* be asked to read (such old standards as *Silas Marner* and *Ivanhoe*, such splendid but currently irrelevant poets as Spenser and Milton, plus the stuffier verse entertainers of the nineteenth century like, say, Tennyson); and what the teachers themselves ought to be reading to have some sense of the group they are theoretically addressing (the obvious New Gurus: Buckminster Fuller, N. O. Brown, Marshall McLuhan, Timothy Leary, etc.)

A reporter for the Washington *Post* was present and moved enough to do a feature piece (marred by minor inaccuracies and odd conjunctions born in his mind rather than in mine) headed: COOL IT ON MILTON, TEACHERS ADVISED, which became, as the article was reprinted throughout the country: AUTHOR: STUDY LEARY, NOT MILTON. And under an even more misleading rubric (ENGLISH TEACHERS TOLD TO STUDY LEARY) the story appeared on the front page of Buffalo's morning newspaper, a journal dedicated to scaring itself and its readers about where the modern world is going, largely—I would gather—to keep mail from the Far Right rolling in. Such readers may not ever have read either Milton or Leary, but they know which is the honorific and which the dirty word. It was at this point, at any rate, that the notion of me as a "corrupter of the young" seems to have taken hold in Western New York at least—spreading as far as the State Legislature, in which a member arose within a couple of weeks (representing as I recall the Hornell District) to ask why my presence was being tolerated in a publicly supported institution of higher learning.

I did not at first pay much attention to all this, nor to the fact that in a pamphlet on pornography, prepared by the same body of New York lawmakers, the cover of a Nudist magazine advertising the reprint of a review I had once done of that unexpectedly amusing movie, *The Immoral Mr. Tease,* had been given a prominent position. On the one hand, the small local furor had got lost in the overwhelming response the garbled version of what I had said in Arlington brought from all over the country—offers to publish my remarks in publications ranging from *Fact* to the *Catholic World,* invitations to run seminars for grade-school teachers, and pleas to join such organizations as America's Rugged Individualists Spiritualistic Entity (ARISE) and the Friends of Meher Baba. On the other hand, I had come more and more to think of what I had to say about young people and where they were (all that had begun with my immensely ambivalent and much misunderstood article on "The New Mutants" in *Partisan Review*) as being directed *not* to the young at all.

To be sure, in spite of their publicly announced contempt for the opinions of the aging, those under thirty desperately desire reassurance and confirmation from those beyond that magical boundary; but it is weakness in them which makes them ask it—and I had resolved not to respond. No, it seemed to me that it was to my own peers that I had to speak, to explain, to interpret—translating for the benefit of teachers what their students were saying in an incomprehensible tongue, deciphering for parents what their children were muttering in a code they trusted their parents to break. What did I have to tell the young about themselves (about Shakespeare or Dante or even Melville and Faulkner I could talk with special authority, but that is quite another matter) which I had not learned from them? One of the things I had learned —something I might have remembered from the *Apology* but did not—is that the young cannot, will not, be "corrupted" or "saved" by anyone except themselves. Out of my own ambivalence, my own fear, my own hopes and misgivings before a generation more generous and desperate and religious than my own, it seemed to me I could make a kind of sense—at least what might be made to seem "sense" to those in whose definition of that term I myself had been brainwashed.

But I found an adult community more terrified than myself, more terrified even than I had then guessed, of the gap between themselves and the young; and therefore pitifully eager to find some simple explanation of it all, something with which they could deal, if not by themselves, at least with the aid of courts and cops. "Dope" was the simple explanation, the simple word they had found (meaning by "dope" the currently fashionable psychedelics, especially marijuana); and once that was licked, the gap would be closed, the misunderstandings solved, the mutual offense mitigated. For such a utopian solution, a few arrests on charges of possession and selling, a few not-quite-kosher searches and seizures would be a small enough price to pay.

Meanwhile, however, some among the young (and a few out of the older generations as well) had begun to propagandize in favor of changing the laws against marijuana, or at least of investigating the facts with a view toward changing those laws; and this seemed to the simple-minded enemies of the young a new and even greater cause for consternation. To legalize pot would be, it appeared to them, to legalize long hair and scraggly beards for young men, new sexual mores for young women, Indian headbands and beads and incense for everyone: to sanction indiscriminate love in place of regulated aggression, hedonism in place of puritanism, the contemplative life in place of the active one. And everyone knew what that meant! At this point, the fight against marijuana with the aid of the police and strategic lies began to be transformed into a *fight against the freedom of expression* (though only in the case of those interested in changing the marijuana laws, to be sure) employing the same weapons.

At this point precisely—it was in March of this year— I became Faculty Adviser to LEMAR, an officially recognized student organization on the campus at Buffalo, dedicated to employing all possible legal means to make the regulations on the consumption of marijuana no more stringent than those on alcohol—and which, incidentally, asked all of its members to sign a pledge not to possess or use pot. I was asked to assume the job, I gather, in large part because I was notoriously "clean," i.e., it was widely known that I (and my wife as well) did not and had never smoked marijuana. Though this may have been in the minds of some of the students who approached me a purely strategic reason for their choice, it seemed to me a principled reason for accepting the position. I would, given the circumstances, be able to fight for the legalization of "grass" not in order to indulge a private pleasure, but in order to extend freedom for everyone. Besides, the situation struck me as intolerable, with exactly the same discrepancy between the actual practice of a community (in this case the subsociety of those under thirty) and the laws which presumably regulated it, as had prevailed in respect to alcohol during the late Twenties.

The same considerations which had led to the repeal of Prohibition early in the following decade, seemed to me to demand a change in the laws controlling the consumption of marijuana in 1967. Certainly I felt this with special urgency as one committed to limiting rather than extending or preserving the possibilities of alienation, hypocrisy, and lawlessness for the young. Moreover, I was convinced that if the University could not provide a forum for the calm and rational discussion of the real issues involved, the debate about the legalization of marijuana would continue on the same depressing level of hysteria and sensationalism on which it had begun. Finally, even if I had disagreed totally with its aims, I would have become faculty adviser to any intellectually respectable group that found as much difficulty in persuading someone to take on the responsibility as LEMAR was apparently having.

As a matter of fact, it depressed and baffled me that a score of applicants for the post of faculty adviser had not already stepped forward; though the student leaders of the organization explained to me that there was real cause for fear on the part of reluctant faculty members that sanctions might in fact be taken against them. *But what sanctions,* I asked in my innocence, *could possibly be taken?* A few anonymous letters to the President of the University calling for dismissal? Another indignant "editorial" on T.V. or in the Press? I began to learn soon enough and in an odd way, when an application I was making for an insurance policy was turned down, though my health was fine and my credit good. The letter from the life insurance company was vague and discreet: "like to be able to grant every request . . . not always possible . . . many factors must be taken into consideration . . . I am sorry indeed. . . ." But private conversations with people involved made it quite clear that at the moment of associating myself with LEMAR I had become to the pious underwriters a "moral risk," unworthy of being insured.

While I was considering whether my civil rights had in fact been infringed, and whether I should make an appeal to the American Civil Liberties Union—the local head of the narcotics squad (a man more vain and ambitious than articulate) had been attempting to argue down the students in public debates organized by LEMAR, and had ended in baffled rage, crying out—according to the student head of LEMAR who was his interlocuter: "Don't worry kid—when we get you LEMAR guys, it's gonna be on something bigger than a little pot-possession," and "Yeah—there are some of those professors out at U.B.—bearded beatnik Communists. I wouldn't want any of my kids to go out there, but that's all right— they'll be gotten rid of."

The issues are clearly drawn—*not* criminal issues at all in the first instance, but differences of opinion and style felt to be critical enough to be settled by police methods, even if this requires manufacturing a case. After all, what other way is there to cope with an enemy who is bearded (i.e., contemptuous of convention and probably cleanliness as well), and "beat" (i.e., dangerously aberrant), and a Communist (i.e., convinced of ideas more liberal than those of the speaker, and—worst of all—a professor (i.e., too smart for his own good, too big for his britches, etc., etc.). Indeed, the case against one bearded professor at least was being "prepared" for quite a while. The statements quoted above were made on April 18 and April 20, and on April 29, the day of the arrest, a spokesman for the police was reported as having said that for ten days my house, watched off and on for "months," had been under "twenty-four-hour surveillance" —a scrutiny rewarded (according to police statements in the press) by the observation of "many persons, mostly young, going in and out. . . ." All of which seems scarcely remarkable in a household with six children, each equipped with the customary number of friends.

What is remarkable is to live under "surveillance," a situation in which privacy ceases to exist and any respect for the person and his privileges yields to a desire to "get rid of" someone with dangerous ideas. Slowly I had become aware of the fact that my phone kept fading in and out because it was probably being tapped; that those cars turning around in nearby driveways or parked strategically so that their occupants could peer in my windows, though unmarked, belonged to the police; that the "bread van" haunting our neighborhood contained cops; and that at least one "friend" of my children was a spy.

It was the police themselves who had released to the press (the unseemly desire for publicity overcoming discretion and reticence) the news that this "friend," a seventeen-year-old girl with a talent for lies, had been coming in and out of our house with a two-way radio—picking up all conversations within her range, no matter how private, and whether conducted by members of my household or casual visitors. She had the habit of disappearing and reappearing with a set of unconvincing and contradictory stories about what exactly had happened to her (she had been in the hospital for a V.D. cure; she had been in jail; she had been confined to an insane

asylum; she had been beaten up by incensed old associates)
—but always she seemed so lost and homeless and eager for
someone to show some signs of concern that it seemed impossible ever to turn her out. For me, the high point—the
moment of ultimate indignity—in the whole proceedings came
at my last Passover Seder when, just after I had spoken the
traditional lines inviting all who were hungry to come in
and eat, the "friend' had entered, bearing (we now know)
her little electronic listening device, to drink our wine and
share our unleavened bread.

The ironies are archetypal to the point of obviousness (one
of my sons claims we were thirteen at table, but this I refuse
to admit to myself), embarrassingly so. I prefer to reflect on
the cops at their listening post (in the bread van?) hearing
the ancient prayers: "Not in one generation alone have they
risen against us, but in every generation. . . . This year we
are slaves, next year we shall be free!" I cannot resist reporting, however, that at the end of the evening, the electronically
equipped "friend" said to me breathlessly, "Oh, Professor, thank
you. This is only the second religious ceremony I ever attended
in my life." (My wife has told me since that the first was
the lighting of Channukah candles at our house.)

Fair enough, then, that the first really vile note I received
after my arrest and the garbled accounts of it in the local newspapers (made worse by a baseless reference to "trafficking in
drugs" in the initial release from the University concerning
my case) should have struck an anti-Semitic note, reading,
"You goddamned Jews will do anything for money." Though
I had not really been aware of the fact, anti-Semitism was
already in the air and directed toward the University of
which I was a member. (Hate mail from an organization
calling itself MAM, or more fully, *Mothers Against Meyerson,*
had already begun to refer to Martin Meyerson, the President
of our University, as "that Red Jew from Berkeley.") It was
all there, ready to be released: hostility to the young, fear
of education and distrust of the educated, anti-Semitism,
anti-Negroism, hatred for "reds" and "pinkos," panic before
those who dressed differently, wore their hair longer, or—
worst of all—dissented from current received ideas.

I should have been prepared by my experiences only a few weeks before the police invasion of my home, by some of the responses I got over the telephone when I had agreed to explain the nature and purpose of LEMAR and to comment generally on the culture of the young over one of those three-hour question-and-answer radio programs which appear to bring out all the worst in all the worst elements in any community. The tone of the whole thing was set by the letter of invitation in which the conductor of the program ended by saying that he could not understand why a man so often quoted by *Time-Life* would agree to act as faculty adviser to LEMAR, or in his terms "would willingly take up the posture of Pied Piper to those young louts. . . ."

Still I was not merely distressed but *astonished* when, just as I was recovering from being mugged, fingerprinted, misquoted, and televised, I received an anonymous letter purporting to be from "a group of Central Park neighbors," which began by assuring me that I and my children were "condemned to a ghetto life," went on to refer to their Negro friends (two of whom were also arrested after the police broke into my house) as "the colored, thieving and prostituting for a rattish living . . ." and concluded: "If Myerson doesn't dispose of you and you leave our neighborhood in a reasonable length of time be assured of total harassment. . . ." What such "total harassment" involves has teased my imagination —though I begin to have a clue or two, since having received only recently a notice that our homeowner's insurance policy was being canceled out of hand (in the extra-legal world of the insurance companies, all men are presumed guilty until proven innocent), which would mean—unless we can replace it—the loss of our mortgage.

In this context of abject fear and pitiful hatred the actual arrest, the charges, the legal maneuvering and courtroom appearances seem of minor importance, however annoying and time-consuming they may be. The elements of enticement, entrapment, planting of "evidence," etc., involved in "the well-prepared case" of the police will be revealed if and when the matter comes to trial (it is now adjourned until September 5), and the charges against my wife and me, my

children and their friends are, as they must be, dismissed.
Meanwhile it seems proper and appropriate only to repeat
a couple of paragraphs from a letter I wrote to *Time* after
they had published an account of the events which seemed
to me to verge on slander: a correction which they shortened
and slightly altered:

When the police recently broke into my home in Buffalo,
after weeks of unseemly surveillance, they did not discover—as your columns erroneously reported—anything
remotely resembling a "pot-and-hashish Party." They found
rather my wife, my oldest son, my daughter-in-law and
me at the point of setting out for the movies, and another
son plus two friends at widely scattered places in a large
and rambling house. That second son—absurdly charged
with "possession of marijuana"—far from indulging in
some wild orgy, happened to be in the process of taking
a bath.

The context of your article suggested that university
students may have been involved in the events; this is
untrue. It further seemed to imply that I was smoking
pot. This is also without basis in fact. Neither my wife nor
I has ever used or possessed an illegal drug, nor are we
charged with this even in the case manufactured by the
police. What we are accused of is "maintaining a premise"
—i.e., keeping up the mortgage payments and maintaining
in good repair our home in which other people are alleged
to have been in possession of marijuana.

Beyond this, legal considerations forbid my going at the
moment, though I suppose two items could be added without
indiscretion. First, I was initially surprised and pleased that
the cops did not tear my first-floor study apart after they
had crashed in on me: I attribute their unlooked-for courtesy
either to a lurking respect for professors (they were only really
rough—as could have been predicted—with the two Negro
boys in the house at the time), or to their being unnerved
at finding themselves for once in so grand a neighborhood
(one of them could not help exclaiming in awe, "You can bet

this is the biggest house I ever seen!"). But I have learned since, alas, that their whole "search" of the premises was a perfunctory sham—except on the third floor, where their young agent had been sent in an hour before the bust to leave a "little present" of marijuana, and where, she had assured them (exiting just five minutes before), it safely reposed. And second, the movie we were headed for was *Casino Royale* —a spy and pursuit film which, for obvious reasons, we have felt no need to see since.

I do not mean to say that even the courtroom is not penetrated by the hysteria that affects the community; at our original arraignment, for instance, a respectable judge was disturbed enough to lose all sense of decorum and to lecture those attending the proceedings (quite as if he were speaking over the heads of a group of condemned criminals) on the folly of considering a university a place where one learns "through the sweat of marijuana smoke. . . . They are taught this is not habit-forming. The records indicate otherwise." There is, finally, little doubt that agencies entrusted with law-enforcement have in Buffalo become instrumental in creating an atmosphere in which not only I, but my wife and children are persecuted and chivvied (largely for the simple fault of being *my* wife and children), my whole life at home and at school harried—quite as if we were all living in a Nazi or Communist totalitarian state supervised by Thought Police.

Even my children's friends have had to pay for their friendship, as the police have diligently tried to shore up their shaky case. One of them, as a matter of fact, was arrested before the 29th of April in the company of the same teeny-bopper spy who swore out our warrant; though it remains unclear whether this was a rehearsal for her, or the occasion of recruiting her for "police work." Since our arrest, there have been a couple more: one of a girl who plays in the same rock-and-roll group as my youngest son—the most shameless frame-up of all, in which, according to her story, the police simply broke down her door, walked into the middle of her living room, plunked down a packet of marijuana on a table, and looking up with a smirk, said, "Hey, see what we found!" More publicized was the second, which involved the arrest in their farmhouse home of what the police called "the operator of an electronic-psychedelic nightclub" and his wife —along with two of my sons and my daughter-in-law who had just come to call.

Quite as interesting to the cops as a "loose substance which will be analyzed to determine if it is marijuana, and several tablets and pills which will also be analyzed" were such other dangerous materials, which they confiscated along with them, as a pack of Tarot cards, some jars of macrobiotic foods, and "a lot of psychedelic literature," i.e., several copies of a volume of short stories written by "the operator of an electronic-psychedelic nightclub." The local press found even more intriguing and, apparently, damning the exotic furniture of the place (". . . there were mattresses on the floor, there were short-legget [sic] tables . . . candles were burning and there was incense in the room . . .") and the garb worn by those arrested ("a long white cotton robe . . . a kimono . . . a black and white mini-skirt with black net stockings . . . "hippie-type" sportswear, including tight-fitting denim trousers . . ."). That the "tight-fitting denim trousers" were nothing more or less than garden-variety blue jeans the magic word "psychedelic" concealed from the titillated readers of the *Courier-Express;* and the adjective "hippie-type" glossed it for others less literate but equally convinced that all who dress differently from themselves are guilty even though ultimately found innocent—*especially* guilty if devious enough to convince the courts that they are less insidious than their clothes declare them.

Yet this is not the whole story; for everywhere there is a growing sense (especially as the police in their desperation grow more and more outrageous) that not I and my family, but the police themselves and those backward elements in the community, whose panic and prejudice they strive vainly to enforce, are on trial. The ill-advised remarks of the police court judge at my arraignment, for instance, brought an immediate rebuke and an appeal to the local Bar Association for "appropriate action" from a professor of law who happened to be present. And my own University has stood by me with a sense that not only my personal freedom but the very atmosphere of freedom on which learning depends is imperiled.

When there was some talk at an earlier stage of the game of "suspending" me pending an investigation, my own department served notice that they would meet no classes unless I could meet mine; the Student Senate voted to strike in sympathy if the need arose, and the Graduate Students Association seconded them. In the end, the President of the University announced that, "on the advice of the Executive Committee of the Faculty of Arts and Sciences and after consultation with the State University attorneys and Chancellor Samuel B. Gould," *no* action against me was warranted. The ground for this decision was, he indicated, "the American heritage of fair play in which a man is considered innocent until proved otherwise"; and for the ground as well as the decision, he won the overwhelming support and admiration of his faculty—some of whom, however, were prepared to go just a little further and insist on the principle advocated by the American Association of University Profesors: "Violations of the civil or criminal law may subject the faculty member to civilian sanctions, but this fact is irrelevant to the academic community unless the infraction also violates academic standards. . . ."

Meanwhile, letters, phone calls, and telegrams had been pouring in to both President Meyerson and me (for the first forty hours after my arrest I received not a single hostile or malicious message) from the faculties of America's great colleges and from many schools abroad—all expressing solidarity and the conviction that at stake was the future of a major university and of higher education as well as my personal fate. Even in Buffalo itself I have begun to sense of late a considerable shift of opinion in my favor—not merely on the part of other teachers and those professionals closest to us, like clergymen and psychiatrists, but from every sector of the population; as it becomes clearer and clearer that the unendurably vague charge of "maintaining a premise" (what high school or university would not fall under it?) has been invented to justify the malicious persecution of dissenting opinion.

Needless to say, my awareness of this growing support lifts up my sagging spirits. I have no taste for martyrdom; I do not know how to find pleasure in suffering even for the best of causes; and I find it harder and harder to laugh at even the most truly comic aspects of my situation. But if the Keystone Comedy being played out around me can be turned into an educational venture (education being, hopefully, an antidote to fear itself) which will persuade the most abjectly prejudiced that everyone, even a college professor advocating a change in the law, is entitled to full freedom of speech—then the shameless invasion of my privacy, the vindictive harassment of my family, and the (perhaps inevitable) misrepresentation of all of us in the press will have been worth enduring.

Appendix One: A Matter of Language

Oddly enough, the very first letter I got reacting to my article concerned itself not with the issues or facts involved, but only with correcting my grandfather's yiddish, or rather, perhaps, my imperfect memory of it. My opening phrase, this correspondent informed me, should actually have read: *Az m'lebt, derlebt men alles:* and he went on—his deep pieties, however irrelevantly, at stake—to reproach me for "carelessness which little behooves a scholar." "Would you not have authenticated," he asked, reproachfully, "the sentence if it were, let us say Greek or Latin or French or German." And at first, I must confess, I was inclined to change it. But who am I to give lessons in grammar to a dead grandfather, on whom, I suspect, the difference between transitive and intransitive verbs was quite lost. And in any case, I am determined—being, I suppose, finally more poet than scholar—to remain faithful not to scholarship or syntax, but to memory. It is my deepest piety.

Appendix Two: The Speech at Arlington

I found it, I'm afraid, rather hard to take any of this seriously, especially since I had delivered an earlier version of the Women's Club talk to a similar group in Montana without any repercussions beyond a heated question or two in the discussion period. My Montana listeners had been, by and large, youngish mothers off the reservation for an afternoon; and though they had not all agreed with everything I said by any means, finding it familiar and relevant in terms of their experience at home, they had been intrigued rather than shocked. The quite different reaction in Buffalo was, in part, a matter of relative sophistication, in part of age, since, as I did not then take properly into account, my second audience was not merely out-of-town Eastern, but chiefly comprised no-longer-youngish wives of professors left over from old U.B.: ladies whose lifelong striving for gentility had at last eaten away the toughness of mind and the healthy vulgarity bred by dealing at close quarters with small children.

More than that, however, the three or four years which had intervened between my talk in Montana and the reprise in Buffalo had seen the conflict between young and old escalate and freeze into a full-scale Cold War. On both sides, therefore, there flourished the paranoia proper to such historic moments: the impulse to search one's own ranks for traitors—and find them. To make matters worse, I had long since grown gray enough so there could no longer be any doubt, even on the part of the most myopic, which side I ought to be on.

In any case though, I was by no means through with the subject twice broached to my contemporaries; after my experience with the Buffalo ladies, and even as my time as a teacher crept past the quarter century mark, I began to talk about it to the young—polishing it and focussing it in talks before student groups at the University of Michigan and the Universities of Amsterdam and Leyden in Holland. And when it assumed what I took to be its final shape only a month or so ago, I sent that version to a magazine more respected by students than by faculty wives, to *Playboy;* from this version I cannot forbear quoting what are, in my own mind, the key passages:

Once the teacher has granted the theory that responsibility equals restriction, restraint, censorship, taboo, he has lost in advance all those "cases" to which he must in due course come. At best, he commits himself to endless wrangles about exactly where freedom—understood as the right to express what he believes without hindrance—yields to responsibility—understood as the obligation to curtail his expression whenever he offends the taste, the conventions, or the religious, political, and moral codes which any effective segment of the community that sustains him adheres to, believes it adheres to, believes it ought to adhere to, or merely suspects someone else believes it ought to adhere to. . . . The teacher . . . has a single overwhelming responsibility: *the responsibility to be free, which is to say, to be what most men would call irresponsible.* For him, in any case, freedom and responsibility are not obligations which cancel each other out, but one and the same thing.

Until a man has learned to be free . . . he cannot begin to be responsible in the deep etymological sense of the word; since the only thing for which a teacher is properly answerable is his own freedom, his necessary prior irresponsibility. A slave or a man under restraint, an indoctrinated indoctrinator, a civil servant brainwashed to brainwash others is answerable for nothing. No matter what charges are brought against him, he can plead innocent; for he is the agent of someone else, a despicable tool, just another Eichmann, dignified beyond his worth by being brought to the dock. . . . It is to the unborn . . . that the free man, the true teacher is answerable; but it is the living, real students, their actual parents, the community which he inhabits rather than the one he dreams, which judge him and can make him suffer. And if that community—parents or students or both—desire to visit sanctions on him, he must not pretend surprise or feel dismay.

It all seems an unexceptionable enough teacher's declaration of faith, almost standard in its commonplaces. So how could I have felt the agitated reaction of the Buffalo ladies anything but an absurd misunderstanding, a silly joke? But that was *my* mistake.

I suppose that now—not quite two years after my ill-omened appearance at Arlington—I would feel obliged to include in any reading list for high school teachers, eager to know what fills their students' heads, the names of political leaders and theorists like Ché Guevara and Regis Debray, perhaps Mao Tse-tung himself, since it is this aspect of the student revolt which has preempted the headlines, as rage mounts over the endless, pointless war in Vietnam. I chose then, however, to emphasize the psychedelic aspect of the youth revolution not because there were no signs—visible even to me—of growing activism on campus and among the young Blacks, but because I knew that people of my own age would have more difficulty coming to terms with a revival of religion among their children and pupils than with a reversion to violence. I suspected, in fact, that they would have been scarcely aware that such a religious movement was in progress, despite evidence everywhere that—in however unorthodox a fashion—some of the young, at least, had raised once more the question of whether the active life was necessarily preferable to the contemplative life; and had dedicated themselves to the pursuit of vision rather than of success or power.

The trend toward political participation and violence, was, I felt quite certain, fully visible to all of them, being more familiar and—whatever their reservations—somehow more acceptable. For all the stupid corniness of the remark, Rapp Brown's observation in defense of the Black Power Movement, "Violence is as American as cherry pie," is disconcertingly true. Americans have beat on each other for the loftiest of reasons ever since our nation began, and the shedding of blood, therefore, seems to most of us compatible not only with manliness, but with democracy and patriotism as well. Did not the author of the Declaration of Independence himself assert that the tree of liberty had to be watered with blood at twenty year intervals? To be sure, everyone would like to reserve the option of force for his own side exclusively.

Unlike violence, religion, certainly when it goes beyond mere church-going in the direction of "mysticism," is regarded as somehow undemocratic, effete, maybe even un-American; since it is caviar to the general rather than pie for everybody. In any case, I was reluctant to discuss with that audience the vexed question of just what the connection really was between the new radical politics and the new mystical sects: between the SDS and LSD—the violent posture associated with the taking of political stands, and the passive one associated with the taking of drugs.

The non-violent resistance movement seems to have served as a bridge between the two attitudes; and perhaps the fact that smoking grass involved coming into conflict with the law of the land may have helped to connect that mild and private pleasure with the more violent and public sorts of civil disobedience, like anti-segregation sit-ins and the burning of draft cards. Moreover, a longing for the irrational and the primitive seems to underlie both: a turning away from the Western tradition, which is to say Christian Humanism, and a preference for guerrilla warfare in the boondocks and parliamentary struggle in the cities.

It is a fact, at any rate, that many New Leftists, Black and White, are on pot, speed, and acid; and that one of the favorite recent books of the young is a work that looks both ways—the content of its first section perhaps sufficiently indicated by its title, "The Politics of Experience," and that of its second, an account of an LSD trip, a little less clearly by "The Bird of Paradise." It is an odd development, finally, but one which must be faced up to, since the marriage of the Drug Movement and the New Left is as much a historical fact and a theoretical puzzle as the development of Military Christianity out of the teachings of Jesus, or the Japanese war code of *Bushidō* out of Zen Buddhism.

In any event, I had plenty else to talk to my teachers about, but I could not resist including in my series of relevant names those of Paul Goodman and R. D. Laing. Laing had moved only a little while before from an initial interest in psychiatry toward one in politics; but Goodman had for a long, long time been trying to define a political stance, pacifist and anarchist, and as immune to the cant of the Classical Left as to that of the traditional Right and Center. As the youth resistance has

moved from a surreptitious flirtation with violence toward an
open advocacy, however, Goodman has become to some an object
of contempt rather than emulation. The "maddies" (more elegantly in French, "*enragés*"), at least, have turned against him;
one of their number wrote in an open letter to Goodman, which
appeared very recently in the *Los Angeles Free Press*: "The most
generous statement that can be made about you is that you
are dead," then signed off "with utter detestation."

Laing seems to be faring better on all sides even now; and
back then I lingered over his example with special affection;
since he is not only the founder of a radically new school of
psychiatry but one of the three signers of a manifesto announcing
the newest of the New Left movements in England. He is, in
fact, the author of *The Politics of Experience and the Bird of
Paradise*, as well as having had decisive influence on that
astonishing film *Morgan*, in which, perhaps for the first time on
the screen, Marxism is portrayed not as a threat or a source of
salvation, but merely an old-fashioned belief of our beloved,
ridiculous parents, and a total psychotic is proffered as a totally
sympathetic hero.

Talking about Laing and *Morgan*, moreover, I realized the
sense in which not merely the young, with whose attitudes toward
books I was primarily concerned, but even I myself approached
books, and had been approaching them since I was a child, with
an imagination conditioned by quite another medium: a newer
medium, and one therefore felt as more immediately relevant
to the problems of my own existence.

I am not sure how clearly I saw all of this in Arlington,
but reading over the transcript of my talk, which I've received
since doing the *NYRB* piece, it has straightened itself out in
my head. It was certainly true, as I remarked at the very beginning of my speech, with appropriate thanks to Marshall Mc-
Luhan, that when "we hand students literature in the form of a
book we hand them something they distrust" initially, since for
them, "children of the television era . . . about to produce a
second generation of children of the television era," books are,
or at least seem, "an obsolete machine."

But it was also true, as I did not manage to say until I
was answering the very last question of the session, that I

was not a pure child of the book either: "I suppose my generation are the children of the movies. They were a ritual part of
my childhood. The notion of having missed a Saturday matinee
at the movies would have destroyed me utterly. It almost became
a primitive charm that held my life together and gave it a
shape and a pattern. And I love still to this day not just some
particular movie that I see but simply the feeling of going
into a darkened house and watching those images on the screen
move through their intended progress, and come to an end. . . ."

In any case, I did not pause to reflect on the meaning of this
fact then; but returning to *Morgan* itself, I went on to speculate
on Laing's notion of madness being, on occasion at least, a
break-*through* rather than a break-*down*. It is obvious on the
face of it, however, that for those of us now middle-aged, books
had already begun to seem obsolete, too; though for us, as opposed to those now twenty, that other medium—our medium
rather than theirs—tended to be thought of as something available only one day a week, as sabbath release or recreation, as it
were. In the world of my childhood, those who went to the
picture show more often than that were regarded as immoralists
and scofflaws, whether they were overindulged kids, or the kind
of idle lady who grows fat on a diet of films and ice-cream
sundaes. Even to stay for the second showing of the two
features, the serial, the short subjects, and the newsreel was considered in those days a semi-sin; since, finally, going to the movies
was neither encouraged nor urged, only permitted and tolerated
under strict ceremonial conditions. But this begrudged and be-
grudging status was precisely what made them intriguing to
us.

I spoke to the Arlington teachers in passing—and it was, of
course, one of the things picked up by the newspaper report,
being already a cliché—about the alienation of the young from
the old, the gap between them and us. But our common allegiance to films and the anomalous relationship to books created
by that commitment places us both on the same side of the
much greater gap between all of us now alive and those who
died before Bioscope. For many in that generation novels were
still, to some degree, a suspicious not-quite-art form, an indulg-
ence barely suffered when not actually forbidden, quite as when

the genre had first properly begun in the mid-eighteenth century.

For all of us now, however, young and old alike, novels have been replaced as a kind of privileged flight to fantasy, an allowed truce with the reality principle, by films and comic books and, most recently, T.V. With the exception of a rapidly shrinking sub-class of "trash": cheap thrillers, detective stories, science fiction, and especially, pornography, the novel has been re-classified, along with poetry and serious drama, as required culture—a duty rather than a pleasure, a confrontation of "reality" rather than an "escape" to dreamland.

In this process of turning a pleasant minor vice into a grim major virtue, teachers of English, themselves often communicants of the Arnoldian Culture Religion, have collaborated by making books another school subject like Algebra and Typing, a part of the standard curriculum. This subject, listed as "English" in high schools and, somewhat more grandly, as "Literature" in the university, included at first just works in another language, preferably dead; then only quite ancient works in one's own spoken tongue; at last, all the "good books"—or, even more chillingly, "Great Books"—including those of the present. In recent times, therefore, it is only those books passed by or despised or even banned by the aging compilers of Recommended Reading Lists (underground literature, as we have come to call it) which seem to young readers in any real sense their own.

The question of what to do about this situation, if in fact anything can still be done, was what chiefly concerned me in Arlington; for I felt, as I duly confessed to the teachers who had gathered to listen, that in the quite near future "work will become not only part-time in a person's life, but can no longer be the justification of it. We can no longer believe in the puritan ethos of work and duty . . . our choice is dying of ennui or embracing an enlightened hedonism . . . anyway, some people are going to be capable of living with pleasure without supplementary aids; other people will die of boredom unless they get chemical assistance of one kind or another, and science is providing that for them, too. Meanwhile, we had better keep providing for those who can use it that staple of enjoyment and extended sensibility, literature. Maybe our great time is coming."

And by the "we" of these statements I meant, despite all my reservations about trying to teach pleasure, precisely teachers of English. Still, as ever, I was full of ambivalence about just *how* we should set about redeeming the "teaching" of literature.

That ambivalence, too, I set about confessing, as is my habit, even though I knew then as I know now that only one side of my double-view ever remains with an audience: that to give both god and the devil their due is to sow confusion among those whose very attention is partisan.

"I have two completely opposite sets of notions in my head on this score," I began, "and sometimes one is up and sometimes the other is up. Let me explain both of them to you. . . . I sometimes think that we should abandon the ancients completely. That we should leave Milton and Spenser for the . . . little core of specialists who work in their own reserved, dusty corner of the library, recognizing that for the mass of people who we hope will be readers, these writers seem irrelevant . . . and the effort of getting through to the point where we could demonstrate their relevance would use so much time and so much energy that we would not have any left for the really fruitful things one should do with literature. When I am in a mood like this, I dream of a hundred-year moratorium on John Milton. A thousand-year moratorium on *The Faerie Queen.*"

But then I added, "Sometimes the thought overcomes me that . . . what we really ought to get rid of is recent literature; that a person should be ashamed to get up in a classroom and teach contemporary literature; that there ought to be something that belongs to the students themselves; that there ought to be something they discover and teach us about, and that it is a little unworthy and ignoble always to be competing with the student to see if we can get out there and discover the new writer before they do."

In the end, however, I plumped in favor of teaching recent literature to high school students at least; insisting further that what we teach should be selected without regard for old distinctions between the trivial and the serious.

"I think one of the other distinctions which is disappearing these days," I told my audience of teachers, ". . . is the line that used to be drawn between popular art and high art. There used to be a notion that there were certain sacrosanct sources of literary satisfaction which not only . . . gave you joy but were somehow good for you. . . . On the other hand . . . there were other kinds, pop culture as opposed to high culture, which you enjoyed fervidly as a kind of minor vice." And I went on to explain "the necessity in a mass democratic society of abandoning the notion of two kinds of art . . . two kinds of pleasure—pleasure for the vulgar, and pleasure for an elite."

This is a point which I have continued to pursue, a clue to one of the basic causes of misunderstanding between the young and the old, the student and his teacher; but the single reporter present on the occasion, plus, I fear, a good many of the teachers, were more interested in the familiar topics of alienation and drugs, for which they had attitudes already prepared and waiting.

Appendix Three: On Timothy Leary

The name of Timothy Leary has, in fact, continued to give me trouble. Merely to mention it is to stir uneasiness at least, often downright hostility, not only in newspapers and the hearts of Faculty Wives, but among school teachers and parents everywhere, and among almost all the editors I have recently been encountering. Looking back over the galley proofs of my *New York Review of Books* article, for instance, I see in the margin beside my second use of Leary's name the query: "author: add something else?" And I remember having been urged, when I called a responsible editor to ask, "Add what? Add why?" to expand my references to him, lest I seem to stand by him too uncritically—or even to confuse my own case with his.

I added nothing, however, considering it churlish and cowardly on such an occasion to dissociate myself from a fellow professor (well, *ex*-professor, perforce) who was enduring indignities and legal persecution which made my own seem pretty mild. He had already been sentenced to thirty years and a thirty-thousand-dollar fine for the possession of marijuana, and was involved in the long process of appeal.

And just the other day, I was telephoned by an editor of *Playboy* to ask if I would not consider deleting or qualifying my remarks about Leary's firing at Harvard in the final version of my Faculty Ladies Talk, since—as I would discover once I had learned all the facts—his case against the University was not as simple and clean as I had presumably supposed. But a case is never simple and clean when one has "all the facts," not even, it would now appear, that of Sacco and Vanzetti, nor, there is good reason to suspect, those of Socrates and Jesus.

Yet when the issues have been drawn, one must, without waiting for a time when all the facts will be in—which is never —take a stand for justice, however approximate, and for the victim, however equivocal; otherwise one ends up like the Sophists and Pharisees, on the side of the prosecution and the hysterics, who, in such cases, always agree.

Out of the four or five pieces of real nut mail which have come to me since my own arrest, for instance, two combine the attack on me with insults to Leary. The first reads, "Hi ya goof ball—Your hero LSD cult Leary is being held—are you going to help him, goof?"; and the second, "For all of your kind really need '*Help*,' you and your family; the O'Leary's [*sic*] and the whole diseased nest. Bathing facilities should be donated . . . your homes should be fumigated. . . ."

Under the circumstances, it has been hard for me to say so, but I have had troubles of my own in coming to terms with Leary because, though I am no snob about victims, I am about the founders of religions and messianic pretenders. And this may, indeed, disqualify me from subscribing to any cult not ancient enough for its first spokesman to be utterly pure, which is to say, a pure myth—like, for instance, Father Abraham. Certainly, I am put off not only by Leary but by most of the other assorted sages, apostles, and messiahs who have moved the young over the past decade or two, from Wilhelm Reich to Meher Baba, Suzuki, Ohsawa, and the Maharishi.

Of the lot, Meher Baba strikes me as the funniest and, there-fore, the most appealing, since despite his claim to be nothing

less than God incarnate for our time, he confesses to a love
for cricket and the movies, looks more like a vaudeville comedian
than a conventional guru, and makes jokes with gestures, having
long since given up ordinary speech. Like some of his fellows,
however, and perhaps despite himself, Meher Baba comes recommended as a worker of miracles: a fence must be built
around any house in which he stays lest animals come leaping
out of the wild to be near him, boughs of trees incline toward
him as he passes, etc., etc. But miracles, as the Rabbis kept
therapeutically advising their followers, can be worked even by
the magicians of Pharaoh.

In truth, Reich and Ohsawa at least seem as much interested
in mere magic as in anything properly described as religion:
promising, in the first instance, a cure of cancer to those who
attain the full orgasm; and in the second, the healing of gonor-
rhea to those who achieve the seventh and most severe of the
macrobiotic diets. Unlike religion, magic is not a way of by-
passing or transcending the science which controls our world,
but only a rival kind of science, more archaic or more naive
than the brand which has created the Bomb and transplanted
the organs of the dead into the living; it is therefore less effective
in all areas, except possibly the healing of hysterics.

Magic, however, constitutes only a part of the New Religions,
and perhaps should be considered merely a kind of window-
dressing or secondary elaboration—at worst, an incidental error
—for, like true religions, they are also interested in conversion
and states of grace. Actually, their avowed end—and in this
sense they resemble the mystery cults of the Hellenistic World
more than orthodox Christianity or modern Judaism—is not
eventual salvation, but *extasis* now: the same sort of exaltation
or "high" which Leary sensed had come to seem, especially to
the young, more attractive than bliss beyond the grave, and
which he promised they could attain by the proper use of
"acid."

The notion of salvation appeals primarily to the wretched,
the excluded, the poor in spirit; exaltation provides an equivalent
satisfaction for the affluent, the comfortable, the bored. Not that
life is at present more boring, much less more wretched, than

in the past. As a matter of fact, a good deal of tedium has been eliminated for most of us with the reduction of working hours and the transfer to machines of much intolerably routine labor; and a good deal of misery has disappeared with the conquest of certain diseases and—for a considerable and increasing minority—the amelioration of poverty and the disappearance of starvation.

By the same token, however, leisure has encouraged the spread of education (both in schools and through the mass media), which in turn has helped to create an acute, even painful awareness of the ennui and pain that still remain—much of it forever unconquerable because essential to our human condition. And to deal with this, we must turn inward: learn to control our consciousness as we have at least begun to control our environment.

This traditional function of religion, Leary—pseudo-scientist like his fellows, a trained psychologist to begin with in fact—hoped to perform with the aid of psycho-chemistry in a setting of ritual and wonder. And his wonder drug turned out to be, predictably enough, a compound synthesized in the antiseptic laboratories of Switzerland: LSD. Meher Baba and the Maharishi, on the other hand, frightened perhaps by the risks involved in taking LSD, or maybe simply more traditional, have attempted to capture those seeking exaltation in drugs by assuring them that meditation alone can produce "highs" superior to any they had experienced before.

More successful than either of the latter, however, has been the Japanese-American inventor of macrobiotics, Ohsawa, who promises exaltation as well as miraculous cures through a kind of selective ritual fasting, justified by pseudo-allusions to Western science and pseudo-citations of Eastern mystical philosophy, particularly the theory of Yin and Yang. Rather depressingly, his popularity with the young, especialy in America, seems based on his appeal to what remains in terms of puritanism, that deep American need to assert virtue through suffering rather than joy, or—to put it more justly, perhaps—through joy earned by suffering. At any rate, he teaches that grace is attained not by self-indulgence but by self-denial: not by legitimizing a formerly forbidden food (the Mexican mushroom, say, or peyote) but by forbidding many foods formerly not merely permitted but highly recommended (including milk itself!).

For better or for worse, then—and on most days, I am inclined to think it for better—Leary was the true initiator of a religious revolution which has already begun to leave him behind; for even Wilhelm Reich, who came on the scene much earlier, and whose madness and trust in magic seem not dissimilar, proved finally too Freudian, which is to say, too European and Jewish, to lead the way into the future. And maybe my own impatience with the perhaps necessary charlatanism of the whole crew of new gurus—their miracle-mongering, asceticism, and sheer goyishness—reflects what is most deeply Jewish in me rather than what is merely finicky. In any case, my admiration for Leary is qualified by a profound distrust precisely because I take seriously his pioneer effort to provide the new religion with a new church.

My Arlington talk already betrayed this ambivalence. "Whether they believe it or not," I said to the teachers, "your students are living on the edge of one of the greatest religious revivals . . . and a man who begins to define it in his own weird way—and he is about as weird as Mary Baker Eddy or Joseph Smith or any of those other American founders of homemade religions —is Timothy Leary."

Since then I have seen him in the flesh for the first time, watched him preach or perform or whatever the proper term is before a convention of the National Student Association. After a false start or two intended to tease us to full attention, he appeared draped in a white robe and accompanied by an utterly stoned Black acolyte, who sat cross-legged throughout, playing a Beatles record on a portable player between his knees. Most of the time he kept the volume low enough so that Leary's words could be heard, but from time to time he would turn it up full blast, drowning out his master's message. Or maybe the real message was in the words of the song: *I get by with a little help from my friends, I get high with a little help from my friends.* . . .

In the end, it all seemed both truly sincere and committed, and utterly rehearsed and false: just such an honest fake as a "genuine medium" will arrange when the spirits fail to come for a scheduled seance—since, after all, who could expect them to appear each time punctually and on demand? In short, it proved nothing, except that it is hard to take any messianic pretender seriously until he is long dead. Meanwhile, I am bugged by the man and, even more, by the stereotypes of him, friendly and hostile, especially when they get in the way of readers understanding what I, as well as he, am trying to say. Yet none of this must be taken to impugn his final importance, or to justify his legal harassment.

Appendix Four: The New Mutants

"The New Mutants" appeared in the *Partisan Review* for Fall, 1965; but I had already spoken it out before a "Conference on the Idea of the Future" held at Rutgers University in June of that year. Sponsored by *Partisan*, whose best period was already some fifteen or twenty years gone, and the Committee for Cultural Freedom, about to be exposed as having been subsidized for a time by the C.I.A. but already on its last legs anyhow, the Conference quite appropriately spent most of its time looking back over its shoulder in search of the future: toward the defunct revolutions of the thirties and even 1848. Not that all the participants were Cold War survivors like me, by any means. There was on hand a youngish leftist poet who had flown in from Germany and one of the oldest prophets of the New Left who had not quite made it from California, but his paper was read by proxy. Yet I found nothing in what they had to say, much less in the interventions of the others present, that had very much to do with what most troubled and stimulated me on the current scene.

In the area of literature particularly, the participants seemed utterly out of touch with anything that mattered: for all their up-to-date spruceness, Van Winkles, every one of them, returners from a twenty-year sleep in the Catskills or wherever. The chief speaker who shared that province with me was, quite elegantly and movingly to be sure, still fighting the good fight for the old

"Modernism," which had triumphed shortly after World War I and had been visibly dying ever since the end of World War II. My own talk, however, began not with long-rehearsed reflections on the literary generation of Eliot and Pound and Yeats and the tradition of the Marxian Left, but with my still raw reactions to the literary generation of Allen Ginsberg and Robert Creeley and Ken Kesey, and the not-yet-traditional modes of revolt foreshadowed in the Dionysiac explosion on the Berkeley campus of the University of California.

I tried to do justice to what frightened me as well as to what attracted me in the life-style of the "mutants," but naturally I pleased no one—not at Rutgers, certainly, nor later after publication. Some of my younger listeners and readers seemed to feel that I had come close enough to what they were up to to understand it, and then had finked out short of total commitment. (A letter from one of them reads in part, "I take it from your recent writing that you're trying to keep up and maybe swing a little with what you've called the shift from 'a whiskey culture to a drug culture.' To make that observation really zing with instantaneity you might have said 'from an escapist *whiskey drug* culture to a reality-pleasure oriented *psychedelic drug* culture! . . .") But at the very same moment, some of my older ones had apparently convinced themselves that having come close enough to understand meant that I had crossed the line, gone over to the generational enemy.

For some, that is to say, understanding seemed not nearly enough, for some too much by far; while for me it seemed all that I could manage or wanted to. Having watched myself respond to my own children's flirtation with peril in sheer panic, as if I had never chosen to run risks myself, or had come to believe all risk-taking wrong, I grew ashamed. And my shame taught me a lesson supplementary to the one I had learned much earlier reading Lenin: that the first duty of the revolutionist grown old enough to be faced with the next revolution after his own is "patiently to understand." Yet to those who insist that their revolution, failed or successful, is the last, just as to those who oppose all new revolutions even as they have opposed all the old ones, such patient understanding seems a crime. "Infantile leftism," the former like to call it; "maintaining a premise" is the name preferred by the latter.

Living in Buffalo rather than Prague, it is the second charge with which I had had to deal, and understanding it I have found much more difficult than understanding the young. "Maintaining a premise" is, even in the notoriously vague context of legal language, a particularly slippery and imprecise term. Applied to running a whorehouse or renting rooms to professional gamblers, it has a semblance of meaning at least; but applied to my own alleged activities—my presumed failure to make absolutely sure that no one was smoking grass on my private property—from which no profit could possibly be derived, it makes no sense at all. Only if approached as a code, whose point is to conceal its meaning from all who do not already know it, will the phrase yield up its significance, which is, after all, simple enough.

Once deciphered, "maintaining a premise" turns out to mean creating a context, a milieu, an intellectual atmosphere in which the habits of the young are understood rather than condemned out of hand; their foibles responded to with sympathy and love rather than distrust and fear; the freedom necessary to their further growth sponsored and protected rather than restricted and crushed by an appeal to force and the intervention of the police. It turns out to mean, in short, writing such an article as "The New Mutants" and having been, in the first place, the sort of man who could write it—rather than the kind who could, in sheer panic, call the cops to arrest his own sons.

Only a couple of months before my arrest, I had read in the *New York Times* a news item headed PARENTS REQUEST ARREST OF 2 SONS, about an ill-advised father and mother who "after serving as complainants against their sons . . . then assumed the role of defenders" by hiring a defense lawyer, who explained to the court, "They were shocked, worried, and sick, and they wanted to do the right thing. They wanted to combat the situation before it could get out of hand, and decided that by telling the police about the marijuana, they would nip the situation in the bud." And reading it, my heart went out more to the baffled parents than to the harassed kids, who had had

at least some notion of what they were doing. It was the old, not
the young, who needed what I had buried away in the *Partisan
Review.*

Appendix Five: Electronic Surveillance

It had only slowly become clear to me how critically important the search and seizure issues, in fact, are. But looking back
now, on the eve of a last-chance appeal to the Supreme Court
of the United States, it occurs to me (I am a slow learner, as
this account has and will testify) that not only does the drug
problem conceal the more important matter of freedom to dissent, but that the issue of dissent itself tends to conceal the
underlying question of whether a society technologically able
to destroy the privilege of privacy will choose to do so or not.

Electronics has raised peeping and eavesdropping to new levels
of efficiency and has made the notion of seclusion and security
behind walls, the ancient distinction between private and public, nearly unviable. The very concept of the inviolability of the
home is at stake, as well as the immunity from improper surveillance guaranteed by the Fourth Amendment. But how hard
it was for me to understand just how much was imperiled (besides my own peace of mind and my attempts to maintain a
dialogue with the young) by the intrusion into my house of an
addled girl with a receiver in her pocket and an aerial down the
leg of her jeans; and by the connivance of the police in her
unconstitutional enterprise.

iii

ONCE THE legal maneuvering had begun, we were clearly in for a long series of postponements and delays, as prosecution and defense plotted strategy and counter-strategy in a game whose ultimate objective, we had to believe, was truth and justice—but which, for many months, was going to be played as if for its own sake, or those of the rules we were never quite to understand. At least this would permit me to go abroad as I had long planned: to lecture at the University of Amsterdam during the fall term under a Fulbright Award, and to teach at the new University of Sussex in England as a Visiting Professor during the spring and summer.

Meanwhile, however, cars full of rubberneckers continued to drive slowly back and forth past our house as the summer wore on. It was easy enough to understand, but a pain in the ass all the same to have become a tourist attraction: the sightseers gawking at us all at work and play as if we alone were visible, they not really there at all. And our immediate neighbors on both sides played it exactly the other way—pretending that they were as real as ever, and that we had simply ceased to exist.

When the article in *The New York Review of Books* appeared, letters of support, many warm and candid rather than merely dutiful or principled, came in from all over the world. And they were not only from the sort of readers I had imagined as picking up the NYRB and responding—preachers and editors, doctors and troubled grad students and professors from Nanterre to Yale—but from the kind of fellow-sufferers I would not have thought would ever find me in that journal—nuts and outcasts and the sort of instructor who gets fired out of his first job—all glad that someone for once had not listened to the voices of discretion advising *don't-wash-your-dirty-linen* or *just-button-up-*

161

and-stay-cool or *keep-your-goddamned-troubles-to-yourself.* To
be applauded by those who have never spoken out because they
have never felt such pain themselves, and therefore long to
share vicariously in that of others, is a satisfaction of sorts; but
to be approved by those who have in fact been abused, but
have not been able to make themselves heard, is a much greater
joy—and an additional grief.

I suppose that is why of all the letters I received the one that
stays in my head is one which ended with the wish, "May the
essence of creation be with you." It read in part: "Being a former
member of the Road Vultures Motorcycle Club I speak for all
my comrades when I wish you all the luck in the world in achiev-
ing your goals. We know how oppressed you must be. Perhaps
you recollect the raid on the Road Vultures clubhouse in December of '65. All the stuff that was supposedly *confiscated* was
planted by no other than them fascist swine themselves. One of
my comrades . . . was beaten so severely by them that he can
not hold a job, every once in a while he blacks out, he has over
100 sutures in his head for *'resisting arrest.'* I myself have many
head scars and memories of kicks in the crotch. . . . Perhaps
someday people will get hip. . . ."

Since that time, a Road Vulture, presumably because he was
identifiable by his garb, was shot to death by a Buffalo policeman when he ran a red light; but whether any more of my
fellow citizens have got "hip" to what is really at stake, I could
not say. And, in any case, that, too, is another black story for
another black day.

Back in July of 1967, I was still licking my wounds and reading my mail, which kept rolling in as if it would never stop.
There were clippings from columnists along with the personal
communications—expressions of real concern, it seemed to me,
and not just of the endless quest for the cause of the week;
there were telegrams, too, from those, known and unknown
to me, who wanted to say it fast: all in all, testimony that a lot
more people than I would have suspected cared that I cared.
Moreover, in fairly short order, translations of my piece had
appeared in Italy—and in Holland, the first place in Europe to
which I had been invited to lecture and the one to which I
was to be going shortly, hoping that this Fulbright would re-

new me as the one in 1951 had done. It was time; I was ready.

But there was still a long month to live through; and, meanwhile, the *Buffalo Evening News* had, astonishingly enough, decided to reprint almost the whole of my article—cutting with appropriate acknowledgment only some six hundred words, chiefly unkind remarks about the local cops and their girl spy, though, in fact, the surveillance aspect of the case was to come to seem to me more and more meaningful and important. As a matter of fact, that newspaper, staunchly conservative but reasonable all the same, has continued—unlike its more hysterical morning counterpart, the *Courier-Express*, to which I seemed from the start its intended enemy—to report calmly and accurately what has happened since, even lending editorial support on occasion.

Its attempt to let me tell my own story in my own home town—rather than to keep on printing the canned PR releases from a Police Department by now eager to save face—created a certain amount of backlash. It did not come to much, but, however limited, it depressed me a good deal. Apparently outraged to learn that three months after my arrest I not merely continued to walk the streets of Buffalo but was even permitted to make myself heard in its press, two anonymous ill-wishers communicated their fury by mail—one in large block letters. The first and milder of the pair, who signed himself "Clear minded individual able to 'get along' without hallucinations in a busy world," advised me a little ambiguously: "Having read the expansive article concerning you and your activities there seems one logical avenue—*Return to the land of your ancestors*, taking Dr. Meyerson for moral support, as well as Leary . . ."

And the second, somewhat cruder but more specific about where he wanted me to go, made clear at least what he took the land of my ancestors (as well as Leary's!) to be. "So you are a professional teacher-author-lecturer-hoodlum-dope-peddler-a low down sneak in the grass," he began, apparently addressing me personally; he went on, it would seem, to my colleagues in general, though still using the impassioned second person, "You are a bunch of the hated Jewish and commie rat nest. Its the 2nd best in the U.S. after the Red nest—U. of Cal at

Berkeley. . . . How come that leftie rats and poisoners of young minds remain at U.B. Why don't you all go to stinking Russia. Or the damned hated Israel?"

Oddly enough, it was *shame* I experienced reading these, in part because I was feeling dog-tired, used up, undone. But it is not, I think, merely the result of fatigue to be embarrassed at having betrayed someone else, a fellow human being, after all, to write indecencies that can be answered only in kind— that *are* answered in kind inside your own head, whether you set pen to paper or not.

In its own miniscule way, it is like being provoked into a war in which the possibilities of dialogue are narrowed down, and violence answers violence until both sides are degraded to a point where the distinctions between victim and victimizer, resister and aggressor, no longer matter. I do not want to misrepresent; I will never learn to love such haters of what I stand for, and I should despise myself even for trying; but I hate having to hate them, hated it especially at that point when I had so much else to do—like packing up and moving to a new country and a new job.

But it began to look more and more as if I might lose my house before I ever managed to leave it. Even before I had been arrested, and certainly before *I* knew that the police had begun to lay a trap for me (though, perhaps, this was already common knowledge in the business community, it occurs to me, discussed among buddies at the Century Club), the New York Life Insurance Company had refused to issue me a special sort of life insurance, into which I had been talked by one of their salesmen, very articulate but apparently as innocent as I of any knowledge about the lesson I was about to be taught for having stepped out of line, i.e., having become faculty advisor to LEMAR.

I had, however, already been fingerprinted and mugged before I managed to extort a note of explanation from the "Vice-President in Charge of Underwriting," under the date of May 8, 1967; and a cagey piece of non-communication it turned out to be.

"We assure you," the Vice-President wrote on behalf of his organization, "that the New York Life is conscious of its obligations . . . and is always desirous of offering insurance coverage . . . if at all possible. However, the Company, in fairness to all its policyholders, has established certain standards which must be met by a proposed insured. . . . There are many factors which must be taken into consideration in evaluating the insurability of any person applying for life insurance. Occasionally, as in your case, the information that comes to us is of a confidential and privileged nature, so that we are not at liberty to divulge the information or discuss the factors on which the Company's decision is based." English translation: *this shady character's about to be busted, so lay off.*

It hardly seemed worth making a fuss about when it first happened, and by the time the non-explanation had arrived, we had other things to keep us busy. In any case, the particular policy I was after, which involved temporary abatement of taxes and an eventual annuity, seemed so clearly a luxury which I had been conned into thinking I wanted in the first place that I decided to forget the whole thing. To be sure, it irked me to have been classified a "moral risk" (this was the further explanation whispered to me, but never put in writing) for having agreed to sponsor an officially recognized student organization; but, after all, I told myself a little severely, an annuity is as out of character for you, as—as a house with a swimming pool in Central Park, Buffalo.

And, indeed, once my arrest was a fact rather than a *sub voce* leak over drinks at the Statler-Hilton, that house became the next item of which I was sentenced to be deprived by a Star Chamber Court, whose very existence I had not suspected until then. That behind the Courts of Law there existed two others before which I must also plead, the Court of my academic peers and the Court of Public Opinion, I had known from the start; but I had failed to take into account the Court-Without-Appeal of the Business Community, those invisible Boards of Directors who, long before I was allowed to defend myself, had already found me guilty of being an insufferable up-start, caught redhanded, and had condemned me to be stripped of all bourgeois privileges and appurtenances.

It all began when the Travelers Insurance Company canceled out of hand (quite legally, it turned out, though without justice or reason) a homeowner's policy which I needed not only for my own protection, but also to keep my mortgage with the Manufacturers and Traders Trust in good order. The time was, as I remember it, early in June, and my policy had a theoretical two years yet to run; but at least I still had a decent period of grace before I was due to depart for the Netherlands and England late in August. But then I discovered, slowly and with growing incredulity, that *no* company was prepared to insure me; in fact, most insurance agents, having read their papers and knowing the nature of the companies with whom they dealt, would not even pretend to try.

The last affable fraud to make the attempt started out with great confidence and loud contempt for his more cowardly fellows, since he, he assured me, really knew what my circumstances were, having read my article in the *News*. In fact, he confided, there was only one thing in it he himself would have changed, for discretion's sake only (he being, of course, a Jew), and that was the first unfortunate sentence in *yiddish,* in a sensitive place where one in Latin, for instance, would have been much classier and more reassuring. But after a while, he refused even to answer his phone when I called, mortified perhaps to discover how tough things really were and determined in any case to let someone else break the bad news to me.

That someone else turned out to be my bank, from whom on August 1, 1967 (less than a month to go before departure time), I received the following letter, headed: "Re: Mtg. #01435," and signed by the Senior Mortgage Officer:

> We are today in receipt of the cancellation notice of your fire and hazard insurance policy of the United States Fidelity and Guaranty Company. . . .
> It will be necessary for you to furnish us with satisfactory fire and hazard insurance coverage by Friday, August, 4th, 1967, as required under terms of our mortgage. . . .
> If you have any questions, please contact the writer immediately upon receipt of this letter.

I had lots of questions, actually, but so strong a sense that those who had the answers lived in another country and spoke another language that all I was moved to say was, "Help!" And I did get some help, temporarily at least, from the Allstate Insurance Company, reachable not through agents, with whom I was done for a little while, but at your local Sears, Roebuck store, which presumably sells everything to everybody, or at least did once. Even they, however, having given me a temporary binder, then apparently consulted whatever blacklist is kept in the Central Intelligence Office used by all insurance companies, and changed their minds.

And all at once, I grew terrified not only for myself but for anyone in our society eccentric enough to be noticeable; and I vowed to place the documents of my own encounter with this Shadow F.B.I. on record, lest the whole thing be forgotten or attributed to the paranoia which after a while it breeds. Certainly, I had forgotten or dismissed cases of which I had heard earlier of people denied insurance, on their lives, their houses, their cars, because they had voted Communist, or refused to sign a Loyalty Oath, or were not properly married.

At any rate, on August 15 (less than two weeks left now), Allstate wrote me, once more in the computerized double-talk I was learning to understand:

> All insurance companies have certain qualifying standards which, together with our judgment and experience, tell us whether we can provide insurance in each individual case. . . . Sometimes because of these standards, we must give up business we would otherwise like to have. . . .
>
> We're sorry we won't be able to accept your application for insurance protection listed above. The temporary protection given you while your application was being considered will expire at the time and date shown below.
>
> As you see, a period of time remains before your protection stops. This will allow you time to apply for similar protection elsewhere. We urge you to do so. . . .

The time and date below read: "August 27, 1967, 12:00 noon Standard Time at the location of the property involved"—all very clear and precise. But we had used up all our "elsewheres," and August 27 was just about when we had planned to arrive

in Europe; so what was there to be done except to stew im-
potently or gripe to friends. Those friends had been rallying
round the whole while, my colleagues in particular offering to
lend me more money than I knew they could afford, or to
switch all of their sixty or seventy insurance accounts to whatever agent would guarantee to cover me—a tidy piece of change,
as we say in the trade. It was convincing testimony to their
generosity and sympathy, which I needed much at that point,
but of little avail in the Court-Without-Appeal, and of no
assistance to the Bank, which seemed not particularly fond
of its old-fashioned role as forecloser of my mortgage.

I knew then that I could not abide Buffalo much longer—
not without a temporary escape at least; for I was beginning to
grow tired of living in a stupid comedy at which I could not
even laugh, most of the pratfalls being my own. And so, assured
by those who claimed to know more about such things than
I that they would enlist the aid of the State Commissioner of
Insurance, as well as certain high officers in Allstate, I determined
that in a few days at most I would set out for New York and
points east, letting the house take care of itself. But before those
few days were out, I received, to my dismay, a new communication from Allstate offering me a grace period of thirty days beyond
August 27, and concluding with the same empty assurance as
before: "I am sure that you will have no difficulty in securing
insurance during this additional 30-day period."

Actually, I was to fly out on the last day of August, though
I did not yet know how to believe it, since it finally came to
me that things could only get better. And in fact they were
destined to, though the news would not reach me in the South
of France where, quite unexpectedly, I was to end up, until two
weeks after my departure. By September 9, Allstate would relent,
and I would make the papers again; what should have been
my private right all along, enjoyed in privacy and peace, by that
time would have become a public issue worth a headline or
two, at least in Buffalo. INSURANCE COMPANY AGREES TO
COVER DR. FIEDLER'S HOME, the *Buffalo Evening News*
would gravely tell the waiting world on the 10th, and at last
I would manage to laugh.

Looking back on it now, however, I realize that it was only

a stopgap victory I was about to win, worth not even a brief truce in the large war which has not yet quite terminated: the war of the credit-controllers against a vulnerable consumer. If only I were what my neighbors imagine, a beatnick pledged to conspicuous poverty, or a mad Head living in squalor, they could not ever have touched me. But quite like those neighbors, I long for the sleek and shiny comforts produced by the miserable world we share; and quite like them, I try to acquire those commodities not by smashing and grabbing, but by buying—at a somewhat faster pace than my current income can cover. And so, over and over, they have had me, and continue to have me.

I did not yet know then, for instance, that Bartlett Buick, Inc., of 3070 Main Street, which had earlier agreed to sell me a car for delivery immediately after my return to the States, would renege—having in *their* turn checked things out with Central Intelligence, they wrote to me in Brighton, England, where I was finally to settle, "We are sorry that we were unable to complete a new car transaction with you." No further explanation offered, of course, and I scarcely needed it at that point, anymore than I did a year later when, having returned, I discovered that I could still not buy a car on credit under the General Motors installment plan, still not borrow money from my own bank to make such a purchase, still not rent or lease a car. I could only get what I paid for cash on the line, taking out my roll of greenbacks like some thirties gangster in a film.

And last indignity of all, even the Diners' Club, whose representatives prowl the airports of the nation handing application forms to anyone debarking from a plane, rejected the one I had filled out—really just to see. I take it there must be others who get turned down, since the form they sent me was printed as if for mass distribution; but who can they be, those other slobs, who alone in a country which guarantees to all the right to overspend, wake one morning to find in their mailboxes the message: "We are sorry to say that there are certain income and credit background requirements that are not present in your application, and at this time we canot issue a credit card in your name."

If, however, I was bugged nearly out of my mind before

leaving the States, it was not solely, or even chiefly, due to
the businessmen, from whom, after all, I expected no better—
each of us is in some sense the prisoner of the role attributed
to us, not without justice, by the other, and perhaps also each
the other's reproach. At least they seem to have found me
theirs; for—they must have figured—if I could make it my
way, bypassing everything they took to be virtue, if my way
was even a kind of virtue, perhaps superior to theirs, then to
what could they attribute their own success except a certain low
cunning, hardness of heart, and narrowness of view, plus a
consummate skill at shortchanging the world?

What really hurt, though, was the thought that my own
colleagues had betrayed me as well: not so much at home, where
those who connived behind the scenes were outnumbered by
the many who stood by me without reservation or fear, but
certainly abroad, particularly at the University of Amsterdam.
The Magnificent Rector of that university had apparently grown
more and more uneasy reading what *Time* had to say about my
case and *Newsweek* and, I gather, the *Courier-Express* as well,
sent him, I have been told since, by a certain self-appointed
and self-styled "Consul" for the Netherlands in Buffalo. The
Rector did not, however, discuss the matter with me—any more
than with his own faculty—indeed, did not ever communicate
with me directly at all, by telephone or mail, but waiting until
the last possible moment, finally decided to cancel my
appointment.

I learned about it first in an after-midnight call from a sympathetic lady, who confided that she had been told it, gloatingly,
by someone at the *Courier-Express,* who had presumably got it
from the pseudo-Consul. It was all part of the Fiedler movement, she assured me, in whispers—a prearranged step, number
two in fact, in a series carefully scheduled: get-my-house, get-
my-leave-appointment, get-my-regular-job even if it meant getting the President of the University first, at last get-me-the-hell-
out! But I refused to believe her, since she sounded, in the
dark and silent house, exactly like the voice of my own worst
paranoid fears. "Don't worry," I assured her—and my doubting
self, "if they were going to do anything, they would have done
it already," to which she replied, "But they *have!*" Not quite
believing her, I hung up.

Her call had come sometime around the twenty-fifth of July, less than a month before I was scheduled to sail for Holland on the *Statendam;* and just at a point where I was beginning to get a little tense over the lack of response from the Secretary of the Fulbright Foundation in the Netherlands, with whom I was supposed to clear final reservations for myself, my wife, and the two daughters who planned to come with me. As a matter of fact, that formerly faithful correspondent had suddenly become as evasive as the Rector himself, unavailable to letters, telegrams, even the overseas telephone. Quite obviously, no one was saying a word (except for my after-midnight informant), and, of course, I *knew,* though I would not confess it even to myself. Certainly I was not surprised when the kiss-off came at last: a letter dated Washington, July 28, and signed by the Chairman of the Board of Foreign Scholarships, who had been up to then and who was to remain throughout quite as solicitous and a little more helpful than I might have expected from one trapped inside that complicated bureaucratic machinery.

It all reminded me in its monstrous indirection (*"You* tell him, man." "No, for pete's sake, *you* tell him!") of my dealings with the friendly insurance agent, the company, and the bank; it ran as follows:

I have just received a telegraphic copy of the following letter which was handed to the Chairman of the U.S. Educational Foundation in the Netherlands by the University of Amsterdam:

From various publications and queries raised with the University of Amsterdam, we understand that Professor Leslie A. Fiedler is presently engaged in legal proceedings relating to the narcotic laws in the United States, which have attracted a good deal of public attention. We are fully aware of Professor Fiedler's excellent reputation as a scholar and teacher and also know he has been eminently successful in carrying out prior Fulbright assignments. We feel, however, that at this time his presence at the University would generate undesirable discussion and adverse publicity. After having given the matter considerable thought, we most reluctantly request you to inform Professor Fiedler that, for the time being, we cannot confirm our invitation to teach at the University of Amsterdam this coming semester. After the legal proceedings are finally terminated we would then like to consider again his coming to this university. We feel that our decision is in the best interests of both Professor Fiedler and the University of Amsterdam.

The Board of Foreign Scholarships is not in accord with the reasoning of the University of Amsterdam. We recognize however, that each university . . . must make its own decisions. . . . We also recognize that this is a severe disruption to your plans, and if you so desire, we will make every effort to place you at another university abroad for the first semester. . . .

With this final note we are back to the correspondence with Allstate; for if my plans had indeed been disrupted (I had long since been granted leave by Buffalo, and the departmental schedule had been reorganized to take up the slack), so would those of any new University which took me on be disrupted —and at an even later, more impossible, stage of the game.

Still it was a lovely and courteous response as far as the Board of Foreign Scholarships was concerned, and my sole quarrel was with the Rector. Rereading the letter which I fired off immediately and in anger, I am appalled at its vocabulary, which seems more that of some rigid germanic defender of *Akademische Freiheit* than my own; as if I had long held, in fact, a Chair of Philology at Amsterdam. Detached phrases represent the tenor of my reply: "maximum inconvenience," "total lack of courtesy and complete disregard for the ordinary rules of academic procedure," "especially indecorous and distressing," "colleagues in the larger academic community," "failure to respect principles of fair play . . . and tolerance of dissent," "ancient and honorable tradition of the University of Amsterdam," "indefensible on the grounds of any principle recognized in the university world," "abject surrender to what you presume to be public opinion," "for the sake of your own self-respect and the honor of your faculties . . . redeem yourself in the eyes of scholars everywhere."

The answer to this came quickly enough and, for the first time, directly to me—but in it, the Rector continued to evade rather than confront the issues, beginning with a demurrer: "The freedom of expression is in no way involved in this case"; passing on to befuddlement: "The only point is, that a professor . . . is presently engaged in legal proceedings. I have not the slightest knowledge how far these proceedings are justified or not. The only point is that we are not prepared to confirm our invitation during the time the proceedings are not terminated"; and ending with an irrelevant compliment: "Personally I may add that I read one of your articles on the narcotics problem and personal freedom, which impressed me very much and which I thought straightforward." Before he had become head of his university, the Rector, I learned later, had been a Professor of Law; and he was, therefore, responding to me in his native tongue, as it were. But this was only one more subterfuge.

What he did not mention at all in his response was the subject of "undesirable discussion and adverse publicity," which had been a main item in his somewhat franker original letter to the Board, and was, in fact, the crux of the whole matter. The word "controversial" did not occur to him, but it sums up precisely enough the charge he was actually leveling against me in his own language of non-candor, quite as if we were both back in Missoula, Montana, in 1958. And in truth, most presidents of most universities anywhere and anywhen seem condemned to that time and place for all eternity.

How easy it is for faculties to remember, and how simple for administrators to forget (even when, as in Europe, they are elected from the faculty) that a university in order to survive and flourish must finally please not its external constituency, which is to say, its trustees and the taxpayers closest to the ear of its officers, but its internal constituency, which is to say, those who teach and are taught within its walls. In the past, universities which betrayed their internal constituency crumbled away quietly, without the headlines accorded clashes with the external constituency; but more recently, as at Berkeley and Columbia and the University of Paris, a baffled student body, backed by some teachers, has threatened to destroy long-established institutions spectacularly and in full sight of the T.V. cameras. Yet many administrators seem to have learned nothing; their backs turned on intramural affairs, they continue to watch and worry about "public relations," which is the customary cant phrase for what-they-are-thinking-about-us-out-there.

What-they-are-thinking-about-us-in-here does not even have a proper name, though it is sometimes referred to as "morale," which in the absence of a better term will have to do. And it is in any case natural for those chiefly concerned with fund-raising and getting budgets through stubborn legislatures, as well as with the kind of press which helps or hinders those activities, to overlook "morale" in favor of "public relations," or at least to convince themselves that to deal effectively with the latter is to insure that salaries will go up and the former automatically mount with them. It is a view almost Marxian in its simple-minded economic determinism, and quite paternalistic in its kindly condescension to those who teach; but it is one widespread enough to have caused me trouble all the way from Missoula to Amsterdam. And I sometimes fear that—should the improbable occur, and the courts believe the case manufactured by the Buffalo police—it may rise to haunt me again.

I want, therefore, to be quite clear about what I find wrong with it in general, before I have once more to argue a particular case of my own; but to do this requires going back to first assumptions. Insofar as those who control a university consider that their *primary* obligation is public service of some kind, immediate, demonstrable usefulness to the community (whether by providing it trained technicians, services, entertainment, or simply by brainwashing students to accept its values without challenge), they have made the community their judge and themselves the slaves of "public relations." This means, of course, that in any crisis, they must join with the community in an effort to identify and punish "controversial" individuals, threats to the *status quo;* must, in short, play the cop against their own dissident students or faculty, or on occasion some unorthodox Dean.

But the primary purpose of a university should be not to

serve things-as-they-are, the oppressive present, but to provide a refuge from its exigencies in the study of an alien past, and to suggest alternatives to it by foreshadowing an alien future. The dream of that past and the dream of that future—for future and past are dreams or they are nothing—the university must not merely teach but live, thus making itself into an anti-community, prototype and forecast, touchstone and challenge. Only in this way can the university lead rather than follow, only in this way become what it must be if it is to exist at all: a model of the permanent and inalienable freedom to be something else, rather than an example of subservience to the demands of whatever group happens to possess power at any given moment.

This obligation of the university is rooted in its odd and impressive history. Coming into existence in the twelfth century, which is to say, still within the limits of the medieval era, it already represented a future which has become our present. It is, in fact, the only institution of its time which has expanded and developed in ours, rather than shrunk and diminished in importance or simply disappeared. The lay clergy, the religious orders, the traditional aristocracies, the Papacy itself have lost power and significance with the passage of some eight hundred years; but professors have come to play an ever more vital and central part in the conduct of affairs, while students are at this very moment just coming into their own.

Whether the university, which helped blow up the closed ecclesiastical order of the Middle Ages in the name of "humanism" and the "restoration of Ancient Prudence," can prevail over the closed industrial-military order of the late twentieth century in the name of "academic freedom" is still an unresolved question. Perhaps we have long since exhausted the uses of freedom as defined, not by parliaments or on the streets, but in the academy, where not poverty and slavery, social immobility or even war, but ignorance and inherited prejudice are taken to be the chief enemies of the human spirit; but perhaps not. So long as the university resolves not simply to do what someone else has decided is its duty, there is a chance.

The Rector of the University of Amsterdam, however, had decided precisely to do his duty as defined by those conservative forces in the Netherlands (their voices doubtless echoed by his

own inner doubts) who had been growing vexed with students
and drugs in general, as well as with the Provos in particular
—those gentlest and wittiest of all youthful revolutionaries, who
had disconcerted their bourgeois enemies by kneeling in public
places to wash their feet. And since he had acted in terms of a
brand of discretion appropriate only to a time already past, the
Rector ended by bringing on himself and his institution exactly
what he had most feared. He himself, that is to say, generated
"undesirable discussion and adverse publicity" from those publics
he had not yet learned to respect; his interior constituencies and
their natural allies throughout the world.

From graduates of his own university, professors in England
and America—including my own colleagues—and (though it
would be a while before I would know it) from his own professors and students, scattered by the summer holidays, cries of
protest began to reach his sensitive ear: "I urge the College of
Curators to . . . apologize to Dr. Fiedler and the intellectual
community to which he belongs. . . . Your action has shamed the
University of Amsterdam and besmirched the reputation of
the Netherlands in the eyes of all Americans with a concern for
cultural freedom. . . ." And to these were added, almost immediately, calls for sanctions against the Dutch university: "A
strong protest is necessary, and an international blacklisting of
the University of Amsterdam would not be without cause. . . .
I hoped American professional associations might respond by
refusing to send any scholars to that institution. . . ."

Naturally, all of this was exploited by the press, not only in
the United States, but by the London *Times* as well, and—to the
special distress of the Rector—many Dutch newspapers: all of
them broadcasting my countercharges against him ("cowardly
and unworthy . . . a betrayal of the principle of academic freedom"), and most of them quite sympathetic to my cause.

The *Buffalo Evening News* was moved to editorial comment
for the first time, taking its stand with the American State Department officials who had backed me against the Rector and
his Board of Curators:

> The American Fulbright people, in disagreeing with the
> Dutch, supported in effect the very correct view enunciated

by UB President Meyerson last May 3, just after the Fiedler arrest. In announcing that UB would take no action pending a court decision, President Meyerson stood on the principle that "faith must be maintained in the American heritage of fair play, in which a man is considered innocent until proved otherwise."

It was in scope and tone a reaction which the Rector had not foreseen; for he had expected me (so, at least, his opinion had been leaked back to me—quite unofficially, of course) to "behave like a gentleman," which is to say, shut up and go away in order not to "embarrass my colleagues"—just as if, he explained off the record once more, I had been involved in some "sticky divorce proceedings, or homosexuality, or abortion."

When, however, I persisted in making noises of protest, not like a criminal caught in the act but like one persecuted for speaking out, and the press echoed my cry, he settled for the next best thing, which is to say, *he* shut up and went away. He was, in fact, overdue for a vacation; certainly I was not about to blame him if he used it as an occasion to disappear, leaving word that he could not be reached—quite, as if he had been caught out in something a little shady, like some "sticky divorce proceedings, or homosexuality, or abortion."

We had reached in any event, a stalemate by the date on which I had originally been scheduled to sail; and suddenly I could no longer bear even the sound of my own voice commenting on my case, much less those of reporters and insurance agents and rectors disturbing the peace I needed to work and reflect, to know who I really was. In a little while, I would begin to believe I was "the controversial Dr. Fiedler"; in any event, I'd had it. So on August 24, though I had as yet no definite teaching assignment until January, when my Visiting Professorship at Sussex began, I headed for New York, planning to take the first possible flight to England. Flight seemed the appropriate word.

Part Four

MONTPELIER ROAD AND AFTER: 1968

i

I HAD NOT LEFT Buffalo a moment too soon; persecution breeds delusions of persecution—minor persecution, thank God, only minor delusions—and everywhere I went I found myself watching the faces I met just a little too carefully, when I was not looking back over my shoulder a shade too suspiciously. Who knows what I expected: to be refused a passport renewal; to be stopped by Customs for some grossly degrading search ("O.K., drop your pants, Buster, and bend over!"); to be met at the ramp to my plane by a federal agent with a new warrant or subpoena in hand? None of these quite, and yet somehow all of them; for I had created in my head at that point the image of the Enemy, tireless and vindictive—though I knew damn well really, that behind my troubles there were only a handful of inefficient jokers, more paranoic even than I, to whom—in odd moments, when they happened to think about it—*I* was the Enemy, tireless and vindictive.

Nonetheless, my heart jumped a little when in the line at Passport Control someone touched my shoulder and said my name: a someone, it turned out, who had watched a television interview the night before in which I had made a valedictory summary of my case and its odd consequences, and who, recognizing me, had wanted to wish me luck. In fact, all of my last-minute arrangements had gone well: the American Council of Learned Societies, for instance, underwrote my fare to Europe, which my Fulbright grant would have taken care of had the Rector at Amsterdam not lost his nerve; and the travel agent to whom they sent me put us on Air India, where the hostess at the door, caste-marked and bowing over her clasped hands, gave me the sense that for the next eight hours I would be sealed into a world alien and remote, and would therefore be, at last, incognito, safe.

Heathrow Airport at London, however, was quite another matter, for the Immigration Officers turned out to be unexpectedly surly. Perhaps the fact that we had come on Air India and exited in a crowd smelling of curry made them particularly touchy; but they are, most of them, a bloody-minded lot under the best of circumstances, and, indeed, it was from their example that I was eventually to learn the meaning of that useful English term.

Still, what was really bugging them, as became clear once we had settled into England, was precisely the flood of Indian immigrants just then descending on Britain from Kenya and elsewhere: the unwanted "Blacks," as both sides oddly conspired to call them. Moreover, I was an "immigrant," too, or the next best thing to one, with my talk (I should have kept buttoned up, but how was I to guess?) of staying for a year and taking over a job at a British university. And more-or-less-White immigrants from outside the Commonwealth were to a certain kind of English mind, for whom the tight little island was not nearly tight or little enough, quite as threatening as more-or-less-Black immigrants from within: both the rough equivalent of invaders from Outer Space.

Well, he had a perfectly valid excuse, that insufferably punctilious anti-Immigration Officer who met me at the gate; I had not received my work permit before leaving America, and there seemed no record of my having been issued one in England. Besides, I can have done myself no good, screwed tight as I was to begin with, and mad as I got after four hours of waiting on a hard bench and thinking: *just what I feared, God damn it, just what I knew would happen, somebody's got the word, or changed his mind, or finked out.*

Finally, we were both rigid, the Heathrow official lost in his nightmare and I in mine. Not that we yelled at each other, of course, as we might have in New York; instead our voices grew lower and lower, as is appropriate to a country scared stiff rather than frantic. "But I tell you," I insisted, leaning toward him from my side of the counter, "the Registrar at Sussex wrote me everything's taken care of"; and he hissed back, leaning toward me from his, "And I put it to you, sir, who's running this country, that's the question, the Foreign Office or some university?"

It was not really a question, however, but an answer; and the hostility in his voice, which was the true point of his statement (neither of us doubted for a moment that the Foreign Office was ahead all the way) seemed to me so depressingly familiar, so finally unbeatable, that I told myself: "Oh, Christ, you've had it. It's back to Buffalo for you, if back is the word. Maybe you never left—maybe you never can."

In the end, however, the stamp he had held poised over my documents for so long fell, granting us permission for a 24-hour stay in England, no more. I had assured him, not quite believing it, that we were on our way to the South of France anyhow; having in my pocket an invitation from a Sussex colleague-to-be who was summering there, and realizing suddenly that if I had an ace in the hole, this was it. It was a Bank Holiday, though, and Heathrow seemed more than ever a trap rather than a way station, a true terminal, with no exits at all. Nonetheless, fighting it out in crowded lines before ticket clerks who kept saying, "No space. All filled up. Sorry, there's just nothing," some way, somehow, the four of us, my wife, two daughters, myself—quite used up before we had properly begun, and more in despair than hope—found ourselves on a plane bound for Nice, with eight of our twenty-four hours still to go.

There was a lion on a leash in the Nice airport, an elephant by the side of the road just outside: both of them there, no doubt, for good commercial reasons, but I preferred to think them inexplicable except as good omens for us. Then we were driven through the gathering dark, up, up along winding roads and between pines, up, up past invisible villages which our hosts named for us all the same, as if they were old friends we would meet later; and at last we were in Seillans.

I had not thought I wanted to be in Seillans really (and where the hell *was* it, anyhow?), but then, I did not know where else I would have preferred to go, given the choice; for I was, for the first time in my life, thoroughly disoriented, unsure where I was or in what direction I was facing. On the plane going over, I had fallen into a half-sleep, and a prayer had come into my head, not like something composed, but rather something recalled "*Oh Lord of Journeys,*" it ran, "*let me re-member that no one ever really knows whence he has come, or whither he is tending, or even what is the true name of the traveler.*"

But our ten days there turned out to be precisely what I might otherwise have never realized I needed: an interval of the only kind of peace possible in the midst of total war, which is to say, a time without word from the front—no letters, no telegrams, no phone calls. I had sent the address only to my lawyer, a man who in the pinch always preferred silence, so discreet that he never gossiped about me even to me, and any-one trying to call through the Seillans switchboard might grow old or mad before reaching his party. Besides, I did not know France at all, certainly not this region, and I loved the sense of unknown hills over my shoulder and the glimpse of an unfamiliar sea on the horizon as I looked toward the south.

It was a world smelling of lavender and rosemary, a world unremittingly green except where the sun touched the red skins of the last, fat tomatoes on the half-stripped vines. The sea was a little remote for swimming, and besides I have no taste— despite secondhand memories out of Scott Fitzgerald—for the pretentious squalor of the Côte d'Azur. But there was a quite satisfactory semi-converted cistern-pool, where the local insects dove to their deaths every evening and past which the local peasants walked toward town each morning—as, evening and morning, I swam back and forth, back and forth. And all the while, the world—unbeknownst to both of us—was slowly com-ing together again inside my wet head.

Like having a toothache or becoming a Trotskyite in America, being harassed by cops and credit bureaus destroys momentarily one's sense of relativity—though in ways more comic than tragic. It is, that is to say, not such a total eclipse of the world by the self as that brought about by a long illness or a bad marriage; but it is quite as likely to debouch in self-pity, and to turn one's pain into an occasion for boredom to everyone else. If, God forbid, only my article in *The New York Review of Books* were to survive a holocaust of all the newsprint in the world, some stranger reading it in the unimaginable future could have little sense of the larger calamities which were in 1967 vexing my contemporaries—and *me*.

Certainly, there is scarcely any allusion in it to the universal conflict, too vast to be contained in a textbook label like World War III, which had set Blacks against Whites in the United States, even as the older war of Whites against Blacks was being exported to Viet Nam. Nor did I find occasion to mention the campaign of Whites against Blacks in England, South Africa, and Rhodesia; of Blacks against Blacks in the emancipated rest of Africa; or of Whites against Whites on the poor, backward continent of Europe, doomed, it would seem, to reenact old battles, in which ghost soldiers rose to charge in response to battle cries in which no one any longer believed.

Moreover, I ignored completely the terror that had befallen us all, huddled inside of boundaries grown meaningless—between France and Germany, say, or the Old World and the New, or even East and West—as developing technology and the pressure of populations had made almost everything that almost everyone had thought of as politics almost totally irrelevant. And yet if that future reader turns out to be sensitive enough to understand my account of Them against Us, community against university, cops against kids, as a parable, he may be able to extrapolate all the rest.

For me, at any rate, Seillans proved to be a place of recuperation from the loss of perspective that had afflicted me when I was writing the *NYRB* piece. There I managed to reach Stage I on the road back to reason, in which my small, immediate troubles, grown shadowy as the vast ones of the world, fell into their proper place. Swimming in the dazzle of sunlight through water, everyone is a mystical philosopher; and so, rising to the surface of my Seillans cistern, I would hear myself cry to the surrounding air and the indifferent birds: "All is *maya*, illusion. All is *maya*, illusion." Then the first gnat would bite, the first pangs of hunger make themselves felt; and I would yell for Surfacain or my dinner, proving I was just about ready for Stage II.

That second stage I reached in England, where I discovered an entire people, behind the flimsiest pretense of maintaining a stiff upper lip, whining louder than I ever had at my worst about their manifold troubles: the brain-drain, the railroad and dock strikes, the sudden onset of hoof-and-mouth disease, the housing shortage, the threat of the New Immigrants, the breathalyzer test for drunken drivers, the influence of drugs and the pill on the young, the menace of pornography, the failure of the automatic signal crossings on railways, the capitulation of the Labor Government to the American War in Vietnam, and the "Americanization of Culture," the insolence of DeGaulle, the decline of the pound and the sinister aftermath being plotted by the "Gnomes of Zurich." Unless I chose to believe a whole nation mad, I had to accept their grief and the troubles which prompted it as no less real than my own; so that walking down streets lined with plaster statues of spastics and blind children, or threading my way among ancient survivors of rickets, crooked as the landscape of a nightmare, I found myself saying after a while, "Nothing is *maya*, nothing illusion. You just wish you were that lucky."

Heathrow Airport served once more as my induction back to reality, though this time, being both rested and in focus, I knew how petty our continuing hassle was; which perhaps explains why, still without a Work Permit, I was able to get thirty days of grace from the Immigration Officer on duty. And once I had made it to Brighton, things began to work for me as they had not for a long time.

It was a matter now not of hanging on to a house, but of finding one, which we did in remarkably short order, since all at once we had become desirable tenants—a well-heeled American family rather than a group of girl students, say, pooling their slender resources for a place large and decent enough to raise posh hell in. It was an elegant house, in fact, our "upper maisonette" on Montpelier Road, rising tall and slender above a tiny front garden full of blowsy roses and revealing through long windows behind the bulge of an iron balcony glimpses of furniture, rickety and raffish at once; old books, including a Fourth Folio Shakespeace; and faded prints, portraying the owner's obviously evil ancestors, whose faces above their ruffs signified a refreshing indifference to who did whatever or got caught by whom.

There was mail as well, a huge stack of it all from America, which is to say, my continuing life ready to emerge, at the slitting of an envelope, from the parenthesis of somewhere-else. And I was hungry enough to begin being me again to have been delighted no matter what those letters said, and charmed besides by the town and especially the street that sloped from our front gate to the sea into which I was to dip a foot only once: the Channel, gray and tarry and oddly odorless, but satisfactorily loud on the rocky beach.

It was a street of refurbished regency houses and the wrecks of large hotels, boarded up and festooned with rusty barbed wire; of seedy roominghouses, called Fredellens or The Squirrels, and bookie joints, pretentiously styled "Turf Accountants"; of pubs, large and small, and squalid teen-age nightclubs, camped rather than established in the basements of abandoned buildings.

But essentially—like everything else in Brighton—its point was to indicate the ocean and the esplanade, along which trippers lounged in the nonexistent sun, even turning brown by faith, and from which they returned to their jobs and their wives bearing dirty postcards and Brighton Rock in the form of fish or babies' pacifiers or girls legs, pink and plump.

To live in Brighton, is, as a matter of fact, not merely to live by the sea, but also to live in a dirty joke which everyone knows, memorialized not only in the Rock and on the postcards, but in scores, perhaps hundreds, of songs and doggerel verses, as well as comic drawings, ambitious novels, and even modern epics. Walking through the tangle of decayed streets quite near our own, I would remember Pinky's obscene record in Graham Greene's *Brighton Rock;* strolling past the Metropole Hotel, I would think of Mr. Eugenides' invitation for a weekend in Eliot's *The Waste Land;* standing before the pseudo-oriental splendor of the Pavilion, I would recall Cruikshank's wicked cartoons of the fat and lecherous Prince Regent who had built it for his *zaftig* dolly; and returning home, I would pass a buttoned-up neighbor walking his dog and dreaming of the next book about Brighton, full of old ladies and middle-aged queers and muscular young men with short tempers.

But I savored none of this properly until much later; for during my first weeks in Montpelier Road I was too busy opening my mail and answering the phone to register where I was. It was on the whole good news.

There, first of all, was the Work Permit I had despaired of ever seeing, but which had arrived in Buffalo the day after I left and then had been duly sent back to Brighton to await me; in a little while, I was a properly registered resident alien, complete with a year's visa and a National Health Certificate. And just beneath it in the pile on my desk, was an Allstate homeowner's policy covering my Central Park house, which we had rented in the last days before our departure. Moreover, word from the University of Sussex had already arrived that there would be, after all, students for me to teach, courses for me to teach them, even a little money to pay for it all; and this, combined with a lecture series at University College in London (also confirmed by mail during that week) would give me the sense of doing something more than skulking in exile.

As a matter of fact, it turned out that I might have lectured in the Netherlands as well, exactly as originally planned; for things were beginning to open up there, too, as I learned the way I seemed fated to get all my news, good or bad, from Amsterdam: first by certain cagey telephone calls from reporters, all quite unofficial; then from actual news items, clipped and mailed by Dutch well-wishers; and at long last, formally and officially from the Rector Magnificus himself. Shortly after the first of September the whispering began; by September 7, head-lines in the Dutch papers were telling their readers that "PROF. FIEDLER MAG TOCH IN AMSTERDAM DOCEREN"; but only on the 12th did the Rector finally bring himself to write, even his English this time lapsing from its former icy excellence:

. . . Just returned from abroad I found out since that authoritative people in the United States . . . ranged themselves on your side and continue giving full confidence in you. . . .

Authoritative sources in your country, are contributing to the impression that in your case the main issue is not the fact, which you are charged with . . . but that other matters are involved of greater significance. . . .

Since we have got the impression that not only the legal action against you, but also other elements are at stake, we appreciate to declare that we regret our decision to postpone our invitation to you. That decision might give the impression—unjustly—that we have taken sides against you. . . .

We are glad to inform you now that on the former grounds the Amsterdam University does invite you once again. . . .

And to cap it all, he managed—despite newspaper reports in his own country about my trip to France and my presence in England—to send this belated communication to my Buffalo address; so that it actually arrived in the same post with a clipping from the *Buffalo Evening News* reporting the "resubmission" of my invitation, and translating in full an earlier editorial from the *Nieuwe Rotterdamse Courant,* which must have had something to do with the Rector's second thoughts, though he did not confess it—preferring instead to claim that the Fulbright Board "did not give us in time full details."

What the Rotterdam newspaper had reminded him about was the fact that "the old American heritage of fair play" is not American alone. "There is no American monopoly here," the editorial insisted. "This rule of fair play is, in fact, a (West) European norm. Indeed, the European convention of human rights signed and endorsed by the Netherlands, states in Article 6, Paragraph 2. . . ." etc., etc. And no lawyer can stand up against so precise a citation.

In any case, as I sat pondering all of these documents, I found myself not quite sure how to answer the Rector, though my first instinct was to say, "No, thanks," out of a sense that, rather than resisting pressure he was now merely submitting to a counterpressure, which, to be sure, I had helped muster against him. At that point, however, another communication arrived, explaining much that had happened between the Rector's two letters, and finally resolving my doubts. This was a different kind of invitation, from the students of Amsterdam this time, or more precisely, from the officers of ASVA, a militant student organiza-

tion, chiefly active in the past in organizing protests against
involvement in Vietnam; and this one I could not reject. It ran
in part:

> We would like to inform you that the University Board
> did not suspend their invitation to you without protest and
> did not cancel their decision without pressure from the part
> of the academic staff and the students. Some staff members
> and the Amsterdam Student Union (ASVA) organized a
> petition against the resolution . . . we succeeded in getting
> some publicity on the affair favorable to our position. . . .
> The regrettable decision of the Univ. Board and the lack
> of alertness in public opinion made us decide to organize
> a debate on academic liberty, and the role of teachers and
> students in and opposite to society under the title: "Critical
> University." On this evening a Dutch Professor, whom an
> entry permit to the U.S. was refused on political grounds,
> will speak . . . two well-informed young academic politicians
> will explain the aim of student movements in Berlin and
> Berkeley, while in all probability the Univ. President will
> expound his principles, practice and policy. . . .
> If there is any chance of you being in Europe about that
> time, we would place a high value on your participation. . . .

"Yes," I said, "yes, by all means, why not," sending my response
off by the next mail. For I quite understood, reading between
the lines, that the meeting they described must originally have
been intended for a protest on my behalf; and that only the
Rector's last-minute change of heart had turned it into a more
general, educational occasion, dedicated not to a living cause
but to two abstractions: the first, "academic liberty," as old as
the time of my teachers; and the second "critical university,"
as up-to-the-minute as the student rebellion that had already
erupted and would erupt soon again in Berlin.

I had no illusions, understand, either about the "debate" or
my role in it. That the "Univ. President," i.e., my old friend, the
Rector, would—despite the firmness of "in all probability"—
not appear at all, I was reasonably certain; and I suspected that

the "Dutch Profesor" would seem to my eye something less unequivocal than a pure victim of State Department discrimination. Both proved to be true, but it made no difference, for what I really wanted was to get to Amsterdam, which I had dreamed for a whole year, without being beholden to the Rector.

Besides, it was high time that I became a real beneficiary of Student Power, so that I could begin biting that tender hand, too, as I was getting bored doing with the considerably tougher ones that had been feeding me of late. Actually, I liked the kids who came to greet me at the airport and walked me tirelessly through the city, since somewhere beneath their surfaces of absolute earnestness, there was a hint of real wit—not easy irony—which would survive their inevitable illusion and keep them from the kind of self-pity and theatrical despair I had watched ruin most of the used-up radicals of my generation. They were types I knew on sight, absolutely international, interchangeable, in fact, constantly on the move across borders grown meaningless to them; so that I was not surprised to learn that the boy friend of the one girl among them was an editor of the student paper back in Buffalo, and that they had met on a *kibbutz* in Israel.

Having said *yes* to the students made it easier and more pointed to say *no* to the Rector, which I did politely but firmly, I thought; though perhaps not quite firmly enough, even in the context of the protest meeting, for in answer to an American who had earlier expressed horror at the withdrawal of my invitation, the Rector then felt able to write: "I received a letter of Professor Fiedler, out of which I got the impression that all misunderstanding between us has been cleared up."

In any case, settled into Brighton for the year, I entered Holland on the morning of September 28, quite like a visiting Briton. The "debate" that night turned out to be in some ways more satisfactory than I had expected; despite the fact that the other speeches were not merely ritualistic, which they had to be, but dull, too, which was optional—dull enough so that I could tell even with my minimal Dutch. My own remarks, however half understood by half of the audience, and understood not

at all by the other half, left them free to cheer themselves for
having stood up for me, which was right and proper, and a joy
to both of us.

In the end, it seemed quite like talking to the Indians in
Missoula, except for the canals and the seventeenth-century
facades past which we had walked between beers and visits to
bookshops, and the astonishingly organized publicity attendant
on the whole thing, the hordes of reporters who had dogged my
steps from the moment I landed at the Schipol airport to the
moment I staggered from our last restaurant to bed.

In the airport itself, I had been hustled from the landing ramp
past exploding flashbulbs to a conference room, where, shoulder
to shoulder around a horseshoe table topped with green baize,
reporters had begun to shout questions at me, each into his
mike, before I had properly settled behind mine. It was a scene
I knew only from movies and T.V., so that thrown into it without
warning, I felt out of character, free to play any role I liked;
though after one giddy instant, I settled for acting the part
I knew best.

Looking now at the newspaper pictures taken that day, I see
the familiar face of a bearded American professor, momentarily
triumphant after long harassment, a little pleased at his own
jokes. There is a particularly euphoric shot of me, looking out
from under the concealment of my own brows with a sort of
half-secret amusement at myself, perhaps, as well as the absurdity of my situation and the seriousness with which all my
questioners are scribbling down the answers I give—one of which
I read in the banner over my head: "*Ik heb een stem en schre-
euw.* I have a voice and I yell."

It was a good day, which is, perhaps, why I was to return
so often to the Netherlands during the following year: to address
a *Lustrum* of sociology students from all over the country (held
in the first Dutch Holiday Inn!); to talk about Red Indians to a
class in American History at Leyden; to read a paper on Shakespeare to the English Club of the same university; to analyze
some poems by Robert Frost and comment on where our newest
poets were going for the students at Utrecht, and so on.

The truth is I came to love Holland, despite its claustrophobic
dimensions and the ridiculous fat solemnity of its citizens, and

its strange addiction to the tulip, most unattractive of all flowers; and I should have felt cheated had I been deprived of it utterly. Its people proved unexpectedly ugly, like the background figures in a Breughel but unredeemed by the benediction of his wit. Yet I was charmed by their unflagging interest in each other: the way in which they sat throughout the week watching each other at breakfast or housecleaning through facing picture windows; on weekends, how they set up camp chairs beside the crowded roads to keep an eye on each other driving, or picnicking on the dusty shoulders.

It was, however, the landscape which justified all the rest, forever immune to the uses to which it is put; since house or houseboat, canal or reclaimed meadow, sea or city street, old ladies on bicycles or cows cut in half by streamers of mist as they stand knee-deep in grass—all, all reveal in the muted X-ray light skeleton, structure, abstract pattern, like a Vermeer or a Mondrian. No wonder it is the best country in the world in which to look at pictures.

For some such reasons, at any rate, I did not stand on my dignity or insist on taking the final trick; I even made eventually an official appearance at Amsterdam, delivering a pair of lectures under the auspices of the Professor of Aesthetics who was originally to have been my Fulbright sponsor—a token 24 hours in lieu of my planned Fulbright term. The Rector did not show up, of course, and to this day I have not laid eyes upon him, which is perhaps just as well; but there was an official luncheon of quite authentic bad food on quite beautiful fine linen, and appropriate formalities from one of his underlings, to which I responded by eating and listening. And what more could have been asked of me?

To be sure, I arrived if not exactly late, certainly not a minute too early, pounding up the stairs of the old University building just as my host was beginning to despair. It was, however, more a contempt for European distances than any desire to annoy those who had invited me which had prompted the split-second timing; it brought me with only minutes to spare (hardly time for a cup of coffee) to my first lecture—the subject of which had been worked out in a comic exchange of telegrams between me and the Profesor of Aesthetics. Eager that I speak to a harmless topic, i.e., one guaranteed not to "generate undesirable discussion and adverse publicity" at this late date, and interested also, perhaps, in having me testify to something peculiarly, even a bit absurdly, American, my host had asked in his final letter of invitation: "Could you give us then two lectures on the Principles of *Creative Writing* and the practice of teaching this subject-matter on *Tuesday, 28, from 11* a.m. *to* 1 p.m."

It was, possibly, only my vestigial paranoia, on guard now for anti-American rather than anti-academic slights, which made me feel like an Oxford-educated Ibo asked to lecture on *Cannibalism* or some other quaint tribal practice, but I was in fact annoyed. And I was not, in any case, about to let them off the hook quite so easily, so I sent back a wire reading, GLAD TO LECTURE ON ROLE OF WRITER IN THE UNIVERSITY; to which the immediate answer was, GRATEFUL FOR YOUR KIND ACCEPTANCE STOP IN OUR CURRICULUM WE PREFER THE SUBJECT CREATIVE WRITING STOP PLEASE CONFIRM THIS TITLE BY CABLE. My final words in response to that: CALL IT ANYTHING YOU PLEASE.

I suppose they pleased "Principles and Practice of *Creative Writing*"; but the couple of hundred students who packed the classroom and overflowed into the hall outside (many of the faces I recognized from my day with ASVA) responded quite as if I were talking about "The Role of the Writer in the University," which I was; or even "Academic Liberty," which I suppose I was, too. On the other hand, the professors and representatives of the Board of Curators present apparently found my lecturing style—my informality of tone, my colloquial language and shameless bad jokes, my soapbox enthusiasm and unguarded gestures—quite charmingly American, and the whole event almost as satisfactory, indeed, as if I had really spoken on *Creative Writing*, or *Hollywood* or *Christian Science* or the *Hopi Rain Dance*. All of which proved to me once more— as if I needed new evidence—that winning, though no easier or more conclusive than losing, is at least funnier.

None of this happened, however, until late in November, a long time after I had sat sorting through and dreaming over that first stack of mail in Brighton; and by that time, I had even come to terms with the piece of news contained in it which had most troubled me, despite the fact that it concerned a project I had approved in advance. There was a considerable difference, however, between a "Fiedler Defense Fund" planned and discussed at a point when I had temporarily exhausted all my resources and was on the verge of losing my nerve, and one in actual being. Yet suddenly there before me was a copy of a letter of appeal signed by a formidable list of literary and academic names, along with news that money had already begun to come in.

I had trouble forcing myself to read it, though it was discreet enough in tone: "You have no doubt read of the arrest and harassment of Leslie Fiedler and his family by a variety of forces in Buffalo. . . . To help the Fiedlers in this crisis and enable them to fight for the due process and freedoms involved, we are establishing the Fiedler Defense Fund. We will be grateful to anyone who sends in a contribution. . . ."

And having read it, I launched into a long quarrel with myself. I had always resented such high-toned panhandling on behalf of others, had I not? What, then, was so different about my own case? I could not even plead dire necessity, could I, since, though I was at the moment broker than I had been in a long, long time, I had to have been pretty rich to begin with, or I could never have afforded to get so deep in debt. That much was evident, was it not? And whose business was my financial plight, anyhow, except mine and my bank's?

Still, I had just given the go-ahead, had I not, to what promised to be a long series of appeals, which would cost me thousands of dollars, whereas—even if reason and justice failed and the decision went against me—I would end up with a fine, in all probability, of no more than five hundred dollars. So why shouldn't a concerned public help foot the bill for a legal fight intended not just to get me out of a tough situation, but to set precedents that would protect others, with weaker voices and less influential friends, against harassment, invasion of privacy, and improper search and seizure?

Nonetheless, I grew uneasy all over again every time an accounting came through the mails, or a bundle of letters that had accompanied the contributions was forwarded: almost all of them too warm, committed, and generous by far to suit the situation of one victimized not so much by his own courage or love of truth as by the small malice of his neighbors and the standard stupidity of the police. Only one joker took the curse off a little by sending in lieu of cash or a check a bundle of losing parimutual tickets. But hard on that antidote came a letter from the colleague at Buffalo who was in charge of the collection, and who, meaning only to be loyal and newsy, succeeded in stirring up again all my old doubts plus some new ones.

"The letter has appeared in the *New York Review* and a variety of college newspapers," he wrote, "but we got the most response from the *Saturday Review*. All kinds of people have sent in money and/or letters: a member of the Road Vultures; somebody in Barry Goldwater's office who says you are fighting for the same freedom 'we' fought for unsuccessfully in 1964. . . ."

"Hey, wait a minute," I interrupted myself, putting down the letter to watch out of the window the queue which wound all the way up Montpelier Road from the Curzon Theater on the corner, where "Bonnie and Clyde" was playing for the third straight week, "you know you've always despised the *Saturday Review* and its subscribers for trying to mitigate their contempt for everything living in literature by a commitment to everything O.K. in the world of Causes, whether it be Ban-the-Bomb or Defend-Academic-Freedom. And what are you going to do with the kooks who, quite uninvited, choose to stand by you? The Road Vultures fine and dandy, but what about those ex-Goldwater fans hand-in-hand with the one-time Stevenson supporters? What have either to do with you, who voted for neither of their favorites; but ended up not by voting for either a rightist or a leftist version of freedom to come, but by exercising the freedom you already had and casting no ballot at all?"

In the end I sighed, folded the letter back into its envelope for filing, and went to see "Bonnie and Clyde" myself—to celebrate having learned at fifty something else I thought I had always known: that just as the victims one supports, the causes to which one rallies are never quite clean, no more are the supporters of victims and the ralliers to causes. Therefore, to see oneself as victim and cause, and come to know one's supporters is to endure the sense of a double corruption.

Well, there was nothing I could do about all that; but at least I would not become a *lost* cause, I promised myself, not if I could help it; for that is the worst indignity of all. And making this pledge, I remembered how indignantly I had pointed to the picture of Sacco and Vanzetti over my lawyer's desk, the first time I spotted it, crying "That's not the idea at all, that's not what I have in mind."

What I wanted everyone involved in my case to know was that I like to win almost as much as I like to be right, and that to achieve both simultaneously is to my mind the best of all possible events. As a matter of fact, I am likely to assume that those who have dealt with me at all begin to know this: I felt baffled and half-undone when the President of the University, in our single private conversation just after my arrest, had said with, I thought, a certain amount of distrust, "The one thing I hope is that you have no intention of becoming a martyr."

I hardly knew how to answer him, for it is a role I cannot easily imagine playing, not even looking the type. I suppose there have been well-padded, florid martyrs with stubborn jaws and cold blue eyes, but no self-respecting movie producer would ever cast the part that way.

Still, from time to time during my last hectic weeks in Buffalo, when a good part of the world seemed inclined to believe anybody's lies in preference to my truth, it occurred to me that I might end up being thus miscast. But the very last item I came to in the pile of mail on my desk in Brighton seemed to eliminate that absurd possibility altogether; it was a report from my lawyer that the liar-in-chief on whom the police were depending, the girl spy with the concealed transmitter, had recanted, had withdrawn her earlier assertions on which the warrant leading to our bust had been based, and had made a totally new statement—all properly sworn to.

The news was not entirely unforeseen, since the day before our departure our lawyer had called to alert us, but his usual caution (he presumed all phones tapped) had made him sufficiently vague to leave me unsure about just what she had said. In fact, I did not actually see the whole record until after my return to Buffalo, at which point my initial elation had been chastened a little by the events that had followed. In Brighton, however, I knew only how to be happy, foolishly certain that whatever new lies might follow, nobody could ever again take seriously any testimony on the part of our young spy.

I have come to find her more and more fascinating, that pudgy-faced, slightly creepy little girl with a transmitter in her pocket and the aerial down the leg of her jeans. She seems, in the tale told of our troubles by stenotyped question and answer, printed brief and counter-brief, the central character, essential to something as never before in her life.

In a strange way, the case behind the semi-fiction of the record seems *her* case, not ours; for we have become involved in it accidentally, as it were, by a series of mischances I have tried to describe in this account. And even the part of the police might easily have been played by another pack of faceless shlemiels, doing bad imitations of the bad T.V. shows in which they believe. Precisely because there is no truth in her, she seems somehow the truth of it all, her sham realer than anyone else's reality. At any rate, it was she who made all the difference.

Yet I hardly knew her before the time of the bust, sometimes, indeed, failed to recognize her when she reappeared after one of her mysterious long absences, since—except for her past appearance at our Passover Seder table—our only contacts had consisted of polite hello's and good-bye's on her part (she was invariably, even disconcertingly punctilious) and answering grunts on mine. I was never quite sure what she was doing on the premises, among those other waifs and strays who came to eat and talk and shoot pool or watch T.V.; for she always had, even to a casual glance, the air of one neither invited nor at ease. It would have been tempting, in fact, to believe her a spy, except that she looked not so much like someone with a mission as someone at a loss: nowhere in the world did she know a place in which she was really welcome, including her own home.

She always seemed to have in hand a present of some sort—a box of stationery, a handkerchief, a trinket for my daughter or my wife—as if, on some level, she had the sense of needing to buy her way in, or to pay for the few minutes' worth of attention they stole from their real concerns to bestow on her. She seemed, I guess I am trying to say, to feel herself irrelevant, to *be* irrelevant in any functioning household. I have come to know her since, reading her testimony and reflecting on her role in our lives, even to think I understand her, as one thinks he understands not a relative or a friend, but a character in a well-studied book; and I am convinced that she could never have become the member of anything as organic as a family. To belong, she would have to join or be enrolled in something: not a community made by love or sympathy, but one defined by uniforms and an oath of allegiance; not one into which you are born or married, but one for which you are prepared by a briefing—like, say, the police. But even in that artificial community, that false *karass*, she remained, the record seems to show, an outsider, a hanger-on, a tool.

I must confess that from the start I found her vaguely distasteful and from time to time would say so to my daughter, who probably estimated her no higher than I did, but tried—consciously or not—to make amends for not being able to feel as sorry for her as the facts of her life seemed to require: her totally fractured family, her constant vain efforts to run away, her aimless and pointless returns, her affinity for minor disaster. People less sensitive and secure, on the other hand, exploited her loneliness as long as they could—for kicks or information—and then brushed her, or beat the hell out of her. It goes hard in any world, but hardest of all in marginal ones, with those who baffle pity; and our poor domestic spy had lived chiefly in the marginal ones.

I suppose that is why she was, in her own muddled way, grateful for whatever warmth she had found or extorted in our open and swarming house, where, at least, nobody beat up anybody else. And, perhaps, it was for the sake of my daughter, whose picture, it turned out, she kept in her purse, that she decided to emerge from where the police had hidden her away and to try to unweave the net of lies she had woven around herself as well as us. Or maybe it was simply that she could no longer remember what had prompted her to lie in the first place: the "sweet talk" of the police, who, for once, had begged her, *her*, for a favor; and her own need constantly to falsify an unendurable reality. Moreover, she had played similar games before—

in one case I knew of for certain, perhaps more—with other victims whom she had first framed and fingered, then exonerated in a sworn statement.

At any rate, quite unsolicited (we had tried earlier to find her, but at this point had temporarily given up), she had called my lawyer's office on August 24 and offered to tell the truth at last; nor had she objected to the presence of a court stenographer when she arrived next day.

The "true" record is, therefore, before me—as much truth, at any rate, as she was prepared or could manage to tell on August 25, 1967, which is to say, considerably more truth than she had sworn to earlier, and a lot more than either she or the police proved able to bear; for in a little while, and quite obviously under pressure, she was to recant and deny it.

Even as pure fiction, her account would be of great interest; and as her closest approximation to truth, it is invaluable testimony in the case behind ours: her case, or rather the case in which, though she and we may sit in the dock, Buffalo, its police, its court, the values it claims and those by which it actually lives, are on trial.

Let me call the participants in the dialogue what they are designated in the legal record, Q. and A., meaning my lawyer and the girl. Q. has asked certain preliminary questions concerning A.'s name, where she lives, whether she knows "the Fiedlers"; and he has learned that before "April 28 of this year, a Friday night," which is to say, the night of the bust, A. had been "co-operating to a certain extent with the police." Quite like a good novelist (he is, in fact, as are many lawyers, interested in the art of writing; he calls me sometimes when I am eagerly awaiting news of my legal situation to ask professional advice from me), he then starts to move from the general to the particular, begins to realize the scene. And suddenly I find myself entranced, not like someone listening to his own troubles, but like one deep in a fascinating book or lost before the screen in the darkened theater. The book before me is, to be sure, one I have read before, but never well enough, I now understand.

> Q. May I ask who had originally contacted you to cooperate with the Police?

A. I don't remember. I was in the hospital.

Q. I see. And what were you in the hospital for?

A. I freaked-out.

Q. I see, all right. And how long had you been in the hospital?

A. About five weeks.

Q. And did a police officer come to see you there in the hospital?

A. Well, several did.

Q. And did they ask you to cooperate with them in terms of investigating narcotics?

A. Well, they talked about it. They wanted me to help them, yes.

Q. And did they at that time mention the Fiedlers?

A. Yes.

The conversation moves off to peripheral matters here, and then returns not to the "freak-out," which belongs to the other case, but to ours.

Q. What did they ask you to do at that time. . .

A. Well, they had gone through my purse, and they had found some pictures of the Fiedlers . . . and they . . . wanted to know how well I knew them and that is all.

Q. All right. Did you tell them you knew the Fiedlers?

A. Well, it was obvious. I had pictures of them.

But there is no way to avoid discussing that "bad trip," out of which, as it were, the police materialized, since to the girl it is the beginning and center of everything; so in a minute or two, we are back.

Q. Tell us now how that developed? What did they first ask you to do?

A. Gee, after I got out of the hospital, they didn't know I was out of the hospital until I called them because I was beat up on and assaulted, and then they took me to the hospital. Then, they asked me to—

Q. In other words, you came out of the hospital? Then, you

were beat up and assaulted? And then you went back
into the hospital.

A. Yes.

Q. Then they came to you and asked you to help again.

A. Yes.

Q. Now, the first time they asked you to help, did you turn
them down. Did you say, "No"?

A. No, I didn't know what I was doing. I was mentally—

She quite obviously hates to admit that, at any point, she
willingly and in full knowledge cooperated with the police; but
she seems doomed to end up in the hospital ("freaked-out," "beat
up on") whatever she does, and once there, inevitably calls the
police. The hospital and the cops, together they constitute for
her the only security she has; but her security is a trap. And
taking her back to the first hospitalization, my lawyer tries to
understand how it all works.

Q. You called the police from the hospital.

A. No, I didn't have a guide, and I freaked-out and I called
the police.

Q. What do you mean by "freaked-out". . . .

A. LSD; I didn't have a guide.

Q. What do you mean, "I didn't have a guide"?

A. Someone that is more experienced to tell me what to do.

So, the language lesson is over; and it is clear that the police
are her "guide," too—that they will tell her what to do soon
enough. And so it turns out.

Q. Now, what did they ask you to do then?

A. Well, they said they were having an investigation of the
Fiedlers, and they were going to see if they can arrest them
on narcotics charges, and I told them I didn't want to help
them, and they said, "Well, they were going to do it anyhow without me." They didn't really force me to do it, but
they—I don't know—they sweet-talk you, you know. They
are very smooth and they—

Q. Yes.

A. I don't know what really happened, but my mother really
   bitched at me, and—

It is the only time a member of her family is mentioned in
the testimony: "my mother really bitched at me, and—" Actually,
I had met her mother once, when the girl was, as she admits
elsewhere, "on Missing Persons." Her mother had come, along
with an uncle of the girl, who was on the Force, to see if we
had some clue to her whereabouts; they claimed she had pinched
her mother's jewels before vanishing.

The combined pressure of her mother and the police finally
persuaded her, and at this point she began making regular trips
to our house, picked up and transported by the cops, and with
quite specific instructions.

Q. . . . What did they tell you to do when you would go over?
A. To observe what is going on, try to pick up things.
Q. Pick up things; what do you mean by that?
A. If there was any grass or anything.
Q. Pick it up?
A. Yes.
Q. And bring it out, in other words?
A. I don't see how they could want me to do that because I
   wasn't searched, so I could have said I brought it out of
   Fiedler's house and I had it on myself before I went in
   there, and I said I brought it out. It's really—they are not
   very good officers.

It is an important point, not because of her judgment of the
police, who at this point she felt had betrayed her in a hundred
ways, but because it relates to the key episode of her actually
having brought in the grass which the police "found" on April
28. On this score, she is very clear.

Q. All right. Now, on the night in question, the 28th, you went
   over to the Fiedler home.
A. Yes.
Q. Were you taken over by the police?
A. Yes.

Q. All right. And on that occasion were you searched before
   you went in?
A. No, I wasn't.
Q. Okay. And you had some marijuana on you; right?
A. Yes.

. . .

Q. . . . well, let me ask you this question: when the police
   came in, I understand they . . . got some, an envelope of
   some stuff.
A. That was mine.
Q. That was yours.
A. Yes.

Yet wanting, I suppose, to be all right with everyone, she ex-
culpates the police of everything except stupidity in this episode,
insisting that they never knew the grass was hers, never searched
her, never asked her, took it as a gift of the gods. It is, nonetheless, a critical admission which, along with a host of others, sub-
stantiates not the official claims of the police, but the story
as it really happened. It is all there in her recorded testimony:
complete details about her intrusions and the nature of the device she carried; a specific denial that I had ever witnessed anyone smoking marijuana in my house; and a further confession
that she was in no position to give any reliable evidence concerning me.

Q. Now, when was the time that you first started going in
   with a transmitter on you?
A. Gee, I don't remember. It wasn't every time I went in
   there.
Q. Can you tell me about that, how that would work?
A. Well, it's about as big as a cigarette pack.
Q. Yes.
A. And it has a wire like that. It's just a wire (indicating).
Q. And where would you carry it?
A. In my pocket. You would have to have the wire dangle.
   It was like an aerial.
Q. I see, okay. Now when you did go in with a transmitter on,
   did the police . . . ever tell you, for instance, "We want to

get the conversations. Try to get in the conversation with
any person like . . . Dr. Fiedler"?

A. Well, Mr. Fiedler was always out of town, and he is really
busy. He is always in his study working; or if he is not
that, he is playing with the kids.

What I had not known and therefore could not report earlier,
since the plan had failed utterly and they had to settle for much
less, was that the police had asked the girl to arrange a "buy"
in our house, however she could manage it. On a couple of occasions, they had even given her money, forty dollars to be exact,
so that it would be the genuine article that was changing hands
when they came busting in like the climax of the Late, Late Show.

Q. In other words, what they wanted you to try to do is set
up a buy so that it would take place over at the Fiedler
home.
A. At the Fiedler's, yes.
Q. So they could get the Fiedlers? is that correct?
A. Yes.
Q. Do you know why . . . they wanted to get the Fiedlers?
A. Oh well, Mr. Fiedler was an advisor for LEMAR and they
thought it would be real good to bust somebody in LEMAR,
and they would get a lot of attention, I suppose.
Q. Had anybody talked to you about this? . . .
A. About why they wanted to bust them?
Q. Yes.
A. I don't know. They kept saying they are "sick people," and
"they are animals."

I must confess that I get a little queasy every time I come to
this place in her statement. And I find myself imagining the
scene: that circle of half-articulate men leaning toward the half-
crazy girl, shot full of thorazine to blur her nightmares or of
opiates to kill the pain of bruises inflicted by God knows who.
I see them tugging at the brims of their immovable hats, perhaps,
or shaking calloused fists in the air, as they growl, "Animals, that's
what they are, and don't you forget it."
Toward the end of her testimony, the girl was to protest for the

benefit of my lawyer and the stenographer, putting on record
what I am sure she had never dared say aloud to the cops, "I
don't like anyone to be called names what they called them,
'animals.'" But at that point, she was recalling a later time when
the sweet talk was over and the police were beginning to threaten
her instead.

A. Well, right after the Fiedlers got busted, I got very upset
. . . and I wasn't using very nice language . . . and they
wanted to put me in some penitentiary.

Q. Oh; is that right?

A. Yes.

Q. Why did you get upset. . . .

A. Well, the whole time I was working—well, helping them,
they lied to me the whole time. They—I don't know—
they just, they are two-faced, and they don't mean what
they say and they only want to use you, you know, a patsy.

BY JANUARY 28, 1968, it was no longer the police she was casting in the role of the enemy, but my lawyer; for discretion had brought her back to the side of the prosecution, who, after all, could threaten to jail her for perjury if she abandoned sworn lies favorable to them for sworn truths advantageous to us.

Moreover, they proved quite willing to provide her with new fantasies of her own victimization in place of the old: fantasies which she, no longer playing the role of a repentant "patsy," echoed in response to the promptings of the "Assistant District Attorney, Appearing for the People." The occasion was a hearing on our motion to suppress the evidence against us on the grounds of improper search and seizure; the relevant exchange went as follows:

Q. Could you tell us first of all why you made the statement to [Mr. Fiedler's lawyer]?
A. Well, I was being harassed and I just couldn't take it anymore.

The harassment consisted, in fact, of three or four visits to her house by an investigator, at a time when she turned out not even to be in town. But this police-prompted distortion of reality was notably less comic and grotesque than the earlier one they had supplied her on April 19, 1967. At the end of a series of statements, made before a magistrate to justify his issuing a search warrant for our house, she was asked (I gather by a policewoman, though the record is not clear on this point), "Do you feel as though your life would be in jeopardy if it were known you cooperated with us?" and she answered, "Oh, yeah." It is hard to imagine the tone of her response, and even harder

that of the policewoman's question, since the cops had intended
all along to release her name and even some details about her
eavesdropping device, as soon as the bust was made. They were
proud of their cunning, eager to make headlines, and, in any
case, never had taken seriously the dangers involved in exposing
her to the revenge of the "animals" she had betrayed.

Perhaps she had never taken it seriously either; for by January
of 1968 she was lying for the police again, in open court and
despite all their former deceits. And they seem to have felt that
they really needed those lies; though they were willing—to the
point of indiscretion, if not downright foolishness—to admit their
use of a listening device without a court order, they were apparently frantic to deny having smuggled pot into our house. It
now begins to seem barely possible, in fact, that the girl, eager
to be of service to them or carried away by a vision of herself
as a full-fledged coplet getting her man by hook or crook, may
have decided on her own to plant a little marijuana where it
would do most good. If so, they must have been doubly flabber-
gasted by her confession to my lawyer.

More probably, however, the truth lies in the vague shadow-
land between an outright request from the cops to make the
plant and a purely voluntary contribution of her own to the
plot against us. The search warrant, issued on April 19, had
only one more day to run of the ten that were its legal life;
and the "buy" on our premises, which the girl had, perhaps,
persuaded them was the easiest thing in the world to arrange,
quite obviously was never going to work, never *could* have
worked. The police must have, therefore, been glancing un-
easily back over their shoulders at the D.A.'s office and beginning
to sweat a little; they had invested a lot of time, energy, and
taxpayers' money, with no payoff in sight.

So they set her up to set us up—more by omission than commission, I would guess, simply by having made a point all along
of *not* searching her under circumstances when they obviously
should have. And having by this time a pretty good idea of the
way in which she strove always to please those closest to
her, whoever they were, they may well have dropped a hint
or two as the critical day approached, casually remarking, for
instance, that it would sure be great if they could be absolutely,

one hundred per cent *certain* that there would be stuff in the house on the night of the bust. Nothing that could be used in court against them, understand, even if they, too, were under electronic surveillance. Anyhow, she could be expected to stay clammed up forever, since it would be her ass that would be in a sling if she spilled the beans.

But they did not understand her well enough, figuring that once she'd done her job, they'd pay her off somehow (actually, they offered to subsidize a course in Beautician's School for her, which she turned down, being allergic to all schooling), and that would be an end to it. What she really wanted, though, was to be of service, of use to somebody, somehow; and when they seemed through with her, she drifted toward my lawyer to get back into the action again. Once in his office, however, her need to oblige present company obliged her, for once, to the truth. So the D.A.'s office and the Narcotics Squad had to lean on her again, just a little, and she was back where she started, with *their* story. Here is the relevant passage from her final lying testimony, my lawyer asking the questions on direct examination:

Q. Did you take some marijuana into the house that night?
A. No, I didn't.
Q. Do you recall coming to my office . . . some time ago?
A. Yes.

. . .

Q. When you came to my office do you recall there was a man sitting in my office with one of the machines like this lady is using now?
A. Yes.
Q. Do you remember me introducing you and telling you that everything you said would be taken down?
A. Yes, I do.
Q. And do you recall that before you started to say anything he asked you to swear to tell the truth, the whole truth and nothing but the truth, so help you, God.
A. Yes, I do.

. . .

Q. Do you remember me asking you in my office that day,

in front of that court stenographer, whether you took any marijuana into the house that night, and do you remember saying, "yes," you took some marijuana in?

A. Yes.

Q. Are you saying now that was a lie?

A. Yes.

Q. And that you lied there in my office under oath?

A. That's right.

. . .

Q. Did you know it was a lie when you said it in my office? Did you know you were under oath?

A. Yes, I did.

Q. And under the face of all these things you say now you lied?

A. Yes, I did.

Having denied bringing in the marijuana, she had, as the police must have explained to her, also to affirm that she had been searched. And this, too, she proceeded to do.

Q. You weren't searched that night before you went into the premises, were you?

A. Yes, I was.

Q. Who searched you?

A. [A] policewoman. . . .

. . .

Q. She searched you on the night of the 28th?

A. Yes.

Q. You are sure of that?

A. Yes, I am.

. . .

Q. How is that done?

A. Well, she goes through a procedure, she checks my purse and pockets, and just my clothing.

Q. Did you take your coat off?

A. I took my coat off.

Q. Did you take any of your other clothing off at all?

A. No.

Q. So her search was made of your coat and your pocketbook?
A. And the pockets on my clothes and shoes.

But this was apparently not enough for the police, who tried in their testimony to make clear that their search of the girl had been total and thorough, not just a perfunctory once-over. They therefore hastened to add details she had failed to provide in her own fanciful account—details which sound more like the appropriate passage in a police manual about how to do it than a description of what was actually done.

Q. Did you witness her being searched?
A. Yes, I did.
Q. What did the search consist of?
A. Her bosom, her privates, her legs, pocketbook, slacks, and pockets of her sweater.

Beyond these matters, she changed very little in her newest version of the events, except that in collaboration with the D.A. and the police, she attributed to her mother a larger role in the whole affair. No longer does that shadowy lady remain only a voice "bitching" in the background, but becomes an active participant, driving her daughter at least half way to meet the police on several of the occasions when the girl was scheduled to enter and eavesdrop.

It is odd, though, how little sense of the girl I get reading the court record, her coached responses carrying almost nothing in turn of phrase or tone which reveals her as intimately as does almost every sentence of the spontaneous and living statement she made to my lawyer. Not only that concluding plaintive cry about how she had been nothing but a "patsy" for the cops all along, but certain quite little things as well: her occasional impatient responses, for instance, sharp and a little condescending really.

I get the real feel of her, too, in her descriptions of her camaraderie with the police before their honeymoon was over, the joy they shared playing Fox and Hare. One scene in particular stays in my mind, though it is rendered only in a brief phrase:

stoned out of her mind in the midst of her duties, she has
lifted from the head of one of her plainclothes playmates that
otherwise immovable hat, worn, I guess, in lieu of a uniform,
and has cocked it on her own.

    A. Because when they came out, I was with some man—
        I don't know who he was. We were driving around in
        front of the Fiedlers', and I had his hat on. I was really
        high, and I didn't know really what was going on.
    Q. Did they [the Police] know you had smoked some stuff. . . .
    A. Well, it was obvious.

I was not present at the proceedings, of course, being then in
England; and even those of my children who were at home
had stayed away on advice of counsel, a fact of which the
Court took official cognizance, observing at one point, "I see
the defendants are not here," and asking that it be "noted in
the record." The newspaper accounts add scarcely anything
to what the court stenographer took down; and though I do
have a letter from an interested friend, who was present throughout the hearing, he reacts too strongly and negatively to the
girl to make a useful witness. "That girl . . ." he wrote, "is a
bloody wretch. I don't mean because of the way she repaid your
hospitality particularly; I mean in general. Feh."

He does, however, provide a description of how she looked
that day, which helps a little: "She is plumpish, frowsy, wearing
a brown and orange checked dress with a blue sweater; her hair
seems to be brown streaked ¾ with silver dye."

And in one place, he describes the fading of her voice (a
stenographic record is tone deaf) as she talked about going to
the police to tell them of the statement she had made to my
lawyer. But I can't *hear* her really, except at a point just after
the almost-disappearance of her voice, when the judge inter-
venes a little unprofessionally, i.e., quite genuinely: puzzled, I
suppose, by the girl's attempts to explain her inexplicable series
of assertions and counter-assertions.

    The Court: What was the reason for you to say that these
        were lies that you told. . . . What was the reason for fab-
        ricating this entire story?

The Witness: It was just getting on my nerves.
The Court: What did you think would be accomplished?
The Witness: Maybe I wouldn't have to go to court.
The Court: How did you figure that would happen?
The Witness: Maybe they just wouldn't have called me.

Not only the rehearsed witness, however, but everyone involved in the case seems to me, as I read and reread the record,
oddly dehumanized by the rigid rules of procedure and especially
the joyless, juiceless language of the law. The judge and both
lawyers, of course, are especially adept at communicating with
each other in the antiseptic, sterile jargon of their trade; and
the others follow their lead, the cops having been through it all
many times before, and the girl a fast learner. And my first
reaction is that in such a tongue it is easier to evade and stall
than to confront any issue directly; easier to lie than tell the
truth; easier even not to know that one is lying than to realize
it.

But on second thought, I can see the point of being able to
neutralize and categorize the terrible and sordid and irrational
stuff of which most police-court cases are made, the advantage
of being able to rehearse, say, the circumstances of a brutal
assault so that the blood drawn once in fact does not seem to
flow again.

Yet that is maddening, too, especially to a writer, used to a
kind of recapitulation aimed precisely at making everything
that has happened, including the language of everyone involved,
more real and more vivid the second time around. And sometimes I find it comic as well, as when, for instance, a quite
ordinary cop says "bosom" and "privates" for a woman's tits
and twat. Or when after a long day of "Your Honor, I am not
ready to enter into any stipulation in reference to . . . ," and
"Now, your Honor, I am objecting that Malinski does not apply
to . . . ," Your Honor must address the quite real human being
(my oldest son, in this instance) who is the defendant in court,
sentence him in fact, and can only fall back on more of the
same, plus a handful of clichés more appropriate at a Boy
Scout Father and Son Dinner:

The conditions of your probation are that you avoid in-

jurious or vicious habits and lead a law-abiding life. . . .
You are also to refrain from frequenting unlawful or disreputable places or consorting with disreputable persons.
Work faithfully at a suitable employment or faithfully pursue a course of study. Satisfy other conditions reasonably
related to rehabilitation. . . .

Now, if you follow all of those directions I feel quite
certain that everything will be satisfactory and you will
again be able to take your place in society as a law-
abiding young man and be of service to your fellow-men.

I do not mean to suggest that there is no evidence of concern
and even of human warmth behind these stale formulae. I
suspect, in fact, that the sentencing judge was a kindly as
well as a decent man; he had merely lost the trick of talking
like a human being, or perhaps, rather, had learned the trick
of not. Disconcertingly enough, the only participant in the proceedings with a human voice was not a nice man at all. He was
the more surly, as well as the more slow-witted, of the two
cops who testified: type-cast as the "bad" partner in one of
those standard Good-Bad cop teams I was astonished to discover
exist in real life, or, at any rate, in Buffalo, as well as in the
movies and on T.V. His more affable partner confined himself
on this occasion pretty much to saying "Yes, sir," "No, sir," and
—when the going got a little tough—"I honestly don't remember"; but the nastier one kept falling out of the dull courtroom
scene into a story by Damon Runyon.

At one point, he interrupted the proceedings to ask for permission to remove his rubbers; at another he translated into
plain English what the girl had earlier called—using, I suppose,
a word taught her by the D.A.—"being harassed." "She told me,"
was his version, "that she was being bothered and she wanted
to get the people off her back, they were driving her crazy."
But my favorite example of his style occurs in an exchange over
what he heard or didn't hear at the other end of the transmitter.

Q. And did you hear words or information concerning
   marijuana?
A. I heard the words itself spoken.

Q. The words itself spoken?
A. Yes.
Q. Did you hear pot?
A. It was all sung, as if to sing.

It is a small poem, shot through with malicious glee, but a real poem at long last: "It was all sung, as if to sing."

iii

THERE HAS BEEN little poetry since, however, in the series of hearings and appeals which have followed the second recantation of the girl-spy; because the human voice has scarcely been heard through the language of symbols and abstractions appropriate to the law as practiced when only lawyers and judges confront each other in a series of strategic maneuvers. Once the girl had deserted us, it became clear that we had little hope in the local courts and must somehow reach first the Appellate Court and the Court of Appeals of the State of New York—and, if these failed us, the Supreme Court of the United States, already on record as opposing total invasion of privacy by the use of unrestricted electronic listening devices. But to reach those upper courts, it was necessary to go through a trial eventuating in a verdict of guilty, or to *plead* someone involved on the case guilty, not as a confession of anything, but as a legal technicality.

My oldest son—the one about to leave with us for the movies at the moment of the bust—was chosen, for reasons which will become clearer later, to bear the brunt of the appeal process; pleading with him were his wife and the two youngest charged (including my second son who had been in his bath), who we hoped would receive suspended sentences—and relieved of the necessity of ever appearing in court, no matter what happened. My lawyer, in fact, proved a canny bargainer, insisting, first of all, that the charge against my oldest son be reduced from a felony to a misdemeanor and, second, that the tactical reasons for his plea be clearly entered on the record.

There was something upsetting about the whole affair; it seemed to me (especially in far-off England) not only morally equivocal, but anti-poetic and anti-human as well. There were not even any witnesses physically present, though the testimony of the girl and the two cops, which had been taken on January 24, and from which I have been quoting above, was made available to the presiding judge. All that was actually heard in the courtroom, though, beyond "Yes," "No," and 'Thank you" from my almost irrelevant oldest son, were the arguments of the lawyers: first, the Assistant District Attorney making his official explanation of the reduced charge:

> It is my understanding at this time that this defendant wishes to withdraw his former plea of "not guilty" to the count in this indictment charging a violation of Section 1751-1 of the Penal Law, a felony (selling or giving a narcotic to a minor), and in its place enter a plea of guilty to the reduced charge of violating Section 3305 of the Public Health Law, as a misdemeanor (simple possession). The district attorney's office recommends to the court the acceptance of this plea in view of the fact that this defendant is 25 years old and was never convicted of any crime. . . .

And then my lawyer, making his official explanation of why we were not contesting the charge:

> I would like to put on the record that one of the purposes for entering this plea is so that we can come under Section 813-c of the Code of Criminal Procedure and proceed immediately to the Appellate Division on a denial of my motion to suppress. That is one of the main reasons of the appeal.

Between them, these constitute all of the truth which seemed from the point of view of law useful or necessary to record.

The complete story, however, is somewhat more complex and considerably less tidy; it goes back, moreover, much further into the past. As early as June, 1967, even before the girl-spy had told her second story, much less recanted her recantation, my lawyer had appeared before a county judge to ask suppression of "certain evidence against Dr. Leslie A. Fiedler, University of Buffalo English professor, and six other defendants . . . on grounds it was obtained illegally by use of electronic listening devices."

It seemed unlikely that such a motion would ever be granted in a local court, certainly not while the indignation of downtown Buffalo stayed at the boiling point and the *Courier-Express* waited in the offing, eager to pounce on anything that could be construed as being "soft" on a professor who was himself notoriously "soft" on drugs. And that, for the moment at least, seemed to the local reactionaries and their genteel wives a crime almost as heinous as being "soft" on Communism or draft-card burners. And I was, after all, on record as favoring a relaxation of laws regulating the use of marijuana, which is to say, *really* guilty, whether guilty as charged or not.

If, however, we could somehow get the case to a higher court in a remoter place, and make our motions to a panel of five or seven or nine judges to whom the protection of the individual against improper search and seizure seemed more vital than the protection of their local college against an invasion of "bearded beatniks," we would have a real chance. So, anyhow, my lawyer stoutly maintained, with a kind of calm optimism I found especially convincing.

How to get to such a court was, however, a real problem, and one that would cost time as well as money. Still, the Defense Fund was about to come into existence, and time seemed on our side rather than that of the prosecution. With time (and a little luck) the passions of the community would cool to a point where we might begin to educate them—not only about the facts of the case (had I or had I *not*, for instance, "trafficked in drugs," or been caught high in the midst of a "pot-and-hashish party"?), but about the nature of marijuana: was it addictive? did it lead to crime? were its dangers so flagrant that only a corrupter of the young would advocate easing the restrictions against it?

Besides, there was the odd chance that somewhere along the line, due process might put us in the presence of a judge, enlightened and unafraid, who could end the whole silly mess by barring the evidence on which the original warrants had been issued. We did not find such a judge in County Court in June, however, but only one who backed and filled about whether the fact of electronic eavesdropping had been established, and maintained that in any case he would have to deny my attorney's motion to suppress, citing in support of his decision "Hoffa vs. the United States," whose bearing on our trial and its issues were far from clear to anyone beside himself. A new trial date of September 5 was set for all of us—the law being, I had begun to learn, a game as little played in the summer as ice hockey.

But in September, we presented two new motions, this time in City Court, where all of us except my oldest son had been charged originally. One of these was an amended form of our motion to suppress, the argument refined and fortified by citations of important new cases in the area of "improper search and seizure." But the second was quite new, being a motion to dismiss the charges against me on the grounds that the statute invoked was unconstitutional. "Mr. Fahringer will argue," the *Evening News* of September 14 reported, "that 'mere possession or use' of marijuana should not be proscribed, because the drug is not inherently dangerous."

We called only two witnesses to say in court what has been known about the relative harmlessness of pot, as compared with, say, alcohol or tobacco, ever since the La Guardia report of the mid-thirties, and what has been suppressed ever since. It is hard to be certain of the grounds for that continuing suppression, though, I suppose, the authorities must do so out of the sense that not every truth works for the good of society; it is the customary argument of oppressors and censors. But many connive in it who are not in other regards censorious or totalitarian; and about their motives I have been speculating off and on for more than a decade.

Despite the fact that religious leaders assure us from time to time that we are saved not by what goes into our mouths but by what comes out, we tend collectively to be more than normally irrational about what we eat and drink. Some cultures, as everyone knows, have banned pork, some all fish, while others have tried to avoid all foods containing more "yin" than "yang"; and there is scarcely one of us without some personal repugnance quite as mad and religious as any sponsored by an organized cult, or screamed at his parent by a stubborn child. It is, however, intoxicants or mind-altering substances, food or drink which heightens or disrupts conventional modes of perception, which are the maximum source of confusion, since no known society has banned or accepted them in *toto*.

But why different societies legitimize some and not others without consistency or agreement (the Moslem World traditionally permitting hashish but not alcohol, the Christian one sacramentalizing alcohol and banning hashish), I cannot explain satisfactorily even to myself. And I am even more baffled by how quickly they change their minds. Food and drink which have come to seem to us the profanest of refreshments—cocoa, chocolate, coffee, tea—were considered elsewhere, and not so very long ago, holy, i.e., too dangerous and valuable for ordinary use; while the opiates, which we prescribe these days with the greatest of caution, were once in every household medicine cabinet. We know that certain eminent nineteenth-century poets dosed themselves with laudanum (ten per cent opium, ninety per cent alcohol, which must have been a real kick); and that certain early twentieth-century babies, including many of us, were given paregoric for the "colic," which is to say, opium once more.

Yet once such a shift has occurred, we regard our outlived vices not with the amusement we bestow on passé styles, but with a horror otherwise reserved for the most heinous of crimes; and how much more so is this true of drug preferences we have never shared. I suppose a basic cause must be the fear we all experience when confronted by the habits of alien cultures, no matter how flourishing and content we know their members to be. And when the alien culture has been invented in our own homes by our own kids, and is practiced there in our despite, no wonder we end by condemning and punishing. Yet this is in a way not only comprehensible but even defensible, since it is our very definition of ourselves as men which we are protecting. The only unforgivable thing is to lie, by claiming that someone else's meat is their poison as well as ours.

And for telling this sort of lie about pot we have not been forgiven by our children, who, having found us out, begin to doubt the most indubitable truths we try to share with them. The only way out of the trap is to cease lying long enough to learn the facts. To those facts my two witnesses testified; and what they said ran somewhat, I trust (the Buffalo press is my only source), as follows. A doctor and pharmacologist from the University of Rochester apparently appeared first:

> He testified that a user of marijuana has a "psychic dependence" on the drug similar to that a heavy smoker has on cigarettes.
>
> Physiological effects, which can be severe in the case of narcotics such as heroin, are "almost nonexistent" for marijuana, he said.
>
> Under cross-examination . . . he pointed out that there has been no "written indictment against marijuana" comparable to the Surgeon General's reports which have indicted cigarettes as a cause of lung cancer and other diseases.

When the Assistant District Attorney, having exhausted the possibilities of psychological and physiological risk, pressed him on the sociological implications of smoking pot, he pleaded lack of expertise.

> He admitted that he could not testify as to the sociological effects of marijuana use but could speak only of its physical and psychological effects.

Our second witness, however, "who identified himself as a sociologist working at UB," though he belonged, as a matter of fact, to our unorthodox English Department, was ready to address himself to this point. And he had, in fact, special qualifications: not only a continuing interest in our case, about which he had written an article in the *New Republic*, but much experience gained while "associated with the study of drug abuses for the President's Committee on Law Enforcement."

> He said that the study indicated that marijuana was not addictive, that there was no evidence that it led to heroin addiction or caused crime.

Even the brief newspaper summary made it clear that there was no current fantasy about grass left unexploded when the two witnesses were through—except, perhaps, its imagined con-

nection with untrammeled sex, which, if mentioned at all in
court, did not make it into print. Yet the decision was to go
against us, since what was being judged was not our specific
guilt but our general role in the community as outsiders and
dissenters. We were not to know it for a long time, however,
since arguments in court have to be followed by briefs, which
judges take a long time to study. Moreover, before any decision
would be made on the first motion, our even more important
second one to suppress was to be heard, too; and the chief
witness at that hearing was scheduled to be the ever changeable,
and—as it turned out—now elusive girl-spy. My lawyer's letters
to me in England tell the story clearly enough, though in brief,
not only of the law's customary delays but of our (also customary, I suppose) fluctuating hopes.

On September 18, he wrote:

> Things have been going very well here and as you can
> see . . . our proceeding on the legality of marijuana got off
> to a good start. The hearing has been adjourned and I
> expect will be continued in another week or so. I have
> high hopes of getting the proceeedings dismissed before
> you return from England.
>
> [The "sociologist's"] . . . testimony was both persuasive
> and beautifully presented. He made an excellent witness.

And on October 13 he sent another account of where things
were:

> We are still in the process of conducting motions to suppress,
> and the case has been adjourned to November 13, 1967.
> Things are going extremely well, and I hope that it will
> be unnecessary for you to return from England before the
> disposition of your case.

On November 4, however, the word was:

> Your case will be adjourned on November 13th because
> the brief on the legality of the proscription of marijuana
> has just been submitted. . . . I hope to set a new date in

1968 before which time we will argue the search and seizure question.

And on December 28, the latest legal news was accompanied by a personal note, a bit of gossip really, though of vital bearing on the case:

> We still have been unable to complete the motion to suppress because of the disappearance of [the girl]. . . . I don't expect that there will be any developments on your case until another couple of months. I might say that things have been looking better all the time.
>
> [The girl] . . . is now married. Her marriage was one of necessity.

At this point, there is a gap in what seemed on the verge of becoming a full-fledged transatlantic epistolary novel, since matters had become urgent enough to require that we communicate by telephone. And when it resumed again on February 11 of the next year, my lawyer was trying to explain that the plea of guilty to a reduced charge, which he had persuaded my eldest son to enter, was in the best interests of everyone: my son's certainly, because he would be assured that in no event would he be sentenced to jail; and our whole family's as well, since my wife and I, on whom a whole household depended, might, if his plea worked, never have to stand trial at all; and even society's, since, following this strategy, we would be able to keep alive the issue of invasion of privacy, important to everyone, rather than of our innocence of the specific charges, important only to us.

Yet to "cop a plea" seems a courtroom ploy proper to guilt at bay rather than persecuted innocence, a kind of betrayal of those who had flocked to our defense. And to let a son (a grown one, to be sure, *en route* from the Fiji Islands to a med school in the United States) bear the brunt of the bad publicity seems an act of cowardice. Perhaps that is why my lawyer argued so hard by mail:

> . . . Needless to say this has been a very painful task for

me because any lawyer worth his salt hates the unseemly
task of securing pleas and trying to protect people from
prison sentences. . . .

However, let me take your questions one by one and see
if I can answer them sufficiently.

First, I believe . . . your son being a member of the
household during the time of his arrest will give us sufficient
standing to raise in the Appellate Courts the question of
electronic eavesdropping. . . . As soon as I am able to
effectuate his plea I intend to immediately expedite an
appeal to the Appellate Division in Rochester, New York,
which is composed of a five-man bench and whose membership is removed from the hysteria which exists in this
community. I have never lost confidence in my theory
which requires a suppression of all the evidence based upon
the Government's intrusion upon your premises with this
electronic surveillance. . . .

As you know, your case . . . will be left open pending the
determination of the appeal.

What we had been discussing over the transatlantic cable
between this letter and the one before was, first, the disappearance and reappearance of the girl-spy; then, the dismissal of
our motion to suppress by the County Court; and finally, the
question of what we must next do to give that motion a second
chance on appeal. That the girl would at some point in the
proceedings take a powder had seemed to me inevitable from
the start; for running away and returning and running away
again was as basic to the pattern of her panicked life as lying
and recanting and lying again, or making it into the hospital,
getting discharged and finding her way back again to a non-
institutionalized world. In her testimony to my lawyer, for
instance, she locates events in time by reference to one or
another of her hospitalizations, or else remarks, quite casually,
"Well, I was on Missing Persons last December"—specifying,
when asked, that she had been during the period in question
"in San Francisco and New York."

Certainly, for as long as we knew anything about her—
and even allowing for her confusion of fantasy and reality—

she seems to have swung back and forth almost frantically between the poles of here and away, false and true, "inside" (which might well have been a jail cell rather than a hospital ward, had there not been police in her family) and "outside." She was, I guess, an authentic recidivist—a technical term whose real meaning I never quite understood before meeting her, not understanding that a zigzag could also be a pattern for a life, quite as well as a straight line or circle or normal curve. This time around she ran the full gamut, winding up in the hospital not long after making her statement to my lawyer, and just before taking off to places unknown.

Those places did not long remain unknown, since the police needed her, and she had made what turned out to be the mistake of getting married. It is possible that she thought of her marriage as a way of washing her hands of the whole case, of becoming a different person with a different name, and no past at all. But her new name belonged also to her new husband, who had become, almost at the same moment as a married man and an expectant father, a soldier caught by the draft; and his whereabouts was, therefore, duly noted in official files.

Consequently, however well or ill it may have suited her plans, our recidivist turned out to be easily retrievable. And once located, served a subpoena, and flown back to Buffalo for the hearing, she had—in her limited view—no option but to play the game required of her by recanting her recantation, and thus destroying for us the last possibility of winning the case in the local courts.

iv

In a way, the question of where to turn next answered itself, since we had come to a place where there was no possibility of retreating except into disaster. But there remained the problem of *how* to move ahead: how to challenge further the baseless assumption that marijuana is a "dangerous narcotic" and therefore to be banned; and how to continue to contest the legality of the total surveillance with which the case against me was established.

We decided to move the first line of attack from the courtroom to the larger domain of public debate in the press, on the platform, over the air, before television cameras, where, in fact, it had all begun; the second we determined to press on through any legal channels that remained open to us, all the way to the Supreme Court if need be.

There is little doubt in my own mind that eventually a decision must be pressed for in the courts as to whether the present laws regulating the use of marijuana are constitutional. But this means persuading the Bench to decide whether or not it is such a threat to "health and welfare" as justifies the severest restrictions and the imposition of jail sentences on mere users and possessors. It seems clear, however, that such a decision by the courts will depend in part on a prior decision by the whole of our society. And the young these days seem more inclined to bypass or challenge by passive resistance the laws they find intolerable than to try to change or qualify them through legislatures or courts. It is especially incumbent, therefore, on those old enough to prefer explanation to demonstration to make the case.

Meanwhile, a considerable minority of the young, perhaps even a majority (quite recently an incensed Buffalo judge has been telling public meetings that "over 50 per cent" of the young people in this area have "experimented with drugs"), has already made a unilateral decision in favor of pot. But making it under present conditions, they define themselves as "criminals" even though they harm no one by the act, and even though they may be in all other respects quite as law-abiding and socially useful as those who cry out against them. As a result, some of them—selected almost at random out of a number so large that there are not cops enough to bust, or jail cells enough to hold them all—end up in prison, occasionally for long terms.

This kind of token harassment, however, like Nazi reprisals against one of ten in the communities that unanimously resisted them during World War II, is a final absurdity. Indeed in, say, the Haight-Ashbury or on the streets around certain college campuses, the police, precisely like unwelcome invaders, find themselves beleaguered in a beleaguered city. It is a situation in which injustice, spying, planting, petty harassment is the rule, and terror threatens at every moment to erupt.

But perhaps such analogies are too extreme to give an accurate sense of the situation of a generation to whom pot is as much a grace and support of ordinary life as Martinis and tranquilizers, coffee and cigarettes to their parents. Let us think rather of a somewhat milder, certainly more American parallel: the twenties and Prohibition.

Certainly for those under twenty-five at this moment, which is to say, for nearly one-half of all Americans, the situation with respect to marijuana is precisely what is was for the whole adult population with respect to alcohol before Franklin Delano Roosevelt delivered us from a law that forbade what almost no one proved willing to give up. Yet the drinkers of the twenties were in a way luckier than the young of today, since scarcely any of them were prosecuted for mere possession of their forbidden intoxicant. But those who smoke grass cannot abide the kind of hypocrisy which, in the period of drinking moonshine, fostered the bootlegger, the hijacker, the gangster, who functioned both as suppliers and scapegoats—providing goods and services which society, having banned, then demanded—and, when caught, went to jail to the loud applause of everyone.

The young of right now prefer by and large to be their own

dealers, rather than open a new territory for exploitation by the Mafia. They are perhaps driven to this by the fact that the mere use of grass is already a crime; and it is surely made easier for them by the fact that marijuana will grow anywhere, in a windowbox or abandoned lot, north, south, east, west.

In part, however, their strategy results from a desire to be their own men and pay their own dues, to have no one else grow fat at their expense or serve time to get them off the hook.

Nonetheless, hoods from the outside—not people who share the taste they supply, but those with a taste only for money and power—even now begin to move into such colonies of the pot-smoking young as New York's East Village, thus providing a second source of woe for those who have chosen to alter their own life-style without intent to harm. It is a grim squeeze to be caught between cops and mobsters, the arm of the righteous and the fist of the outlaw; but it is not an inevitable consequence of smoking grass. Indeed, it could all be changed overnight with a single stroke of the pen—millions of "criminals" removed from those disheartening statistical lists with which good citizens like to scare themselves, as well as millions of victims protected from the power of the underworld. All that is required is to replace present rigid laws with others less stringent, like those, for instance, which presently regulate the consumption of alcohol.

I used to think that some day soon some enlightened legislator would rise, without any interest except the welfare of the young, to initiate the change. And I was convinced that any moderately reasonable legislature would hasten to support him once the issue had been brought out into the open, thus setting an example that would be followed by state after state. More recently, however, I have come to believe that, though there are doubtless legislators who use marijuana themselves, even they do not now dare to expose themselves.

No, it is not, I now believe, in legislative assemblies, so sensitive to community pressure, but in the more protected atmosphere of the courts, perhaps only in the United States Supreme Court itself, that the first step to end the Cold War against pot will be taken, by declaring all laws which define marijuana as a "dangerous narcotic," or which treat it as such, unconstitutional. For a while, as a matter of fact, we considered trying to move our own case up for review by that body, with the question of constitutionality our grounds of appeal. At the very moment, however, that our own pair of witnesses was testifying to the nature of grass in Buffalo City Court, some twenty-five or thirty experts were making a similar but much more formidable record in another pot-possession case in Boston. And we have finally been content to let the Boston lawyers see if they can get to the Supreme Court—with the hope, perhaps, of entering an *amicus curiae* brief in their support, if and when they do.

Meanwhile, I refuse no invitation to testify or debate on the subject of pot and the law anywhere in the world I can reach; and I turn down none of the requests which come to me by phone or letter because of the association in the press of my name and marijuana. Some of those requests are weird, some merely banal; and the pleaders are as various as the pleas: a high school debater in quest of data; someone who has not made it with whiskey or women still looking for a religion cheaper than God; a sociologist in search of a case to demonstrate a theory; someone busted and fired without protest or publicity, looking for a fellow victim; a mystic proselytizer eager to offer me visions superior to those I presumably enjoyed on pot; a weary editor in search of what he has learned too late is up-to-date; a long-lost friend sure he has found me again in my distress, and wanting to talk about *his* troubles. Wisdom and love are what they ask for, nothing more than that; and how can one brush them off without seeming unsympathetic, or respond without sounding pretentious? To reveal oneself as a boor, or to set oneself up as hero and sage: these seem the uncomfortable alternatives.

And there is no way out; for once being chosen, by circumstances or fate, one has no choice any more. It is just such a trap (after a while you even *like* it, which is the worst) as being a Jew or a Negro. I carry my story with me not like a record but like an identifying feature, a hook nose, nappy hair. My mere presence, the sound of my voice, triggers prejudice and counter-prejudice, which is to say, reminds old and young that they are engaged in a continuing war: a war whose immediate occasion is marijuana, but whose ultimate cause is a conflict

of religions, each utterly incomprehensible to the communicants
of the other, and neither quite understood by its own. And so
to step out of my role, I would have to step out of my skin
and my name.

Yet I cannot help resenting the new identity that has been
imposed on me more by chance than by my own design; for
I know that if it does not falsify me totally, it robs me of a
dimension. I am not just, not even primarily, the professor who
was busted for pot and maligned, much less the pot-happy corrupter of the young, but a refugee from the urban East, as well,
who lived in Montana for nearly a quarter of a century; a thirty-
years married father of six kids; a critic, teacher, and committee-
member; a writer of fiction and verse; a maker of jokes, good
and bad; a translator of Dante.

But what can I do? A student runs for the presidency of the
student body at the University of Oslo, pledging that if elected,
he will bring me to speak, and it seems a sufficient program;
at the same moment a lady in the process of returning from
suburbia to school drops out of her Humanities Course at
SUNYAB because, she says, I am still on the staff. There is
something more than a little comic about the disproportion,
the skewed scale of these events.

Others, more customary, are also more dully depressing. POT
PROFESSOR ARRIVES IN BRIGHTON read the headlines in
the *Evening Argus,* a week after I have moved into my house
in Montpelier Road; and a month later, a popular English magazine called *Nova* defines "bust" in a hippie glossary for squares:
"Arrest by police, as in 'Leslie Fiedler, the noted literary critic,
has been busted at fifty.'" At just about the same time in
America, *Variety,* under the heading, "1967 Lingo: 'Conglom-
erate' and 'Psychedelic,'" has got me sandwiched between
"credibility gap and generation gap" on top, "Twiggie, Alfie, and
Georgie Girl" on the bottom. It is an odd conjunction, but even
odder is the immediate context in which they place me: "tune-in,
turn-on, drop-out, viz., Timothy Leary, Leslie Fiedler, et al."

And there is no end; returning to America, home, and school,
I discover in the September 1968 issue of *Esquire,* under the
general rubric of "The Beautiful People: Campus Heroes for
68/69," my picture peering in a window at a Last Supper of

New Testament Gurus, and beneath, the identifying description: "*Leslie Fiedler* (profile), hip literary critic, got busted on pot charge." Moreover, in a quite recent *Buffalo Evening News*, there I am again, mentioned prominently in an article on "The Lively Arts," the tone friendly enough in general. But tacked on to my name, once more and still, is that dreadful-silly adjective which has haunted me for so long: "the controversial novelist-critic, Leslie Fiedler." How can I help feeling that in the single word "controversial" it is all waiting to be reborn: the history of three troubled decades of my life ready to repeat itself— not as comedy perhaps (though we have it on the good authority of Marx that second times in history are always comic), since that is what it was the first time around. But as what, then, *what?*

Well, the journalistic stereotype in which I am trapped as far as the adult world is concerned serves me as a passport into the realm of the young. But by now that word has got around, too, to the other side; the writer of the article in *Esquire* which accompanies the picture of the Last Supper announces it to the few who have not got the word yet, with the sort of protective irony appropriate to his craft and that magazine:

> Picture your old man sitting at home wondering who you *do* trust. Not *him,* and certainly not your college president. Cut out this painting and send it to him. These, for his information, are twenty-eight people he might not listen to, but you would—if they were around to tell you anything. Provided you still can be told a thing or two.

Twenty-eight, including Ché Guevara, Buckminster Fuller, Dr. Spock—and Fiedler. Silly as it is, it contains a grain of truth: I am, from time to time, invited into the world of the young, on the basis of two errors.

In the first place, young people are likely to assume that because I have been busted, I am not merely *Kosher,* but a real Head in professor's clothing; just as their parents, on the basis of the same evidence, may assume that I am not merely a member of the marijuana lobby but some sort of unreconstructed, if aging, swinger. And in the second place, they tend to conclude

that I must have something to teach them more real and true
and dear than how to read Dante or Dickens or Mark Twain;
though, in fact, to me there is nothing more real and true and
dear than this—or if there is, I have it still to learn from *them*.
And this leads to all sorts of absurd misunderstandings, which
I should, I suppose, resent, but which in truth I relish and even
consume with all the writer's insatiable appetite for material, all
the comedian's hunger for the play of cross purposes.

After a talk to a spiritless, scarcely responsive group in a
prototypical midwestern college, from which an instructor has
recently been fired for smoking a Camel in class, I walk toward
my host, no longer quite sure he is proud for having been brave
enough to invite me in the first place, and think, with a sinking
heart, of the room in the Holiday Inn Motel toward which he
will whisk me as quickly as possible.

But I never quite reach him; for out of the crowd of square,
tight students—the remorselessly crewcut, obviously beer-drink-
ing boys and their dates—appears a freckled, graying lady who
might be the spinster aunt of any of them. She asks if I'm too
tired or would like a cup of coffee with "her and some of the
folks" before going to bed; I would, with excuses to my host.
But once I have got where she is taking me, once through the
door of a frame house which looks like something left over
from the last Booth Tarkington movie—there are the strobe lights
flickering on a further wall; and the young man who takes my
coat flips open a poison ring on his fourth finger and asks would
I like some hash that he just happens to have. And he thinks
I am joking or playing it super-cool when I protest that that is
not the idea at all.

Sometimes, however, this particular misapprehension backfires.
I went once to Washington, D.C., for a Conference on Drugs
organized by the National Student Association, and thought I
had discovered that acceptance by one minority group opens
up all others, since I was taken, as soon as our own meetings
were over, to a convention of all the "homophile" (i.e., male
homosexual and lesbian) associations of America. For a half-
hour or so I sat in the dim basement room of a Catholic College,
if not accepted at least unchallenged, listening to the clicking
of a mimeograph machine behind me and the drone of the

chairman's voice before me, as one more group maligned by the righteous, as well as harried and set up and enticed by the cops, tried to find a public voice and a program of self-defense.

It was another world of interior exile, another underground American community I might never have penetrated without having been arrested myself. Yet this time I began, after a while, to feel to myself an interloper (though I was not, I kept protesting inside my own head, just a tourist, a sightseer), and —it turned out—to the others, too. At any rate, a large, fierce woman, who may have been eavesdropping over my shoulder, suddenly arose to challenge my credentials and, I suppose, my motives.

After a brief flurry of discussion, I was asked to wait outside while the delegates talked me over in earnest and in privacy so they could decide whether to welcome me back or exclude me permanently. I knew I was sunk, however; for once a question has been raised under such circumstances, there is no chance. And I was not surprised, therefore, when at last the official messenger appeared: a genuinely troubled young man, who said, laying a sympathetic hand on my arm, "Well, we did our best—but you know how those goddamned dikes *are!*" And he was gone before I could remind him, myself, the world, that though I might be straight, I had written "Come Back to the Raft, Ag'in, Huck Honey." I had been busted. I *knew*.

The second error also leads to endless misunderstandings, not nearly so funny by and large, but intriguing in their own right. I am, for instance, invited for a brief term as what is called a writer-in-residence—teacher-in-opposition, really—by a student group inside of some large, shapeless university, which they try hard to believe oppressive instead of merely disheartening. They have found funds of their own (being richer as well as more disgruntled than students have ever been before) to realize their own desires; and they have no trouble, consequently, in by-passing their President, their Deans, the Chairman of the Department (who have lost their nerve anyway, no matter how loud they talk) that should by traditional protocol have sponsored me; and which takes its small revenge by pretending officially that I am not there, do not, in fact, exist.

I scarcely have time to notice the snub, however; since the

students, ignorant or contemptuous of normal academic sched-
ules, are running my ass off twelve or fourteen hours a day with
appearances in classes, at coffee houses, at special showings of
underground films, plus scheduled individual conferences and
informal discussions on street corners and in cafeterias.

The organizers of the enterprise have taken the word of the
cops and popular press that I am a spokesman for an adversary
culture more progressive, more revolutionary than the one to
which their standard curriculum subscribes; and they therefore want all of me they can get in the short time they have
me—as an antidote, presumably, to the mind-poisoning which
most of their fellow students do not even suspect, much less
resent.

But I am in fact aware, and am compelled to say so cir-
cumspectly, that such antidotes are not very effective; that most
of the concerned organizers as well as the majority of their
unsuspecting, unresentful fellows will end up as understrappers
of a not-very-much modified social system: doctors, lawyers,
librarians, school teachers, organizers, mayors, congressmen—
and professors like me. Besides, though I am an adversary to
the politics of most university administrations, theirs included,
so, too, am I to that of most student activists, including some
of them.

I am, in fact, adverse to politics itself as ordinarily defined;
so that when I am not, like my favorite models Rip Van Winkle
and Huckleberry Finn, on the lam, I am neither pledging
allegiance to the red-white-and-blue nor chanting, "*Ho—Chi—
Min,*" only saying with Bartleby the Scrivener, "I would prefer
not to," which is good unmelodramatic American for the satanic
Latin of "*Non serviam.*"

In general, I guess, this must be apparent; since most S.D.S.-ers
seem to find me less sympathetic than do the boys on motor-
cycles (less audible, but no less present on most campuses),
who are likely to invite me to to some in-entertainment of their
group, say, a concert of "grease," i.e., vintage rock-and-roll, on
records; then display to me the swastikas they wear around their
necks—though in some cases they are Jews themselves. And
once again it is time to say, "That is not what I meant at all."

Nonetheless, at least I am there to say it; they are present to hear me or not, as they prefer; and in a time of maximum tension and distrust, this is worth a good deal. It is not merely that the war of the generations (there is no longer a "gap," as the newspapers tend still to insist, but a meeting on the battle line, a "confrontation," to use the currently fashionable term) has reached a new pitch of fury concerning drugs, as well as student power and the draft and the conduct of political conventions, but that being a civil war, in which enemies and allies are not always as easily distinguishable as both sides pretend, it depends on espionage and counter-espionage, subversion and treason, quite as much as on direct conflict.

The facts of the matter are clear enough to any reader of the newspapers, no matter how biased or obtuse. All up and down our land, bust follows bust ever more rapidly, although without visible effect—by now, they are an end in themselves. And we do not stand alone in this respect among the nations: England, used to the game of follow-the-leader in economics and the Cold War, emulates us in the campaign against marijuana, too, busting film stars and pop singers and ballet dancers, as well as students, even though their scared parents still have the prosecution of pornography, which we have apparently given up, on which to work off their baffled aggressions.

Meanwhile, the Soviet Union closes ranks with its theoretical class enemies, hunting down the smugglers of hashish on the borders of Tashkent; and in Ceylon itself, the potheads are driven from the slopes of the Holy Mountain of Katmandu, just as earlier they—or their counterparts—had been hounded from the streets of Athens and Paris and Rome, for being short on money or long on hair.

Confronting the threat of a cultural revolution which no traditional ideology explains, old political enemies find themselves embarrassingly on the same side—the leaders of the governments in Prague and Havana and Calcutta concurring with the mayor of Paterson, New Jersey, in their opinion of the poet laureate of the potheads; and the young in all of those cities taking to the streets in rage and despair.

America, however, surpasses all the rest; for there repression has achieved a degree of efficiency which seems a last caricature of the "American Way" that on almost every other front has broken down. But it is, of course, the "American Way" turned on itself in a kind of cannibalism, since it is the sons and daughters of the Establishment, where disaffection and ennui are greatest and the shift from Whiskey Cult to Drug Cult most rapid, whom the watchdogs of the Establishment pursue. No longer are the riotous offspring of the most recent immigrants, but the heirs of the first families the prime prey of the fuzz: the children of those who compose the College Boards and the National Merit Exams busted in the panicky East; those of reactionary politicians and police chiefs, as well as well-to-do liberals and successful novelists, arrested in the ultimate West; a daughter of a contender for nomination to the presidency charged with possession in the flattest and most arid stretches of the mid-West; and, finally, the son of the Jailer of the Year caught smoking in God only knows where.

But such injustice is not as even-handed and fair as it seems at first glance; for there is one institution in American which is immune to harassment, and one particularly susceptible to it. Army camps are, as everyone knows though few trouble to remark, never busted at all—certainly not in Vietnam, but not even in this country, though the incidence of smoking grass must be higher among draftees and professional soldiers than among students, and it is by no means kept secret. And just as soldiers are scarcely ever troubled about pot from without, so are they protected from within: the practice is apparently tolerated, if not downright encouraged, at all levels of command, as was booze earlier, and whorehouses. But this is, of course, precisely "maintaining a premise" in the full legal sense.

In colleges and universities, on the contrary, especially in the most distinguished of them, the campaign of repression is intensified quite out of proportion to the occasion. Schools are fair game in all seasons, and, in particular, schools that cost money to attend; for here are gathered together, in the view of the police, the privileged children of privileged parents—asserting with their McCarthy and Dick Gregory buttons, their "Fuck for Peace" stickers, and the blast of Bob Dylan or Big Brother and the Holding Company through their open windows what must strike the cops as an insolent assumption of their right of asylum.

When, therefore, provoked—it seems to them—beyond patience, the police act not in cold impartiality but with all the class fury, the *ressentiment* of the worker and petty bourgeois confronted by the coddled upper-bourgeois lovers of Negroes and burners of draft cards. The war on pot and students is not class war as foreseen by classical Marxism or as preached by campus radicals; but it seems the closest we are likely to come to genuine class struggle in the United States, though the wrong side wears the uniform of the State. Precisely because the new "criminals" are separated from the police by class lines, unlike the ordinary junkie or thief, the world they inhabit proves difficult of access. Besides, there is a long tradition—heritage of the upper-class paternalism which, when they were a much smaller elite, kept all university kids out of court short of murder or arson—of deans and college presidents as protectors of "their" students.

Past the vigilance of such administrators, certainly, it would be impossible to infiltrate the campus with informers and stoolies and professional spies would be as visible and out of place in the company of students as the police themselves. It has, therefore, proved necessary to send a new kind of undercover agent, recruited from among the students themselves, into the dormitories to peek, take notes, report back to Headquarters, and —on instruction—bug, make plants, arrange buys: in general, finger and frame. To make this possible, however, administrators have to be persuaded that times have changed, that in a period of moral crisis it is honorable as well as necessary to connive in such enticement and espionage—or at least to look away, to close one's eyes just a little.

It is not just "cooperation" which is demanded from University authorities by the police, though this is the polite name they give to what they are after, but total abdication of all judgment and control. At 5 A.M. of January 17, 1968, for instance, a large, well-organized squad of cops—too many and too well organized really for the kind of job they were about to do, though not for the kind of publicity and public acclaim they were seeking—swooped down on the dormitories of the Stony Brook branch of the State University of New York and arrested twenty-one students on drug charges. They had conducted for months, apparently, an elaborate surveillance, and so were able to provide the reporters who, of course, accompanied them, a book-length manuscript compiled from the dossiers of the chief users they had in view.

Any raid on any large college dormitory mounted at random and without any prior preparation would probably have netted in the neighborhood of twenty pot-smokers; it seems, as things go these days, a standard catch. But legal questions of establishing "probable cause" for the issuance of a warrant aside, such incursions have to be preceded by large-scale espionage because their chief end is not the arrests, which are real enough though incidental, but *exposure*.

They are, in fact, "demonstration raids," quite as the elaborate trials with predetermined verdicts mounted in East European totalitarian countries are "demonstration trials": intended not to bring anyone to justice, but to demonstrate the vigilance of the state and the obduracy of its enemies. Similarly, "demonstration raids" are supposed to make clear to the largest possible public that students in college prefer grass to Kents, and that their administrators refuse to crack down on them with the rigor that such lawlessness would seem to require.

A "heroic" exploit, certain state legislators called this comic-pathetic raid in an initial burst of euphoria; but it was apparently not equally satisfactory to the police, since they had caught no faculty in their net at all. To make amends for this, they, along with their sponsors among the politicians of Suffolk County, have been trying ever since—largely by innuendo and unchallenged hearsay "evidence"—to implicate twelve junior members of the staff.

In addition, they have turned with special vindictiveness on the President of Stony Brook, who, they have pointedly informed the press, had not even been alerted to their pre-dawn swoop; since, they contend, he had previously proved himself unworthy of such confidence. More specifically, they charge that he "had refused to cooperate with the police" on an earlier occasion when, according to them, an anonymous tipster had informed them a campus "pot-party" was in progress; but when, according to him, an attempt was being made "to frame an associate dean, who found a packet containing marijuana slipped under his door."

In the end, no one is satisfied by the statements and counter-statements, the charges and countercharges. The cops and politi-cians consider that they have found new warrants at Stony Brook for seeing "drug addicts" (practically anyone under thirty) and "corrupters of the young" (anyone over that age with a beard or a doubtful allegiance) everywhere; while the students have been confirmed in their suspicion that they are surrounded by finks (practically anyone over thirty) and undercover "narks" (an indeterminate number of quite indistinguishable people under thirty).

As a consequence, ranks are closed, first of all in terms of age, and manuals are issued on both sides for spotting and dealing with traitors from within: the adult community satisfied with newspaper summaries or briefing speeches on the narcotics menace delivered at Service Club Luncheons; the young sup-plied with more detailed kinds of information (since not merely their sensibilities but their freedom is at stake) in their own underground press.

A recent, presumably much-reprinted article called "Freak Your Nark" is attributed to "A Federal Attorney" and lists a number of possible ways to counterattack:

One. Take photographs of undercover narks, as it destroys their psychological stability. . . .
Two. Anyone holding should make a point of always having some crabgrass on himself suitably wrapped . . . refer to "grass" and sell him that at regular pot prices. . . .
Three. Use counter-blackmail. A nark is likely to break a couple of laws. . . . A fine recent example is of a country nark who slept with an underage girl. . . .
Four. Growing pot on your own property is an offense. . . . Therefore get some seed and plant the stuff in the yard of cops, narks, judges and legislators. . . .

There is more, some of it rather silly, in fact, but the whole chilling in its revelation that among many of the young at least, police persecution is simply accepted as a part of the pattern of

existence, like the nightly bombing raid by the victims of our
other undeclared war; and we know how embittered and in-
durated a conflict must become before such attitudes are possible.
But how can any sort of dialogue flourish under these circumstances? In truth, of all things not impossible, it is the most
difficult. Yet not *impossible*, in any case, as long as anyone,
young or old, can stand up in the No Man's Land between the
opposing forces, and not be shot down forthwith—even if he
screams his head off to draw attention.

No Man's Land is precisely where my bust put me, and I
have been making noises from it ever since. Yet though there
has been occasional sniping from the side of the old, it has
been sporadic and inaccurate enough to make me suspect it is
half-hearted (after all, I am unmistakably past fifty); while
from the side of the young, no one has either fired in malice
or contemptuously suggested that I go away and die. And profit-
ing by that fact, though rather unnerved by it, too (I am not,
needless to say, without reservations about the young, any more
than I am about the old), I have been tickled to walk up and
down in their world—and learn. Not teach or preach, understand,
for what they ask and will listen to from those older than they
is confirmation and flattery: a declaration of love and commitment which I am too ornery and weary to give, though love at
least is a large part of what I feel contemplating them.

So instead of offering advice or support or sympathy, I make
jokes, recite my dreams, and let them overhear me talking to
myself, all three of which they seem to like, especially when my
jokes are wicked, my dreams mad, and my soliloquies what they
take to be irreverent, that is, my kind of prayer.

But chiefly I have been learning from them: who their gods
are and how they worship them, who their enemies and how
they hex them; but especially how it feels to be when and where
they are, and how they have learned to say it to each other. I
have in short been learning their language, the last language I
expect to learn ever (unless, after all, I keep my many-times-
broken promise to myself and get to Ancient Greek before it
is too late), in order to qualify for the last time as an interpreter
in what I hope is my last war. I want not merely to be able to

say to those who hold power and sit in judgment over the young what it is they are after, but to say it in something very like their own words—the cadence and flavor preserved in any case, and even much of the intent; though all of it translated down (or *up*, no matter) to make the kind of sense to which those of my own generation alone can respond.

Such translations, I assure myself, may eventually have their effect in courts and legislatures, since in the world of judges and lawmakers, quite like any other, passion and rhetoric may carry the day when facts and reason fail. But even more importantly, they can make a difference right now for those baffled parents, those two-time losers who use up the little spirit that has survived their own delusions in bewailing their defeated hopes for their children. To learn a new language, an old saw has it, is to find a new soul. How lovely it would be if one could persuade parents to reverse the educational process of their own schooldays by learning this time not Latin or Hebrew, which is to say, "dead languages," but rather a language not yet quite born; thus infusing into their fading selves the souls of living sons rather than those of extinct grandfathers.

This hope, at any rate, has sustained me as I have listened with special attention (my own immediate fate as well as that of my kids being involved) to those of the young who have gone out of their way to consult me; and I have eavesdropped quite as attentively on those who have not.

I have heard out, that is to say, though most often not answered, my own students, first of all, when they have turned to me for something more than the catalogue promised, and which I was in no position to give them: seeking me out in office hours not to check on the week's assignment, but to ask why the hell there is no Anarchist Club on campus; or where can they get really reliable advice about beating the draft; or how do I explain the fact that the people in this school who *look* like Heads aren't, and maybe even vice versa; or don't I think Bob Dylan is really out of his old hang-ups in his newest album; or how come I don't realize that the President or Rector or Vice-Chancellor is a fink, above and beyond the standard finkiness of people in his position; or—in exactly the same tone—

couldn't I recommend some graduate school where someone, you know, not exactly *straight*, could make it without selling out *too* completely.

And I have also endured, even enjoyed, being caught at home after hours—though maybe writing again for the first time in weeks—by a campus journalist learning to use a tape-recorder; or a campus radical on the verge of rustication who begins by giving me the word (not quite the *whole* truth, of course, but as much of it as he thinks I can bear, which is to say, a wee smidgeon more than he is about to reveal to the bourgeois press) about who it actually was, or *wasn't,* anyhow, who threw the red paint on the American apologist for Vietnam—and who ends by asking if I would read and criticize, with a candor equal to that he has felt free to use with me, the first fifty pages of a Maoist interpretation of *Piers Plowman.*

Moreover, I have tried to listen and remember, whether an interloper or an invited guest at public meetings in Amsterdam and Leyden and Sussex, in Washington, D.C., and Evanston, Illinois, and Manhattan, Kansas, the sound of the voices crying from the rostrum slogans and names and holy words: Black Power and Student Power, victimization and confrontation, Enoch Powell and DeGaulle, McCarthy and Teddy and Bobby, Rudi Dutchke and Danny the Red, Ché and Regis Debray, gerontocracy and alteration of consciousness, LSD and pot.

Lying between sleeping and waking afterward, I have played back in my own head not only what the speakers said but the noises of the audience as well: the groans of protest and sighs of assent; the Black kid in his Malcolm X sweatshirt rising to heckle Tim Leary's companion and assistant, who happened also to be Black; the hippie humming some tuneless reminiscence of a song to himself while he combed out some girl's long yellow hair draped down the back of the seat before him, sure that vision was there rather than in the words that assailed him; or the American students in an English auditorium chanting together to drown out a speaker from their own Embassy: "L.B.J., L.B.J., HOW MANY KIDS DID YOU KILL TODAY?" —a crummy slogan, I have always found it, but recited this time in the beautiful sort of unison they had all learned Pledging Allegiance to the Flag.

It is, on the face of it, a strange way for a grown man to spend his time, but I kept feeling uncomfortably mobile, oddly disponible during my stay at Sussex. Certainly, I have never been more restless in my life, moving not only up and down, back and forth across England itself, but on to the continent as well, five, six, seven, eight times (after a while, I lost track); even to America twice, where I felt not like one returned home, but a visitor in transit still, tempted to whip out my passport every time I bought a souvenir, a genuine root beer or hamburger or hotdog.

Not even in America, however, was I tempted to look for El Dorado; I had no sense at all of myself as a man on a mission or in quest of anything, only of being a collector with plenty of money and the impulse to shop around for mementos of whatever alien place he is in at any moment. In the end, just like such a well-heeled fool, I bought everything, planning to sort it out later and at my leisure; bought frantically, too, since I knew by then that I was a traveler in time rather than through space, and that, therefore, my schedule was not in my own control.

At any rate, it finally came to me that if I was really traveling in time rather than space, it did not matter in the least where on the map I was; because wherever I found myself might well be the "there" I was seeking: the place where the young were at home, the next place, the absolute future. And having learned this, I persuaded myself that I could hear the voices of the young saying things they had not yet spoken aloud to anyone. I had, that is to say, what used to be called a "vision" of the young playing out in the occupied theaters of our world (which include the lecture halls at Columbia and the Sorbonne, as well as the Odeon itself), while old actors and professors sulk in the wings, the unmediated Happening of their own lives. It is a performance, like any other, destined to last not forever, as the actors perhaps believe, but only for as long as *their* forever is—which will surely be no longer than ours, which itself seemed so limitless in prospect only a short time ago.

This vision, at any rate, I have been trying to communicate in recent articles and interviews—and, for a final time, in this book. Yet rereading just the other day a series of answers which I gave originally to questions posed by an English magazine called

The Running Man, but which have recently turned up again in *The Village Voice,* I found myself more than a little dismayed.

It is not, please understand, the journal which seems inappropriate, despite the fact that I do not ordinarily read it or think of it as an especially sympathetic forum for my views. Its editors and typical readers these days, though somewhat younger than I, are already old enough, far enough from the moving center of events, to be a fit audience for what I have to say—to need, in fact, to be reminded by one even more removed than they of how wide a gap has opened between them and their younger brothers and sisters, their older nieces and nephews, who read the less literate but more relevant *East Village Other.* To be the parental voice in the avuncular ear may not be a customary role for me, but it is one I rather enjoy. I only wish that what I had to say in my responses to the interviewer (or at least what was left of them in a version edited by him) did not seem on the page, and in America, so obvious: so close to the kind of truth any hack journalist can see, which is to say, yesterday's truth at the moment it is becoming today's lie; and so far from the poetry which defeats him, which is to say, tomorrow's truth, which from the vantage point of today we still cannot ever imagine becoming a lie.

"The one way," I seem to have said, "in which the student, like everybody else in urban industrial society, feels he lives in nature or has some notion of non-bureaucratized, non-industrialized life is in terms of his own sex life, or at least an ideal of his own sex life. So it is natural that . . . in students' minds the model for a good society is to be found in some ideal of a free sex life. . . ." And I went on to observe that "the demonstration is somewhere in between the orgy on the one side, and the Organized Political Party or Army on the other. . . ." After which I moved from *eros* to England, a long, sad trip, and concluded by observing what should go without saying: "The university is based upon the traditional assumption that age and experience lead to a certain kind of wisdom or useful knowledge which can then be imparted to the young . . . this holds up in times of relatively slow change, but when you get a time of revolutionary speed . . . the young have a distinct advantage over the old. . . . The university is changing from a place in which the old instruct the young to a place in which the young will instruct the old."

And this conclusion, though banal enough for a Dean, is true enough for its occasion, true enough for those who do not yet know even so much. Somewhere or other Sigmund Freud remarked that he had been forced to spend his life telling people the kind of things they could have learned from any normally observant nursemaid; and I have from time to time intrigued myself by speculating on what he would have said *on the next level*, if he could have assumed such minimal wisdom in those he addressed: his actual colleagues and his potential patients. I know, at any rate, what *I* would have said *on the next level* about universities; and, indeed, have written this book in part in order to be able to do so, in context and with all the ironical qualifications provided by life itself: "The university is changing from a place in which the old are permitted to pretend that they are instructing the young to one in which the young will be encouraged to believe that they are instructing the old."

Not to attempt the impossible is craven, but to believe it possible is foolish, which may be worse, and philosophers have always been able to demonstrate that in theory instruction is impossible. The university, therefore—like any authentic institution, the church, for instance, and the parliaments of the world —exists to demonstrate the impossibility in practice of its own goals, thus sparing us from the twin indignities of premature despair and utopianism too long endured.

I had not really meant to write this book though, only to think about it, to put down notes for it inside my head; partly because it is too predictable a response, partly because inevitably it falsifies the experience it purports to preserve and communicate. I know the trap, for I have watched others fall into it. "I was the man, I suffered, I was there," is the boast with which they begin; but having committed it to print and clapped it between covers, they deserve the response they get: "Don't kid us, you're only somebody who wrote a book!"

It had all been laid out for me clearly enough the day after my arrest, in a telephone call from a woman I had long known (which was fine), but who also had long known me (which is rather more disconcerting)—known me in fact since I had *not* been arrested in 1933. "Well," she began, claiming immediately all the privileges of that knowledge and the love that had earned it, "I never would have thought it. Not in a million years. You're the kind, Leslie, who always gets away."

Silence from my side, since under the best of circumstances, I'm an idiot on the telephone.

"You know *that*," she insisted. "I mean everyone does."

Another silence, which, knowing me, I take it she read as an assurance that I was still there, even listening.

"I just wanted to tell you that—" She could not quite finish it, preferring to leave the essential message unspoken, unspoiled. "Oh *hell*, you'll just write a *book* about it and make lots of money."

Then she was gone; which left me, of course, saying over and over to myself—and writing to the publishers, my own as well as strangers who approached me out of the blue asking for such a book—what I had not managed to tell her, "I won't, I won't, I won't, I *won't* . . ."

I HAVE WRITTEN that book, however, since it is what my whole plea demanded to become, if I was to appeal it from the courts to the world. Besides, there seemed no other way to come to terms with a larger piece of my life than had been touched by the Buffalo Narcotics Squad, but whose real shape and meaning I perceived for the first time only after those cops had entered it, so tangentially and so late.

My case has, in fact, produced not one book but two; for besides this one that I am finishing even as I apologize for it, there is another, already published though in an extremely limited edition, and already read by fourteen men: by the five judges of the Appellate Division, Fourth Department of the State of New York Supreme Court, which sits in Rochester, plus the nine who sit on the Court of Appeals in Albany. And before we are through, hopefully it will be read by nine more, the nine justices of the Supreme Court of the United States, to whom we have referred our plea.

Just as my own book has grown out of the plea that the laws restricting the use of marijuana are instruments to suppress dissent, so the other one, written by my lawyers, is the product of our motion to suppress the evidence against us on the basis of improper search and seizure. A modest volume of thirty-four pages (with a somewhat longer appendix in the form of a "Record of Appeal"), it is entitled like a million others simply "Appellant's Brief," and was first announced in a news story dated September 17, 1968, which ran as follows:

A new delay in the trial of Dr. Leslie A. Fiedler and other remaining defendants in a marijuana case occurred

247

today in City Court because of an impending appeal of a
motion to suppress evidence. . . .

Dr. Fiedler, a State University of Buffalo English professor at the time, and others were arrested in a police raid
of their Morris Avenue premises April 18, 1967. Police
charged Dr. Fiedler . . . and his wife . . . with allowing the
premises to be used for unlawful use of narcotic drugs.

. . . a son was charged with a felony of giving . . . and
a misdemeanor of possession . . . His wife was charged with
possession . . . [a younger] brother . . . and an eighteen year
old youth and [another of] 19 were charged with possession
of marijuana.

All pleaded innocent on arraignment. Their lawyer . . .
subsequently brought pretrial motions in both County Court
and City Court to suppress any alleged evidence on the
grounds that police unlawfully planted a police agent in
the Fiedler home and there was unlawful electronic surveillance of the premises.

The motions were opposed by [the] Assistant District
Attorney . . . and his arguments were upheld by [a] City
Judge . . . and then [a] County Judge . . .

Both entered what are known as an intermediate order
that isn't appealable unless there is a conviction or a plea of
guilty, which is equivalent to a conviction in the lower court.

[Their lawyer] . . . stating he was doing so to achieve
an appellate review of the search and seizure question
involved, then entered guilty pleas for [some of the other
defendants] . . .

Dr. Fiedler, his wife and [one of the] youths obtained
adjournments of their jury trials. . . . The new trial date set
. . . is November 4.

This describes where we stand now, and the legal maneuver-
ings which have brought us there, with sufficient clarity, I think;
though quite like the court record, it leaves out the human ele-
ment completely. It tells nothing of the strain during those long
weeks, for instance, in which my lawyer and I discussed whether
it would be prudent, however legally useful, to plead anyone
at all guilty, and if so, whom. Obviously, I could not plead so

myself under any circumstances, since such a plea would doubt-less compromise my situation in the University. But the District Attorney insisted it be one of the principals rather than one of the lesser accused; and at the worst juncture, it was even sug-gested that my wife make the plea.

In the end, however, this seemed mere deviousness on the part of the Prosecution in which it would have been sheer folly to acquiesce, since to the court of public opinion constituted by our neighbors decisions arrived at by due process elsewhere bore less weight than our own posture, our own apparent judgment of ourselves.

That judgment was and remains "innocent": collectively and individually innocent, not only of the absurd police charges (about which there was never any real doubt), but also of having in any essential way failed our own personal codes.

To make this clear to everyone, my wife and I intend to keep insisting not just that we are "not guilty," which is a legal formula only, but that we are "innocent," in the full sense of the word. We will make this assertion in conversation, bugged or not bugged, in writing public and private, as well as before any judge and jury we may eventually have to face—if our mo-tion to suppress fails in the highest court.

No doubt the District Attorney's office will be offering us new deals before we are through, because they begin to lose faith in their case even as we grow more confident in ours. But we shall refuse to bargain, since, first of all, we trust that we shall prevail even in their terms. And, in any case, we are convinced of what we could not quite manage to believe in the early days when we seemed to be losing our war of nerves with the world: *that the final decision of the courts does not really matter.* How-ever a judge may decide, we will stand or fall by the verdict of quite another tribunal in which all are equally plaintiff and defendant, judge and jury and expert witness: the court in which we not merely judge our fellows, which is not so difficult after all, but also ourselves.

Yet the Court's decision on our motion to suppress matters a great deal, too, and not only to ourselves; for, as I have learned reading and rereading my lawyer's brief, our plea has taken us into a contested area of the law, where what is at stake goes far beyond a fine or a jail sentence, my wife's amicable relations with her neighbors, or my job at the university.

What is involved is that which any man of good will, reading the most garbled and biased accounts of our case, perhaps sensed from the first: the survival or extinction of what Justice Brandeis, a dissenting voice even in 1928, described as "the right to be let alone—the most comprehensive of rights and the right most valued by civilized men."

Since that date, however, and especially during the last few years, there has been a mounting assault on that most comprehensive of human rights: an attack made possible by advances in technology and prompted by growing panic on the part of the more recent and insecure beneficiaries of our society. Such late and uncertain beneficiaries tend to respect technology, by which they have immensely profited, more than privacy, which they have scarcely experienced and therefore neither cherish nor quite understand.

The threat they feel is to property, not freedom, especially as the discontent of other elements in the population, still excluded and expropriated, erupts into violence directed more against the goods they do not possess than the men who do possess them: arson and looting in particular. And they call in response for counter-violence, though the acts which terrify them may well have been prompted in the first instance by repressive measures aimed at making sure that America's last poor remain poor forever—lest no one be able to tell ever again who has made it and at what point.

"Law and Order" is, as everyone now knows, the name for such repressive counter-violence, just as "Power"—whether in "Black Power" or "Student Power" or whatever—is for the disruptive violence it answers. And though that honorific name is intended primarily to conceal the real nature of what it purports to describe, it inadvertently reveals an essential difference between the two sides who currently gut our cities: one imagining it does not want to do so at all, the other reasonably sure that such destruction is what it wants and needs.

In fact, both sides lust for the flames that only one cheers aloud—the victims in order to destroy the evidence of their indignities, the victimizers to blot out the proof of the price demanded by their prosperity. Cautious as well as hypocritical, however, the exponents of "Law and Order" do not, like their opponents, go into the streets themselves to do battle, but send the police on their behalf. And watching it all on T.V., they can applaud their surrogates with an easy conscience, since their legitimacy is attested by the uniforms they wear, the warrants with which they are supplied.

Recently, however, even the watchers of T.V. have begun to grow uneasy over the excessive zeal of the cops: their uncalled-for private pleasure in their public duty of breaking heads, as well as their willingness to break those not only of their actual challengers but of anyone else who looks as if, under proper circumstances, he might become one, or who merely takes pictures of what they are doing, or who happens to be within range when their anger is up. Indeed, the scandal has grown so public that certain responsible government officials have begun to detach themselves from their constituencies, speaking out for the benefit of the press against what they do not quite call "police brutality," like those who suffer it directly, but what they are willing to label at least force applied misguidedly and out of all proportion.

But clubs, along with tear gas and mace, constitute only one half of the threat of repression, the least efficient half in fact. Even more menacing, because silent and largely unsuspected, and when challenged still defended as necessary or proper or both, is legitimized stealth: in particular new methods of eavesdropping on the excluded, the rebellious, and the merely suspect by means of electronic devices which make possible a kind of Total Surveillance quite as terrifying as Total Force.

It can be argued, indeed, that electronic surveillance is potentially a greater threat to the health of the community, certainly to the possibilities of development and change, the very notion of a future, for it is directed more often than not against dangerous thoughts rather than dangerous actions; it overhears and registers speculative solutions, audacious theories, fruitful heresies not yet shouted from street corners or posted on walls, but tried out in the presumed privacy of a home.

But police have used stoolies and spies, the counter-argument runs, and will continue to need them as long as the continuing war against crime and subversion is waged. So why the sudden agitation? What's so different about our situation right now, except its greater urgency? Every war, hot or cold, employs agents; and though we despise those in the hire of enemies, particularly turncoats from our own side, we celebrate those on our side, glorify them in popular fiction and on television. Who does not know and love the Man from Uncle or 007 or the Black and White buddies on "I Spy"?

True, modern means of spying employ not such heroic figures but machines backed up by machine-tenders; yet why *not*, if machines prove more efficient at overhearing, just as they have long proved more efficient at breaking codes? It is as much a part of the progress we all love, the movement toward one-hundred-per cent effectiveness, otherwise demonstrated in the H-Bomb or the contraceptive pill.

And yet, hard as it may be to believe, something not merely new but finally sinister has been added to the ancient practice of spying with the perfection of an invisible, unsleeping, incorruptible, indiscriminate Ear by which the police can attend to everybody, everywhere, all the time. Eventually, it begins to be clear, the information collected by thousands upon thousands of such devices, data miscellaneous, random, universal, will be fed into some central computer that will digest and classify it, then sound an alarm in the appropriate precinct station—not immediately after, but just *before* someone steps over the line of crime, sin, treason, or heresy. And at that point, our police will have become instruments of crime prevention through thought control, rather than clumsy investigators after the fact, threatening pointless reprisal.

Even now we seem to have moved almost to the state of affairs foreseen some twenty years ago by George Orwell in *1984*, from which my lawyer quotes in his moving brief:

> There was, of course, no way of knowing whether you were being watched at any given moment. . . . You had to live— did live . . . in the assumption that every sound you made was overheard, and, except in darkness, every moment scrutinized.

And this he follows immediately with a quotation from the record of our case:

> [The Narcotics Chief] . . . said police had kept the Fiedler residence under twenty-four-hour surveillance for the last ten days.

It would seem as if no one, no matter how ill-willed or obtuse, could fail to register horror at a situation in which, after a scant twenty years, what seemed a grotesque prophecy of totalitarian repression can scarcely be differentiated from a story in today's newspaper. Recognizing the real horror of it all would, however, mean deciding to do something about it—take a stand, draw a line, perhaps even mount a counter-attack. Yet the Courts themselves, right up to the Supreme Court, have instead been responding with a kind of caution hardly distinguishable from indecision, only slowly and tentatively, sometimes inconsistently, beginning to set limits on Total Surveillance.

Over the past weeks, I have been reading through the relevant cases, with their inconclusive or contradictory decisions, as adduced in my lawyer's brief—moving deep into that strange semi-fictional world of the Law, in which accused and accusers alike seem to function not as men but as instances and examples, which is to say, as shadows and ghosts. All the same, they have grown very real to me as I, too, come closer and closer to turning into one of them: another name identifying another case in the limbo of legal records. And I have got to be fond of them as well, that whole dim crew which includes Katz in his "bugged" telephone booth; On Lee in his laundry, confiding in a faithless former employee called Chin Poy; Lopez in his tavern offering a bribe to an Internal Revenue Officer with a tape recorder; and Osborn trying to make a deal with "a Nashville Policeman called Vick."

Osborn is, however, far and away my favorite, not because I can see him in his trap any more vividly than the others, but because in deciding his case, the Supreme Court took a real leap ahead, defining unequivocally two limits on surveillance, two hard and fast principles upon which our own appeal is based. First of all, they made it clear that in order to be legal, electronic surveillance must be preceded by "an antecedent justification before a magistrate" (the listening device had been brought into our house without a court order); and second, they insisted, it must be conducted under "the most precise and discriminate circumstances which fully met the 'requirement of particularity'. . . ." (our own girl spy had kept her channel open to anyone who happened to be in our home when she made one of her calls).

Finally, I have come to feel that the questions about the use and control of marijuana on which our case bears, pressing and important as they are, may be less pressing and important than the larger legal issues of proper search and seizure and the protection of Fourth Amendment rights, which seemed to me at first intolerably abstract and remote from real men suffering real pain, real kids harassed by real cops; I have even dreamed of writing a courtroom brief, for the sake of making the issues clear.

Every novelist, I suppose, dreams on occasion, lost inside of his own head or staring at the blank sheet before him, of being a lawyer instead, which is to say, not just the lonely inscriber but the public performer of his own words to a living audience: an applauded actor in the archetypal theater of the courtroom. Similarly, every lawyer (including my own) seems to love imagining himself a novelist in total control of just such a plot as is customarily imposed on him by circumstance—a drama rehearsed for admiring posterity rather than twelve semi-literates, all more likely than not wishing they were not present. But my lawyer has had to content himself with writing a brief, that is, *my* story, and I with reading *his* words in the privacy of my own study; though I must admit that I did speak his conclusion aloud late one night to a quite noncommital audience of two cats and a dog:

It is self-evident that man can only retain his individuality and personal beliefs if there is preserved for him some degree of privacy. A person's right to choose how he will privately live his life cannot be made to depend on the popularity of his beliefs. We must have privacy for all or we will have it for none.

The awesome police surveillance conducted here, so destructive of privacy, offers an ominous omen of what will come if these practices are not judicially controlled. If we approve this unauthorized secret watch over a college professor, who advocated an unpopular idea, in exchange for a handful of evidence to secure several misdemeanor convictions, we will have paid an enormous price. A price we simply cannot afford if man's individuality is to survive.

But, alas, the decision in the Appellate Court went against us, the five-man court splitting three to two, and the Chief Justice writing an eloquent dissenting opinion on our behalf. And just the other day the highest court in the State upheld the majority opinion, leaving us only the option of asking the Supreme Court of the United States to hear our plea and, hopefully, reverse the earlier decisions. Win or lose on that level, however, I know I will never get the issues out of my head. Yet I also know that really to win, somehow I must learn to forget, learn to live as if whatever cops do, my privacy is unbroken, my life my own.

My next door neighbor, who had not spoken to me for two years, recently provided me with a clue as to how I must live—surprising both of us by saying a cordial hello to me when we met face to face. He was no longer able, I suppose, to figure what else to do with someone who is simply *there*, rooting up his dandelions and turning brown in the sun.

And that was a victory for both of us, a victory for everyone, though no headlines announced it, or ever will.